DANNY'S BOYS

A Novel

CHARLEY HEENAN

North Carolina

Danny's Boys: A Novel
© 2022 Charley Heenan. All rights reserved.

Published in the United States by BQB Publishing
(an imprint of Boutique of Quality Books Publishing Company)
www.bqbpublishing.com

Printed in the United States of America

978-1-952782-76-3 (p)
978-1-952782-77-0 (e)

Library of Congress Control Number: 2022943620

Book design by Robin Krauss, www.bookformatters.com
Cover design by Rebecca Lown, www.rebeccalowndesign.com
First editor: Olivia Swenson
Second editor: Allison Itterly

*For
the sad
and the mad
and the Nones*

Acknowledgments

I offer my heartfelt gratitude to my writers' group: Lynn Rosen, Ann Stolinsky, Robert L. Brown, Deborah Drezon Carroll, Chris Brady, Margaret Sayers, Tom Durso, Anne Boagni, Carol Moore, and Juliana. Each reviewed my many (very rough) drafts with patience and kindness. Their encouragement, insight, and advice helped me immeasurably, and I am blessed to be able to work with them.

Many thanks to Elise Juska for her review and analysis, I learned so much, and I truly valued her positive feedback. Thank you to Terri Leidich of BQB Publishing for taking a chance on me and my story, and Olivia Swenson, of Olivia Edits, for her suggestions, diligent review, and careful explanations. Thank you to Rebecca Lown Design for the cover artwork and Susan Baker for all of her input.

Most of all, thanks to my amazing, always helpful husband and my darling son who make my life complete.

CHAPTER 1

Wholly Thirsty

Freshly showered, after working the early shift in Acme's produce department, I put on clean jeans and a long-sleeve Eagles shirt, pulled a Jeff cap from the top of the coat closet, and adjusted it in the beveled wall mirror above the living room sofa. Mom wanted me to wear something nicer in case that lazy-eyed girl, who she liked for me, was there, but I was already wearing the hat. From the kitchen, Mom was saying something about not drinking too much and not being late.

"Lock up after I leave," I called, hurrying out the door. "Love you."

Shenanigans had been on a decline. In our mid-twenties, school, work, and girlfriends had distracted all of us. Not me so much, but most of my friends. Danny Cunane, my best friend, was three for three. There were fewer late nights, fewer epic stories, and an overall lack of hilarity. Even our Thursday happy hours at McRyan's, which after twelve years of Catholic school we'd called Wholly Thirsty, had taken a hit. Sometimes, only a couple of guys showed. Tonight, at least, everyone promised to be there.

It was a short walk to McRyan's, only two blocks up and three over from my house. Our neighborhood was a small chunk of Northeast Philadelphia, a concrete plaid of rowhouses, strip malls, churches, and corner bars accented with parks and rec centers. Inside the bar, the polished wood-paneled walls held

Guinness signs, the tricolour flag, Celtic crosses, and assorted Irish crafts hand carried across the sea. The décor matched that in most of the finished basements in our neighborhood and felt homey, like the only things missing were a few sofas. I sat in our usual spot at the bar's curve nearest the door, and Vizzie, the bartender, poured a lager without me needing to ask. The first sips worked their magic like a full-body sigh.

Unlike other parts of Philadelphia, where the city required bars to be a mile away from churches, McRyan's served as an unofficial extension of ours, with St. John's parishioners stopping in before or after church and school events. Danny sat at one of the long tables in the back with Gav, Terry, and Ray. The four had recently been named to the St. John's Catholic Youth Organization Board. They huddled over a laptop, hammering out all the details for our CYO basketball teams: rosters, uniforms, referees, gym reservations, and the like. I didn't interrupt—the sooner they were done, the better—but Danny called to me.

"Yo, Tommy Dunleavey. Everything okay? You're early."

"I don't want to miss anything," I said, and he smiled.

I did my part, keeping everyone connected. Once a year, I organized an outing to an Eagles game—scouting the tickets, ordering for the tailgate, hiring the party bus, and collecting the money. We were going that Sunday. While I waited for everyone, I reviewed my tailgate checklist and watched the Phillies play the Padres in the last game of their season, pacing my drinking so as not to get too far ahead.

I was on my second beer when Jack, Danny's younger brother, wandered in. I'd known him so long that he was practically my little brother too. He even looked like me. We were both five-nine and thin with longish dark brown hair. Today he was wearing a shirt and tie, probably his brother's since the oversized collar exposed the neck of his undershirt, and iron-creased khakis that bunched around shiny new tasseled loafers.

"Look at you all dressed up, fancy-schmancy. What gives?"

"I had a thing downtown this afternoon. I'll tell you later." He looked to the back and gave a chin to his brother before sitting with me.

"You aren't interviewing, are you?" I asked. Danny had used his parish connections to get his brother a job on the city's Graffiti Abatement Team.

"No, I like the work. Good pay, nice bennies. I go into a place that's filthy, make it nice." Jack stretched out some wrinkled bills and laid them on the bar. "My boss is a tough read. Some days he says I'm his best worker and stuff, then today . . ." He frowned. "I had to leave early, that's probably why, right?"

"Well sure, he lost production, that's all." I signaled that his first drink was on me and said, "I'm proud of you, man. You really got your act together."

He turned away, hiding a blush, and made circles in a cocktail napkin with his pint. In a quiet voice, he asked, "What's new with you, Tommy?"

Before I could say same old, same old, a breaking news banner scrolled across the bottom of the television screen: "Sexual abuse allegations in a Northeast parish. Details following the game."

"Jeez, you hate to see that again," I said. "That's tragic, really tragic, you know?"

Jack looked up and kept his eyes on the television. "Yeah, it is."

Battling car horns outside the bar reached a crescendo and made it hard to hear the game. I wandered over to the front window. Angry traffic jammed the two-lane one-way street all the way down to St. John's. Drivers yelled out of car windows, hoping to force a miracle parting of the gridlock, and a synchronized flipping of the birds ensued like the wave at a game. The traffic lights were out again. It'd take forever for everyone to get here.

I sent a group text, giving options for avoiding the jam. Someone responded, *Thanks, Mom*.

At the top of the inning, my friend Eddie Shields, ran in. The broad-shouldered ginger jumped ass-first onto the barstool next to us and said mid-spin, "A shot of Jameson and a lager, stat."

Even Vizzie laughed.

"A tree limb fried the cable lines at the over-fifty-five development. I had to explain how to reboot servers and televisions to old people all day. Then I hit the damn traffic. Need I say more?" Eddie downed the shot and sucked down half of his beer. Once he was off the clock, his Comcast customer service filter disappeared. "What's new at the Acme, Tommy? How's your zucchini hanging?" So funny. He gave Jack the once over. "You running for office?"

Jack grinned and shook his head.

Dez Regan, the gentle giant, lumbered in next and leaned his elbows against the bar between Jack and me. A six-eight fireman, the stools were too small for him. We peppered him with questions about a recent multi-alarmer.

"I'll tell you, my guardian angel needs new wings after that one," he said. Someone of Dez's size swinging a hose or an axe inside narrow rowhomes or centuries-old structures demanded a lot from an angel.

Jack asked, "How do you . . . not be afraid?"

"Focus," Dez answered. "People are depending on me. I have my training, my faith."

"A shame you're a coward when you're talking to chicks," said Eddie.

"Well, it'd be unfair to the rest of you if I had it all." Dez smiled, then pointed to the Jameson and motioned that he was buying a round. Jack passed, said he had a big job tomorrow and wanted to get in early. I feigned wiping my eyes, lamenting that our little man was growing up.

As Vizzie poured three shots of Irish, the breaking-news banner about the clergy abuse scrolled across the TV again.

"Which parish do you think it is?" Eddie asked.

Including the parishes bordering the city, there were at least twenty. We knew all of them either from attending Mass or competing against the schools in CYO.

"Might be St. John's. You never know, might even be Father Farrell," Eddie said. He imitated our parish priest's habit of clasping his hands and tilting his head, then stuck his tongue out Gene Simmons-style.

"Knock it off, Eddie," I warned.

A quiet man with a ready smile, Father Farrell had been a major part of all our lives for the last fifteen years or so. He was there for Mom and me after Dad died. Mom said he was classy, someone for me to emulate.

"Ignore him," said Dez

It was easy to do just then, as two cute St. Hubert alums entered, and we all sat up straighter. Dez smiled at the women and waved, flicking an empty shot glass at Vizzie in the process. Beer almost came through my nose.

We were still laughing when Stevie Behan, a.k.a. StevieB, slinked in and tapped me on the shoulder. A Mass-every-day Holy Roller, he was more at home at a novena than a bar. StevieB shook our hands, saying, "How ya doing? How's your family?

Me? Staying out of trouble." Jack offered him his seat, which he took and then sat with his hands folded on the bar like it was an altar rail. It wasn't his fault; I blamed his parents.

"I assume the four in the back will finish sometime this century," said Eddie, pointing to Danny and the others still working on CYO business. "Besides them, who are we still waiting on?"

"Brendan and Matt. Probably stuck in traffic."

To pass the time, the five of us shot darts. It was early, so we all shot well, until Eddie dusted one of his shots. "Fuck, fuck, fuck."

"Watch the language," said StevieB.

In all fairness, Eddie probably didn't even realize he cursed. Then he muffed another shot. "Goddammit, what the fuck is wrong with me?"

"Apologizing for taking the Lord's name means nothing if you keep doing it," StevieB said. "Seriously, you lower yourself."

Eddie side-eyed him, had to have fun with it, and dropped a few more choice words "by accident," apologizing and swearing in the same breath.

"Knock it the fuck off," StevieB blurted.

We all howled. StevieB, of course, buried his face in his hands and then apologized to everyone within earshot.

"C'mon, man," I said. "It's nothing." The poor guy needed to drink more.

Brendan Sullivan and Matt Asher finally showed. They walked in together, Brendan mid-rant about the traffic lights being held together with duct tape and chewing gum and questioning what the city did with all our tax money. Matt, still in his scrubs, teased him by suggesting with a straight face that the city's charter schools needed the money for their water polo teams.

As Brendan sputtered, Dez slowed his roll by toasting "To Wholly Thirsty."

Everyone at the bar joined. Drinks flowed and conversation moved onto finer things, like offensive lines, over-unders, and whether my coworker's allegiance to the Dallas Cowboys demonstrated a form of mental illness.

"You guys hear about the clergy abuse story?" Brendan asked. "Wait till you see, someone'll have their hand out, wanting money from the church."

"Ironic. Since these things start with a priest putting their hand out," said Matt.

"Not funny." Brendan frowned. "With all the fundraisers we have, you know all the money ends up with the lawyers."

Paying tuition at Catholic schools was a hardship for all our families. Most of us had been pulled into the principal's office when our parents were late with a tuition check, or had our grades held up, or were suspended from a team, or were threatened with expulsion. Being one of six kids, Brendan was pulled in more than any of us. I was even pulled in after Dad died.

"It's too early to get so serious," I said. "Besides, we were having an important conversation here. The Eagles are playing Dallas on Sunday."

Between us and neighborhood folks wandering in, poor Vizzie needed an extra pair of arms to keep the pints filled. The late arrivals ordered a round of shots, and this time Jack joined them.

"Yo," I said, "you're supposed to be taking it easy."

He waved me off. Ah well, best-laid plans.

While we partied, the illustrious CYO Board continued their work. I finally yelled back to them, "Hey, how much longer? It's like I'm at a party where people are doing homework." It was for their own good that I hounded them to take a break, plus their table blocked access to the good dartboard.

Danny walked over to us. "All right," he said. "We hear you. We're almost done. We're clashing over the rosters."

We all headed to the back and grabbed seats at their table. St. John's had enough kids to field two high school boys' basketball teams. The question at hand was whether to put the two superstar Mallory brothers on the same team or not. On the same team, they would dominate but leave their teammates with little to do, and then the other St. John's team would be lucky to win any games.

As president of the board, Peter Gavin, a.k.a. Gav, could have made the decision, but he wanted some consensus. Gav was our local success story. He'd set up Gavin's Insurance after college and had the whole neighborhood as clients. He'd sometimes wear a suit jacket to a keg party, but he was still one of us.

Danny suggested that it was more important for each boy on the team to contribute something so they'd all have skin in the game.

Terry Joyce, at six-six and an all-city basketball player back in our day, wanted a winning team come hell or high water. He suggested that kids would rather put their skin in some championship jackets.

Ray Naulty was short, but he carried himself as if he were tall, probably because of his smarts. He attended grad school and was Mister Go-To in the neighborhood for anything requiring serious intellect. In high school, a teacher had once said he was a ray of light, and we reminded him of it from time to time.

He asked, "You ever play with guys who do it all, call all the shots on the court? This is bad for the Mallorys. They'll turn into egomaniac little assholes."

It was a tough decision, and analysis commenced. Some debated nurture versus nature, whether the Mallory brothers could be turned into assholes if they weren't assholes already. Danny made the best argument: It sucked to endure hours of practice for a team with a few standouts who'd hog all the playing time. But opinions favored having the Mallory brothers set an example for the other kids and teach them what winning felt like.

Terry reminded us, "It's good for the school; it helps our rep to have players who know what they're doing. Plus, how great would it be to beat St. Mark's?"

The debate ensued. Tempers simmered. In the end, Gav called executive privilege. He said, "We have talented, dedicated players, let's use them."

Then, Matt got us all laughing with a story, and any lingering tension dissipated. He and his fiancée, Brigid Keller, and her mother had left a Beef and Beer at St. Bart's, and a passed-out bum lay in the parking lot. Mrs. Keller insisted, at the top of her voice, that the scruffy man was either City Councilman Tyson or Tom Waits, "or I'm a jackass."

"Now how do you answer that?" he asked. "It was not the councilman and it was not Tom Waits. I love Brigid, so of course, I had to smile and say, 'Yes, Mrs. Keller, I've heard Tom Waits likes to spend time at St. Bart's.'"

With everyone relatively sober, I reviewed the logistics for Sunday's Eagles game. Ray, who mastered the perfect ice-salt-and-water ratio for icing the keg, would pick up the beer, and Brendan, who worked at Greenberg's Deli, would bring the hoagies. I reminded everyone to be on time—the bus would pick us up at 10:00 a.m. at the rec center.

I also slipped in a mention that the local band Scooby Dudes was playing at Towey's bar tomorrow night if anyone was interested. I wondered aloud if there would be any surprise guests, and all eyes went to a suddenly shy Jack. He knew a guy, and the last time they played, he surprised us, ending up on stage singing lead on the Chumbawamba song with the "I get knocked down, but I get up again" lyrics. Everyone in the crowd had gone nuts, cheering and singing. Schedules were tight on Friday nights, but I got three takers, plus Jack, who was a maybe.

Vizzie brought pitchers of beer to the table, and the conversations and laughs continued. I would have been fine if the night never ended. At the far end of the table, Dez and Matt drank a round of shots. Jack joined them, another hit to his take-it-easy plan, but he was young, and it was that kind of night.

Danny, next to me, tore the label off his Miller Lite and said in a low voice, "Jack say why he's all dressed up?"

"No. He said he was downtown," I said. "Maybe checking out venues for your bachelor party?" Danny and his fiancée, Megan McFadden, were planning a spring wedding and Jack was the best man.

"That'd be cool. Megan's worried that he's unreliable. He's been on a couple of benders recently. Drinking legally is still new to him. You know what that's like."

Megan was alright, but she was a bit of a drama queen. I looked over at Jack, who'd wrapped his tie around his head pirate-style.

I said, "She's overreacting. He'll do fine. I've got his back."

The Phillies lost, and the evening news show, delayed by the game, finally aired, leading with the church scandal. Every seat in McRyan's had a view of a large screen television, and the room quieted with territorial interest.

After a warning to viewers about the sexual nature of the story, the anchorman reported, "The District Attorney's office has announced a new investigation of a Northeast Philadelphia parish priest for the alleged sexual assault of a child. The DA's office is not releasing specifics at this time, except to say that the claim is within the statute of limitations and that the priest has been active in the community for some time. The DA is asking that anyone with any information to please call their 1-800 number. There will be a more detailed statement next week."

Discussion ran the gamut.

"Why'd they lead with this and not even say what parish it is?"

"It's the cool thing in some circles to beat up on the church."

"Ever notice that they always make the priests out to be the pervs, and those preachers get caught being sleazy all the time."

"At least those preachers get caught with people their own age."

"There's really only a very small number of priests who are freaks."

"One is too many if you're the little kid getting raped."

Matt joked, "Take this bread and eat it, for this is My body . . . literally."

Most laughed, but StevieB put down his half-empty beer and walked out. I hadn't noticed him getting upset. I should have.

We all shouted out a serious chorus of "Come back. Ignore Matt. He's an idiot."

Matt ran to the door and called out to the street after him, "C'mon, man, you know I'm an idiot." He returned to the table shaking his head. Then he called StevieB on his cell and left a one-sided apology. "Ugh, I feel so guilty," he said.

I did too. "You know how he is."

Danny added, "Our uncle's the same way, isn't he, Jack? The church is beautiful and all the priests are holy. He covers his

ears and leaves the room if anyone even hints at the scandal."
Jack nodded with a slight whiskey wobble.

Tugging on the collar of his Oxford shirt, Gav said, "Hey,
I'm with him. I hate to hear the church get trashed."

"StevieB'll get over it," said Ray. "C'mon, let's play some
darts."

Everyone was in. We played Around the World, a perfect
game for a large group after a few beers, as neither the ability to
compute and track scores nor absolute sobriety was required.
To make it interesting, each person either anted up a dollar a
round or folded, and the pot built until someone won.

Each of us brought our own style to the game. Matt took
forever to shoot, Eddie was slam-bam, and both were out after
the first round. Matt acted as a smarmy play-by-play announcer
for the rest of the match. He lamented that he and Eddie were
"forced to be content with the important things in life: good
looks and great wit."

"Speaking of great wit, you know this church thing? Maybe
they missed something last time around. Maybe a bad priest
slipped through the cracks," Eddie said too loudly.

"You're disgusting," I said. "I'm disgusting?" he asked. "It's
what the priest did."

"Knock it off, Eddie," said Brendan.

"What? StevieB's not here." Eddie rolled his eyes. "Sor-ree."

My lean-in move failed me in the third round, and Dez's
size, as usual, hurt his finesse, so we both folded. Jack missed
shots too but stayed in the game, despite Terry busting on him
that he was throwing his money away. After that, Jack waved a
dollar in the air like a conductor when he anted up each round.
By the end of the sixth, Ray crossed into the wrong wedge one
too many times and was out, as were Terry and Brendan.

In the final round, three competitors remained: Gav, Danny,

and Jack. Of the three darts each would throw, Gav only needed two to hit, Danny needed three, and Jack needed three plus the others to miss to force another round.

Matt pointed an empty beer bottle at Jack like it was a microphone. "A win looks impossible, young man. What's your strategy against these dart icons?"

The dim bar lights reflected off the sheen on his face. With his tie still knotted around his head, his shirt unbuttoned to mid chest, Jack leaned back in his chair, smiled, and said, "I've got God on my side." Everyone laughed.

"The kid is in it to win it," Matt said, and cheers and hoots erupted.

With his beer bottle mic, Matt reported, "This is it—for the big money." All eyes focused on the shooters. "Danny Cunane, will he, or won't he?"

Danny positioned himself, then threw; two of his darts hit, and the third missed.

"He'll move forward in life, but probably not in this game," said Matt.

Jack was next. We all rooted for the crazy knucklehead; stranger things had happened.

"Will this young upstart show us how it's done?" Matt asked.

I did a drum roll on the tabletop as Jack took aim—one, two, three perfect shots! The crowd went nuts, and Vizzie had to tell us to keep it down. Then Gav took the line, and two shots later won it all. It was a huge letdown, but we all congratulated him. Jack stared at the board with a numbed frozen look like he really believed there would have been a different outcome.

Matt said, "Shake it off, Jack. You're a true Philadelphia sports fan. You never gave up."

After darts, there was a consensus that we needed to order

food. I got my usual: hot roast beef sandwich with horseradish and a side of fries. Conversation meandered from CYO, the Eagles, next year's Phillies' prospects, and then eventually back to the clergy abuse story.

"The church has had issues, but they've made changes," I said. "The fact that they mentioned the statute of limitations must mean that it's old news. When the archdiocese got investigated that last time, Father Farrell said that the victims were a pretty screwed-up lot—might not even be a real thing."

"Hey, I did a rotation in the psych ward back in nursing school. Just because someone's messed up doesn't mean they're lying," said Matt.

"What I don't get," said Danny, "is why those victims don't report it right away?" There were murmurs of assent. He added, "By not saying anything, they're letting more kids get raped."

"That's not fair. Don't blame the victim," said Ray.

"Well, one good thing is we know it isn't Father Farrell," Brendan said.

Danny said, "Yeah, the guy works like eighteen-hour days. He doesn't have the time."

Father Farrell was always helping someone in the parish. He was at my house plenty over the years. As a kid, he intimidated me with the man-in-black thing—thick black hair, eyebrows, black suit, and seemingly so serious—but then I got to know him. As busy as he was, his door was always open.

Gav pointed a French fry at us. "That's how I would know somebody was full of shit, if they named Father Farrell. You can tell he's all right."

We raised our glasses. "To Father Farrell."

Eventually, folks started finding their way home. It was a great night—all of us together, some drinks, some laughs, some stories, good food. It was ordinary, like so many other nights. And it was our last Wholly Thirsty.

CHAPTER 2

Mr. Helper

Fuzzy-headedness intruded at work the next day—nothing too bad, I'd had worse hangovers—but on Fridays, we unloaded the trucks. Sometimes the warehouse down at the port slipped in a case of something decayed, which was always difficult on shaky mornings.

They did it for fun. I didn't know that when I started as Assistant Produce Manager at the Acme. Too intimidated to complain, I let it slide, until they sent stomach-turning mushy, moldy eggplant that reeked like the leftovers of a missing mobster. I called, all earnest and indignant, while snorts and giggles came through the line, and the voice said, "Tell us what the problem is." The men at the warehouse worked long hours in unheated buildings and took simple pleasure in breaking in newbies. They still sent up a box of something disgusting every once in a while. I only called them on the really foul stuff and thanked them for thinking of me, but not today. If anything whiffed in the slightest, I'd toss it without even looking at it.

Thankfully, they spared me. After unloading the trucks, I posted the receipts into inventory, and then tagged one of the high school kids, who worked stocking shelves, to help me rotate the produce and set up the displays. This was the best part of the job; I was like a coach. I focused on what made the kids tick—were they ambitious, needy, tired, anxious? Nine times out of ten, it was one of those four, and that told me how to manage their work. They cracked me up, more often than not, they constructed a Jenga-like overloaded display of apples or potatoes or whatever, either to save a trip back to the walk-in or because their creativity got the best of them. The other part of my job entailed explaining slip-and-fall lawsuits. The fruits and vegetables changed with the season, but not much else.

This was Mom's dream job for me. I had Dad's same calloused hands, but unlike his construction job, I worked in the neighborhood, indoors, with year-round hours and benefits, plus she liked telling her friends that I was in management.

"It's job security, Tommy," she would say. "People have to eat."

My mom never asked what I wanted to do with my life, but in her defense, I had no clue. I tried community college and finished some general courses but could never decide on a major. My career was something I would have talked about with my dad. I was fourteen when he died. The gaping hole in my life left by his passing swallowed me up any time I ever contemplated career stuff. I remembered him saying that his coaching CYO baseball and basketball was more important than his regular job. That never made any sense to me. CYO was a volunteer gig. I coached, in a way, and at least I got paid for it. Career-wise, it was easier to go with the flow and let the Acme pay my bills.

After work, I swung by Manyon's Beer near Sheffield Avenue. Their employees, mostly gym rats, lifted and moved kegs all day. I chatted with my buddy NoNeck and placed the keg order for Sunday's tailgate. NoNeck mentioned that Jack was his first customer of the day and, already tipsy, had bought two cases.

"Who was he with?"

"By himself, as far as I could tell."

Last night, Jack had mentioned a big job he had to do early this morning. Did he blow it off? Danny would be so pissed.

I pulled out my phone and composed a quick text to Danny: *Jack not working today?* But then I deleted it. Who was I to tattle? Maybe the job got canceled or something. I didn't know everything going on in Jack's life. Still, what was with the drinking so early . . . hair of the dog?

I drove over to Greenberg's Deli and parked my car. I texted Jack, *Saw NoNeck—2 cases? Where's the party?*

Jack texted back immediately, *I was thirsty . . . jk. Private gig. Does she have a name?*

Thanks for always looking out for me, Tommy. You're the best.

That was a polite mind-your-own-business answer. I texted back, *Hey, you're in for Towey's tonight, right?*

Not tonight. Staying home—thx, he responded.

What did he mean by "private gig"? Maybe Jack met someone, friends of those St. Hubert women? If so, he was doing way better than some of us. Sure, Danny and Matt were engaged to their girls, and Gav did okay, and Ray, the forever student, was surrounded by college women, but the rest of us, not so much. Our jobs were not the most exciting or high-paying, and we still lived at home. It was hard to look good on dating sites. Our strategy involved hitting the local bars and clubs where we played the odds that there'd be some friend of a friend who might be dazzled by our charm and good looks. Somehow, we were still unattached.

I texted Jack again. *Lunch tomorrow? Mayfair Diner, maybe 1-ish?*

I waited a bit but got no reply.

Entering Greenberg's Deli, I soaked in the aromas of pickles, fresh rolls, meats, and cheeses. Even though I got an employee discount at the Acme, I still ordered our tailgate sandwich trays from Greenberg's. The food was five-star awesome—great quality and generous portions. Mr. Greenberg, the owner, was the only Jewish person I'd ever known personally. A big man with bright blue eyes, he was part of the neighborhood but also separate. Jews didn't believe in Jesus. Over the years, he'd patiently endured questions from newly confirmed kids whose parents frantically shushed them. Everyone liked him.

Mr. G and Dad liked to talk baseball. They'd discuss the merits of the roster, the latest recruits, and debate the root causes of the Phillies' less-than-stellar record, usually centering on the farm system or the latest manager. Whenever the Phillies made a trade, Dad looked forward to getting Mr. G's take. On the day Dad died, Mr. G delivered trays of sandwiches to the house, at no charge. He sponsored a couple of the CYO teams each year and knew all our names. Brendan had worked for him since high school; Jack worked for him too, for a short while. Mom and I would stop into the deli for dinner sometimes, and Mr. G would notice if I was having a bad day, even if Mom didn't.

Mr. G stood at the red Formica counter manning the register. High school kids hustled in the back to set up for the dinner rush. I couldn't stop thinking about Jack. What the hell was he up to drinking solo before noon?

"Tommy, great to see you, kid. How's your family?"

"The Eagles are playing Dallas, Mr. G."

He stared at me. "I asked how your family is."

"I'm sorry. We're good. Same old, same old."

"Something's on your mind, kid. Have a seat." He pointed to a booth and carried over a cherry Coke for me.

I told Mr. Greenberg that I was worried about Jack. "Who am I to say, but he might have a drinking problem."

Mr. G sighed. "Sometimes it's hard to know how to help a

friend. If you think he's drinking too much, then he probably is. It's pretty bad if he's not showing up for work. There'll be consequences. Let him know that you care about him, that he's a good person."

"He is a good person. I do care about him. We all do."

"He's always seemed to me to be kind of . . . I guess sad is the word." He hesitated. "Maybe he needs to see a professional?"

"I don't know if he's sad. He's just drinking a lot. When you say professional, do you mean a shrink?"

"A counselor, a psychiatrist, psychologist. His issues might not be something you can help with. Some people need an outside opinion."

If I told Jack he needed a shrink, he'd probably deck me. There were no shrinks in our neighborhood. Where would he even find one? Catholics went to priests, not shrinks.

I placed our game-day order and, preoccupied with Jack, headed home.

Later that night, Eddie picked up Brendan, Terry, and me for our big night at Towey's. As we passed the Cunanes' red brick rowhouse, I barked at Eddie to stop. They complained because they wanted to arrive early and get the choice seats at the bar, but I promised I'd be quick.

I ran up the steps to the door and rang the bell. With one hand on her hip, Mrs. Cunane cracked open the door. She scanned me over her shoulder with a look that told her if my socks were clean.

"Tommy, what are you up to? Danny's at Megan's," she said.

"Is Jack here?" I waited, and she opened the door all the way.

"He's in his room." As I stepped into the living room, she asked, "Did you have anything to do with the condition of himself earlier?" She tilted her head toward the upstairs.

"No, ma'am."

Her glare lasered my back as I climbed the steps, walked down the hall, and knocked on Jack's bedroom door. It took a couple minutes before I heard the hardwood floor creak from his footsteps and the light switch click on. Then he slowly opened the door. Jack had the small room. It was furnished with a twin bed, a side table, a small bureau, and a desk. A poster took up most of one wall, the one with that quote that I liked from Bobby Sands, the Irish political prisoner who died on a hunger strike: "They have nothing in their whole imperial arsenal that can break the spirit of one Irishman who doesn't want to be broken."

He peered at me through reddened eyes. His hair stuck out at angles like a punk rocker wannabe, and his clothes were disheveled like he'd passed out in them. He backed away, sat on his bed, and said in a raspy voice, "Yo, Tommy, what are you doing here?"

I leaned against his bureau. "Checking in. How much of that beer is left?"

"All of it." He pointed at the nearly empty fifth of vodka on his desk. "I did some damage to that, though."

Jesus.

Talking to friends about big stuff was easier than talking to family. I mostly ignored my two older sisters and their husbands, who loved telling me how to do life. Still, I chose my words carefully.

"You've been pounding pretty heavy lately," I said. "Everything okay?"

I waited, as he concentrated on smoothing the blanket on

his bed bit by bit. He nodded. A non-answer. I tried selling him on going out with us, but he focused on that blanket like it'd save the world.

"C'mon, it's the Scooby Dudes. They're your guys."

A hint of a grin. He turned me down. I asked about the job. With downcast eyes, he shook his head. "I got fired."

"Damn. That sucks." That explained his going on a bender. "It's just a job though. We'll get you hooked up with something."

He sat stone-faced.

"Drinking's not the best way to deal, you know? I'm worried about you, man," I said. "It might be a good idea to talk to someone. I'm no StevieB, but the church is a good place to get your head together. Maybe you could talk to Father Farrell? Priests are pretty good at helping people."

Jack stared at me and said nothing, like maybe he was considering it, and I left.

––––––––––––

At Towey's, the four of us—me, Terry, Brendan, and Eddie—paid the cover, got our hands stamped, and took seats at the bar with a bird's-eye view of the stage and the dance floor. As the room filled, I spied three women seated at a round pub table talking and checking their phones. They were overdressed: black pants, silky tops, jewelry. My eyes stayed on the redhead with the wild, curly hair and smiling eyes. She must have sensed me staring. She turned toward me and peered through her mass of curls. She turned away fast and then peeked at me and smiled. I held her gaze as long as she let me, and a choir of angels sang in my head.

My friends caught my line of sight, and Terry said, "Those girls are so far out of your league, you'll get shot down on your way over."

Her two friends—oh yeah, they were stunning, model-like. But that redhead? I called dibs.

Terry said, "Are you sure? There's something wrong with her face."

"There's something wrong with your face."

"Oh, come on," he said. "I'm only looking out for you."

Brendan checked her out, rubbed his chin, and said, "I know her. Well, I talked to her. We catered a luncheon for her office. I arranged the menu with her." He remembered that she worked in a medical office building, but not her name or any other details. Still, he offered to introduce me. She had two friends—I needed a third man.

Terry said, "I pass. I'm not getting shot down. I'll sit back and watch you all strike out."

Eddie put his hands on his hips and said, "It's a difficult mission you're asking of me—charming a beautiful woman. I may not be successful, I may not make it back, but I'll do it . . . I'll do it for Tommy." Laughing helped calm my racing heart.

The three of us neared their table. Brendan approached solo and said to the redhead, "I know you from somewhere, but I can't place the name. I catered a work party . . ."

The women disengaged from their phones. Once she and Brendan were chatting, Eddie and I moved closer, and introductions were made. Her name was Eileen Cowan. A nice Irish name. Brendan and Eddie moved around the table and talked with her friends, and I stood next to her.

Eddie asked her friend to dance, but she explained the three were waiting for a limo, due shortly. They were headed to Atlantic City for a weekend bachelorette party.

"You need any dancers for your party?" Eddie asked with a smile. "I'm happy to oblige." He showed them some of his moves.

They laughed. Eileen's cheek crinkled from a small scar. She caught me looking and covered it with her hand. "Car accident," she said and turned away.

I hated that something might have hurt her. "You don't even notice it."

She rolled her eyes. "You sound like my parents." But she removed her hand and grinned.

"So how did Brendan do, catering?" I said.

"Good." She smiled. "Very good. How can you go wrong with Greenberg's, right?" Her eyes met mine and stayed there, never wandering to her phone, her friends, or around the club.

Despite trembling on the inside, I managed to hold up my end of the conversation. "Oh yeah, the food's always great. Mr. Greenberg's a great guy; he's a family friend." Her eyes widened. I added, "Really. I just talked to him a couple hours ago. I'm running an Eagles outing for my friends and placed an order for Sunday. Are you a fan?"

"Love them." She turned in her seat toward me. "You think this is their year?"

"I'm an Eagles fan. I think that every year," I said, laughing. "Why don't you let me find a ticket for you? You can go with us."

"Ugh. I'll still be in AC."

"Maybe the next one?" I asked, and she nodded.

Everything faded into the background: the warm-up DJ and his light show, the drunk girls in the corner singing along to "Play that Funky Music," our friends sitting around the table laughing. There was just her.

I asked, "Is this your first time here?"

She twirled the end of her hair. "Not really . . . I've been here once or twice. My office comes here sometimes on Fridays for happy hour. What brings you here tonight?"

I explained about knowing the band, which I hoped made me sound cool.

And just like that, a wayward dancer tapped the tabletop and sent Eileen's glass of wine into a wobbling dance of its own. It toppled over and the contents spilled toward her. I put both my arms down at the edge of the table in front of her. She jumped from her chair. My shirt sleeves acted as a barrier and a towel, saving her from being drenched. I moved closer, smiled, and said, "Part of the service."

She grabbed some napkins and patted my sleeves, sopping the wine. She held my arm in her hand, pressing it with a bar towel supplied by a busboy. My heart raced. I thanked her, and she thanked me. We gazed into each other's eyes. Electric. I asked her if she might skip the bachelorette party.

She paused. "I can't. It's for my cousin."

I understood, but I was over the moon that she'd even considered it. I picked up her empty glass and pushed through a crush of people at the bar to get her a refill.

The bartender asked about the wine. "A pink one?" I said. He disappeared into a back room and retrieved a dust-covered bottle and made a show of wiping it before twisting its cap. Short on glasses, he had to rinse the one I handed to him. By the time I returned to Eileen's table, she and her friends were putting on their coats.

"I'm sorry, but our limo is here."

"Can I get your number?" I blurted.

Her green eyes sparkled as she said, "I don't really know you. Maybe I'll see you at a Friday happy hour?"

"Okay. It's a date." I beamed. I stood with my beer in one hand and her wine in the other, transfixed, watching her walk to the door. She put her hand on the push-bar, and before she left, she turned back and smiled with her deep dimple.

Eddie came up behind me and imitated baseball's Harry Kalas elongating, "And she struck him out. That girl is . . . outta here."

Maybe, but I had hope. She turned back for that one last look, which meant she liked me. Eddie took the wine from me and offered it to another girl, pretending he'd gotten it just for her, but she was having none of it, so he drank it.

I sat on a barstool and checked social media on my phone for Eileen Cowan, but nothing came up. My friends checked, too, but nobody could find her. Weird.

"She gave you a fake name," Terry said.

We had a connection; there had to be a reasonable explanation. I was an idiot for not asking what parish she was from.

"I'll get her deets from the office," Brendan offered, but that seemed stalker-ish.

Eileen had said that her office sometimes attended Towey's Friday happy hours. If I had to go every week to see her again, I would. If I had the car, I'd have left right then. I met Eileen, and there'd be no topping that. But Eddie drove. Might as well have a good time.

CHAPTER 3

Jack

Early Saturday, Mom knocked on my door, popped her head in, and told me that she needed an escort to Mass. A blinding hatchet-head hangover from last night's beers and Jell-O shots prevented my forming a coherent sentence to ask why. In a floaty, shaky mindset, I stumbled out of bed, dressed, and made it to the kitchen. I sipped the tea she had poured and begged my body not to gag as the hot liquid hit my acidic stomach.

While she waited for me to come to life, Mom rubbed the Miraculous Medal that hung over her cardigan-wrapped turtleneck. In the years since Dad died, she'd adopted a nunnish fashion sense: sensible shoes, ever shorter hair to best control those stubborn grays, and dark clothing to reflect her permanent state of grief. She knew I'd had a late night, but she insisted we walk: "It's too lovely not to, Tommy."

The beauty of the chilly morning's pink sky only amped up my anxious hangover guilt. The rays of the rising October sun hit my eye slits no matter how I angled my head. My punishment for a late night. I was an idiot not to have grabbed a hat or some shades. She spared me any chitchat as we strolled, and I encouraged my stomach contents to stay where they belonged.

Mom attended Mass every morning at St. John's. Most people I knew switched it up. I usually went to the five o'clock Mass on Saturday at our church or slept in and went at noon on Sunday. Worst case, I would drive over to St. Katherine's on Sunday night for Mass with everyone else from Northeast Philadelphia who'd missed earlier services. Not Mom. And she always arrived fifteen minutes early to talk to Dad, who we knew sat up in heaven, maybe not right next to God, but in the general vicinity.

"Thanks for coming with me," Mom said. Roger and Betty Hanlon, our next-door neighbors, usually went with her, but they were down the shore. "I wouldn't have even asked, but Mrs. Keller told me that there's some famous musician on hard times sleeping in the church parking lots. Better safe than sorry," she added.

I clenched my jaw and fake-smiled.

St. John's, built into the side of a small hill, had a retaining wall across the front, and two wide stairways cut into the wall on each end. We climbed the rough-hewn fieldstone stairs to the wide patio-like landing that wrapped around the front of the building. In the middle of the landing, a Sacred Heart of Jesus statue faced the entrance. The statue depicted our Lord in His robes, with His sacred heart exposed, smiling down with His arms extended in a pre-hug pose. Hand chiseled by Italian artisans from white Carrara marble, the six-foot tall Jesus standing on a two-foot-high platform towered over the tallest parishioner and served as a backdrop for special occasion photographs: First Holy Communions, Confirmations, graduations, and weddings.

My beer-battered body had one simple goal: to get Mom into the church and myself home and back into bed. I fast-walked to the closest door and held it open for her, but she wandered over to the Sacred Heart statue where three heavy-set elderly parishioners, all bundled up in full-length coats, stood with their backs to us and their heads bowed in prayer. Mom was chatting.

I usually waited until Mom entered the building, but she usually never dillydallied like this. I mind-messaged her: *Get in the church.* If I went over, I'd have to chat, and I was so tired. I stared at Mom, trying to get her attention, but she wouldn't look in my direction. My head pounded. I felt dizzy.

Looking down, I noticed the soles of a man's sneakers peeking through the gaps between the old people's legs. Jesus, there really was a bum. Mom turned to me, extending her arms to block my view.

Information in my booze-marinated brain processed in slow motion. There was a man kneeling in prayer in front of the statue. Hard on his knees, the hard stone. Blue sweater, jeans, and Converse sneakers. His hair stuck out punk-like. Not praying. Not sleeping. Not some man.

It was Jack.

Jack was . . .

No. No. Please, no.

Jack was dead.

He was kneeling at the foot of the Sacred Heart statue, sitting on his heels. Jack's forehead was pressed against the white statue base, but his head twisted to the side at an odd angle exposing his face, closed eyes, and a crooked grimace. His sleeves were rolled up to reveal a cross sliced deep into each forearm. A blood drenched rosary was wrapped around his hands and bound his fingers together in prayer. Black-red blood pooled around him like a moat and painted the base of the statue with red smears. Next to his right knee lay an old-time straight razor.

"No!" I screamed until I ran out of air.

Mom wrapped her arm around me and pushed me away from the scene.

"Mom! Please . . . make Jack get up. Jack, please!" I held my fist in front of my eyes, then punched my forehead to push away what I had seen.

Mom hugged me and whispered, "Get ahold of yourself, Tommy."

I pulled out my phone and held it at arm's length, handed it to her, and croaked, "Danny."

Mom called him. "It's Jack. It's bad. St. John's. Get here now . . . with your parents."

Time slowed. I grabbed the phone and texted Dez. Impossible to say the words out loud: *Jack dead at SJ.*

People arriving for morning Mass gathered near the body.

Led by the custodian, Father Farrell exited the church. He hurried over to Jack's body and bowed his head for a quick prayer. He then pursed his lips, visibly steeling himself, and asked everyone to step back. He knelt next to Jack, raised his right arm, made the sign of the cross, and blessed him.

The crowd grew. Each new arrival repeated the same devastating words:

"Oh my God."

"It's Jack Cunane."

"He's dead."

Somebody started reciting the Rosary, and the crowd prayed in unison. The volume grew in my ears and in my head. The wail of a police siren pierced the resounding monotone of Hail Marys. My stomach heaved.

Then the Cunanes, with coats pulled over their flannel pajamas, running down the street toward the church, yelled in panicked voices.

"Jack! Where are you, Jack?"

"We're coming, Jack!"

They climbed the steps two at a time in slippered feet. They pushed through the small, numbed crowd to the statue.

Unshaven with bed hair, Danny turned away from the sight of his younger brother and wailed, "No, no, please no."

Unable to look away from their dead son, Colin and Sheila held each other and alternated between keening and sobbing.

My friends appeared one by one. We all stood together on the landing. Each one of us cycled between looking ahead, looking away, trying to look strong, and then covering our faces and losing it.

The crowd continued to grow—old people, kids, neighbors. There were whispers of suicide. Whispers that Jack was mental. Whispers swirled around me, everywhere and nowhere.

Two police cars with lights and sirens pulled up to the curb. Two linebacker-size Black policemen walked up the steps armored with a holster, gun, a taser gun, billy club, flashlight, and pepper spray. At the top of the steps, the crowd quieted and parted a path, and the policemen walked the gauntlet over to Jack. They shook their heads.

The taller officer said, "Aw, son, why'd you have to do that?"

If the cop hadn't been large and armed, any one of the Cunanes might have taken a swing, even Mrs. Cunane, that was the look in their eyes. "That's my Jack! No way he did this," Mr. Cunane said. Then he crumbled and cried.

Danny said, "You can't go by how this looks. Someone did this."

Father Farrell introduced the Cunanes to the policemen. "This is the young man's family."

The policemen exchanged a look, and the one with loose lips said, "I am Officer Williford. This is Officer Carter. We're very sorry for your loss."

Officer Carter took a few steps away from Jack, turned to the crowd, and yelled, "This is a possible crime scene. We need everyone to leave this landing area. If you have information about what happened here or have talked to the young man in the last twenty-four hours, we ask that you move into the church so we can take your statements."

The officers herded folks away from Jack, but only a handful of people left the landing. By now, most of the neighborhood had gathered. Officer Carter repeated the order, but no one moved. He turned and said, "Father?"

Father Farrell bellowed, "The policemen have a job to do. Let's respect their efforts. Everyone needs to get off the landing now."

All of the kids left the landing as soon as Father Farrell spoke, and more adults did too, but there were still hangers-on. Those of us remaining had our eyes on the Cunanes, waiting to take our cue from them. They hurt. We had their back.

Officer Carter spoke again. "A terrible thing happened here. We can tell that this young man was very much loved. There are questions you all have. There are procedures we have to follow. Let us do our job. These folks," he said, pointing to a trio exiting the Medical Examiner's van that had just arrived, "will take care of your friend."

Two men and a woman emerged from the van. They were wearing navy blue windbreakers that said "Medical Examiner" in big gold letters. The woman had a long black braid. She marched up the steps carrying a briefcase. The two men removed a gurney from the back of the van, carried it up the steps, and waited for her direction.

Officer Williford approached her and spoke to her in a low voice. "Parishioners arrived for Mass and found him. The priest called us. Kid's well known. Family says it's murder." She looked at Jack and then at Officer Williford. He shrugged and said, "I know."

The Cunanes held each other so tight that they became one person. Mrs. Cunane, so small and pale, wiped her face with her hands, then glowered at Officer Carter with a mother's fire in her eyes. "I don't want them putting our Jack in one of those bags you see on TV. I'll go get his blanket from home."

Officer Carter took her hand and put his hand on hers and said, "I'm sorry."

She sobbed. The Cunanes remained rooted. Officer Carter tried again to convince them to move.

Mr. Cunane countered, "Officer, I'll wait here with Jack if you'll help Sheila into the church. If you need me to go inside, I will, but send Danny or Sheila to take my place."

Officer Carter repeated, "Y'all need to go into the church."

Mrs. Cunane challenged him. "We have to stay with our Jack." The policeman faced her and said nothing. "Please," she squealed again and again, and then blushed for begging in front of everyone.

Officer Carter put his arm around Mr. and Mrs. Cunane and introduced them to the woman from the medical examiner's office. She was the case manager and spoke in a soft tone, "My team has to recover all of the evidence and we need to work without interference. I promise we will do a complete and thorough investigation. Please go inside. I assure you that we will treat your son as if he were one of our own."

Danny and his parents, with scrunched faces, backed away from Jack, holding him in their view until almost to the church door.

Once the Cunanes were inside, Officer Williford shouted to

those of us milling around, "If you have information for us on their boy, move it." He pointed to the church. "Otherwise, get off this landing or get arrested."

As the landing cleared, the policeman secured the landing with crime scene tape.

With small steps, a procession of folks entered the church through the lobby, including Father Farrell, Mom, and me. We all blessed ourselves with holy water. Father Farrell held Mrs. Cunane's hand and escorted her family to a pew. The rest of us sat in the row behind them.

I wanted to pull out the cushioned kneeler to pray, but I was too wrecked. Jack was gone. How could this happen? Why would he do this? I told him he should talk to someone; maybe that upset him, made him feel like a loser or something.

After only a few minutes, the woman from the medical examiner's office entered the pew in front of the Cunanes and knelt on it facing them. In a quiet voice, she explained that her staff worked closely with the police department. Her team gathered and analyzed the evidence, the police took statements, and any additional investigation depended on those results.

"Grief is a hard thing to get through, even more so with an unexpected death. Our office can recommend grief counselors that can help you. I urge you to call them." She handed them a card. "This is all of our contact information."

"When will we know what happened?" Danny asked.

She explained that the unexpected death of someone young mandated an autopsy. The body would be released in a day or two, but the final autopsy results took six to eight weeks. She said, "I am your liaison to the office. You can contact me at any time with any issue or question. I am so sorry for your loss. If you'll excuse me, I'll get to work. Officers Williford and Carter will take your statements."

The policemen split the interviewing tasks between them, calling us up one by one to the front of the church. Father Farrell and Danny were the first to be interviewed.

Mom sat next to me and held my hand. Danny alternately argued and sobbed, and it killed me. Tears fell from my eyes, and I wiped them away quickly. Mom hated to see me cry. Officer Williford interviewed the Cunanes together. It would have been physically impossible for them to separate. While I waited, my gaze wandered around the interior of our church—the wood-carved Stations of the Cross, the ten-foot crucifix over the altar, and the mural of our Lord emerging from the tomb—images I sought after Dad's death that promised triumph over tragedy. The bright sun shone through stained glass, illuminating the room as if God was reaching out to comfort us.

Mom nudged me. It was my turn.

At the front of the church, I sat across from Officer Carter under the Blessed Mother's watchful eyes. He asked me how long I had known Jack. I told him we lived on the same block. I was six years old when I met Danny and his family. Jack had been learning to walk and liked to hold my hand. I locked down emotions that fought to escape. He asked if anything or anyone had been bothering him. *For Chrissakes, something must have.*

He asked if Jack did drugs, did he have any new friends, any girlfriend or boyfriend issues. I answered all his questions. No drugs, no new friends. I didn't know if he was seeing anyone, but it wouldn't be weird for him to have kept that secret until it was serious.

I realized I was talking fast, so I slowed my speech, but he said, "Keep going." I mentioned Jack's drinking—a little more heavy-handed than usual, but nothing crazy. Jack wasn't an alcoholic. Officer Carter asked specifics about what time I arrived at the church, what I saw, when I last talked to Jack. I mentioned that I'd stopped by his house last night. I asked the policeman if I should have noticed something or said or not said something. He shook his head.

"Your friend died at church," Officer Carter said. "Was he real religious?"

I hesitated and shrugged. It was honest. Jack was an altar boy for a time back in the day like Danny, but he was no StevieB. He didn't go to the Masses I went to, but that didn't mean anything.

At the end of the interviews, we all sat silent in the pews.

Officer Carter addressed everyone and said, "We're very sorry for your loss. You each have our business cards and the contact information for the medical examiner's office. If there's anything you forgot to tell us—anything that we should know— please give us a call."

Officer Williford walked over to Cunanes and put Mrs. Cunane's hand in his. He said in a quiet voice, "Colin, Sheila, Danny, how about you let me drive you home." Danny declined, then hugged his parents and assured them that he wouldn't be long. He gave me a look, and I stayed.

Everyone else left through the side entrance following Danny's parents. Danny and I ran to the lobby and peeked out the window. The team from the medical examiner had already left. Jack was gone.

Danny pressed his cheek and his palms against the glass. "My little bro." He then turned around, slid down the wall, and sat on the floor. He cried. "Tommy, this ain't right. I want my little bro back. I want to take him home."

All the times Danny had been there for me, I tried not to cry, but I failed. I said, "He's home now, Danny. He's home." I squatted next to him and put his hand in mine. Through tears,

I managed, "Let's get some air." With all the strength I had, I pulled my friend to his feet.

All of our friends had waited for us—everyone who was in McRyan's for Wholly Thirsty. Everyone except Jack. They stood on the thin strip of grass that bordered the side of the church. With swollen, blotchy faces, they surrounded Danny and hugged him. Danny blubbered into syllables. We hovered until he had nothing left inside, then in a silent procession, we guided him home.

CHAPTER 4

Mass

I was ten when my Nan, my mom's mom, moved in with us for two months while cancer killed her. I'd come home from school, never knowing if it was a good or bad day, but I tried my best to cheer her up—telling her stories and neat things I learned. Mom usually cut it short, wanting me to go easy on her. After a couple weeks, Nan stayed tired. She would sleep until it was time to wake, then took the medicine that put her back to sleep. I remember asking Dad endless questions about death and crying at night in the dark. Dad reminded me more than once that God sent His only Son to show us there was more than this life, but I still begged God to let Nan stay with us.

One night, Dad and I walked to the rectory after dinner, and he asked Father Farrell to open the church for us. Father greeted us warmly; he was happy to accommodate us, wished more parishioners took their faith as seriously as we did, and I walked taller with a sense of nobility. Coming from our sad home into St. John's, the majestic space, with its hundred-foot ceilings, elaborate stained glass, and statuary, just us two—it was transcendent. We lit candles and prayed a Rosary together in quiet voices, and the repetition of the Hail Marys calmed my Nan-panic. God would take care of her. Afterward, Dad flashed a ten-dollar bill and said that all of my praying warmed Nan's heart so much that she wanted us to have a treat. At the

Ice Cream Shoppe, I got a scoop of vanilla with jimmies and Dad got a black-and-white milkshake. Nan hadn't slipped him any money—she was too sick—but I went with it. My prayers cheered up Nan. I did good.

I was in high school when Dad was diagnosed with cancer. Not one to see a doctor regularly, he was already Stage IV when they found it. I challenged him every day—have a catch with me, shoot hoops with me—and he did, until it hurt too much. It was so unfair. I yelled at God in my prayers. "Why are you doing this?"

Once Dad took to the bed, I stayed away, spending time with friends, at school, or throwing stones in the Delaware River, and always breaking curfew. One night, after creeping up the stairs to my room, I turned to close the door, and there was Dad, shrunken, slouched in my desk chair, waiting. I considered escaping, but he pushed off on the wheeled desk chair and blocked my exit. The effort exhausted him.

"Tommy, if I could fix this, I would. I don't want to leave you. Sometimes, a bad situation, you just have to face it. I only have so much time, and I want to spend it with you."

After that, I sat with him at every chance. He talked to me about how life was short and to make the best of it, how much he loved me, how proud he was of me, and I told him what a great dad he was . . . but mostly he slept. I was so lost, so angry, sad, and helpless. Father Farrell visited often. He talked Mom and me through some serious discussions—always patient, assuring us that we were never imposing.

"Growing up without a dad will be difficult," Father Farrell warned. "I'm always available if you ever need to talk." It was kind of him to offer, but I never took him up on it; I had my friends.

Near the end, Danny coordinated with Ray, Dez, Matt,

Eddie, Brendan, Gav, Terry, and StevieB to come to my house after dinner and then to church to say a Rosary. They showed up and reminded me that I could help Dad—in the best way, with prayers. I loved them all for being there, and especially Danny for arranging it. Afterward, I told them Dad slipped me money to treat them at the Ice Cream Shoppe as thanks because their prayers helped comfort him.

So, I was not surprised when the gang showed up at the Cunanes' house a little after 4:30 p.m. Like most of my friends, I switched up what Mass I went to, but not Danny. On Saturdays, he was Five-O'clock Danny, always. I arrived there first, and the rest arrived soon after with the same unspoken plan to accompany him to Mass. The Cunanes welcomed us into their home. Out of respect, button-downs and khakis replaced the normal casual dress code for Saturday Mass, and none of us wore sneaks. If Danny skipped Mass, it would nag at him, make him feel like he'd forgotten to do something. He didn't need that. Jack needed our prayers, and Danny needed to pray.

The Cunanes' house had the same straight-through layout as every other rowhouse in the neighborhood. A living room opened to a dining room and then the kitchen. The kitchen opened to a small deck that hung over the alley. Bedrooms were upstairs, and the family room, laundry, and one-car garage were basement level.

In the living room, the gilt mirror by the front door had been turned to the wall, and the Belleek mantel clock on the end table had been stopped. Mrs. Cunane was old school, being second generation from Donegal. Jack was not wrapped in white linen lying in the living room with her standing watch, but a window was open somewhere in the house in case his spirit was here and needed to get out.

A sofa and loveseat slip-covered in light brown microfiber

anchored the corner walls of the living room. Mr. and Mrs. Cunane sat on the loveseat, leaving the sofa for guests. Mr. Cunane draped his arm around his wife, keeping them both upright. With faces rubbed and ravaged from crying and shock, they surveyed all of us crowded into the small room, leaning this way and that, like they were still looking for Jack. But there was no Jack. Just us, red-eyed statues, stoic and not so stoic, with only our broken hearts to offer.

Danny thanked us all for coming. His voice cracked as he spoke, but a part of him was somewhere else. "Megan's a wreck. I thought maybe I'd skip Mass today and go with Mom and Dad tomorrow, but you made a special trip and all . . ." Speaking to his huddled parents, he said, "I'll go tomorrow too. I can say some extra prayers for him."

That was Danny, trying his best to bring some light into a dark room.

Mrs. Cunane asked if she could get us anything, and everyone declined. In the quiet, she asked, "Our Jack, he had a good life, didn't he? We gave him a good life, right?"

Through tears, we all gushed yes, that he had had a good life, he had more laughs than most, he had so many friends— almost babbling.

Mrs. Cunane said, "The detectives went through his room looking for evidence. They'll find out who did this thing." She turned to me and said, "Tommy. You stopped by last night to talk to him. What were you up to?"

I was five years old again. "He seemed a little down, so I . . . tried to convince him to go out with us," I stammered.

"You're wrong," she said. "He was happy as ever. Mr. Cunane, Jack, and I had a nice night, didn't we? After you left, we watched *Back to the Future* and ate Entenmann's chocolate cake." Her eyes were fiery. "He wasn't sad at all. I would know. I'm his mother."

"Yes, ma'am," I said. "I was wrong." I would have agreed with her if she said the sky was green.

"Of course you are. I would know," she said.

"We'll have the funeral after the medical examiners complete their work," she said quietly. "There will be a wake, of course."

Mr. Cunane cleared his throat and said, "That policeman asked the Medical Examiner's office to give Jack's autopsy priority. But we told him that they should take their time and get it right. Sheila and I know from watching the TV crime shows that if they rush their investigation, they might miss something important. So, you know, it might be a while."

Danny's head bobbed, agreeing with his dad; he was in denial too. The rest of us nodded slowly so as not to challenge the Cunanes. They would hear the suicide verdict soon enough.

As we walked down the sidewalk, I imagined the eyes of our neighbors peering through lace-curtained windows at us, that we were changed, having been touched by death. We gathered at the midpoint of the retaining wall at the church. The back of the Sacred Heart statue towered above us. Each of us touched the retaining wall and said a quick prayer.

As we turned to go, Danny cried and whispered, "I can't."

We all froze except for Gav, who grabbed Danny by his shoulders and said, "There will be worse things than this. Take one step—one foot in front of the other, and then do it again and again. C'mon, you can do this."

Danny looked to me. Tears rolled down my cheeks. I put my hand on his back and said, "You're not alone, man. We got you.

We'll go to Mass. We'll have a little talk with Jack and the Big Guy, right?" His shoulders slumped, and he let himself be led.

At the top of the steps, the crime scene tape flapped in the breeze and protected the death site like a macabre valet rope, funneling attendees up the side of the building to a rarely used entrance. Passing through the door brought it all back. I wanted to curl up in a pew and cry, but I had to be strong.

Each of us took holy water, blessed ourselves, and followed Danny to the first pew. None of us ever sat in the front row as a rule, but Danny whispered, "I want to make sure God hears our prayers."

Walking up the aisle, friends and neighbors, who likely showed up special for the Mass, blessed themselves, extended their hands to us, and wept. Their anguish and tears hit my heart like hammers. Kneeling, I prayed hard with everything I had. I imagined Jack looking down on us, and I used all my restraint not to call out to him.

I had not anticipated how hard it would be to go to Mass. When Dad died, cancer had ravaged his shriveled body, so I expected death. I hated it, but I wasn't surprised. We said our good-byes, and Father Farrell gave him last rites. The last time that Dad was conscious, he squeezed my hand and said, "It's okay, Tommy. Be a good man. I'll see you on the other side." I was gut-punched, heart-ripped-out devastated. But going to Mass with my friends and family had softened the blow, had helped heal my broken parts, and provided a solace I had never found anywhere else.

But Jack's death . . . was a blindsided attack, no chance to brace for the punch. A fight lost before it began. Everywhere, something or someone reminded me of him, and his death hit me again and again like a merciless boxer. I had wanted to help Jack, tried to. He was hurting, and I told him to talk to Father

Farrell. I should have done more—dragged him there or stayed with him, something. I had to help Danny now, but how? I was a staggering blob myself.

The organ music signaled the start of Mass and everyone stood. As usual, the cantor sang the entrance hymn a few octaves above everyone else, and two altar boys escorted Father Farrell up the center aisle from the lobby to the front of the church. After the priest took his place at the altar, he led the congregation's recitation of the "I Confess to Almighty God" prayer. We confessed our sins in a general way with "Lord have mercy," followed up with "Glory to God in the Highest," and then sat.

In high school, when I grew too quiet after Dad died, Mom would hand me the Bible and tell me to randomly pick a passage. She hoped it might have a message or provide an insight. She did it herself and said it had helped. I teased her by calling it Bible Bingo. I'd grab a candlestick and mimic a bingo caller, saying, "Ladies and gentlemen, we have John 8:32, 8:32 . . . what? What's that? We have a bingo." I made her smile.

In the early days, I was keen on Bible Bingo. Sometimes I read a passage and it was exactly what I needed to hear, like Dad had guided me to the particular passage, or that God was making up for taking Dad away from me. My heart would fill up, but then it would break again if the passage didn't apply. The readings today came from Job 1:6–22 and Luke 9:46–50, and I prayed that they offered us all some kind of lifeline.

In the first reading, God bragged to Satan about how holy Job was. Satan blew Him off, saying Job was only holy because God made his life easy. To prove Satan wrong, God gave Satan power over Job's possessions, and Satan, being a dick, destroyed them all, even his kids. Job reacted by shaving his head and falling to the ground and worshiping God. In the reading from

Luke, the apostles argued about who was the best among them. Jesus sat a child next to Him and said whoever welcomed this child welcomed Jesus and God the Father, and that the least of all of them was the greatest.

I found little comfort in the readings. Terrible things happened under God's watch, no shit, and God loved those with an open heart—people like Jack. So then why? I wanted Father Farrell to put it together for us.

"We had a terrible thing happen here today," he began. "A dear and beloved member of our parish died. In times of tragedy, we look for answers. The easy answer is, of course, that there was an unbalanced mind at work, an embattled soul, but in getting through our own pain, we must look to Scripture to tell us how to deal with tragedy. Job lost everything—everything he loved, everything he owned, and still he praised God. He will always provide for us. When we have troubles, trust God. How do we honor this all-protecting God? Jesus tells us. When His apostles wanted to know who was greatest, Jesus pointed to a child and told them that the one who empties himself of pride and takes the position of a humble servant or a child best serves God. Let us honor God best by serving Him with the humility of a child."

I needed Father's homily to talk to me, to help me, but my attention wandered. Why did Jack do it? Was this some kind of test for us? Would God be disappointed that Jack lacked Job's strength? Should he have trusted God to ease his troubles? I prayed, "God, I will do anything you ask of me. Please welcome Jack. Please help us get through this."

After the readings, everyone professed their faith in the Nicene Creed. Father led the prayer where we petitioned God for the needs of the church, for public authorities, those burdened, and then for the local community, in that order. After each, we responded with "Lord, hear our prayer." For the latter two, we shouted the response a little bit.

The bread and wine were carried up to the altar by Brendan's sister's kids, Timmy and Katie. As they turned to go back to their pew, they spied Danny, their CYO coach for various teams. Katie broke down, crying big, messy sobs; Timmy too. We all lost it. Danny, mid-pew, tried to climb over us to go to them, but Brendan got to them first and walked the kids back to their seats.

We knelt and cry-prayed "Holy, Holy, Holy" and then implored God with the Our Father. For the Sign of Peace, congregants, as a rule, turned to their neighbor and said a variation of "Peace be with you," but not today. People rows behind us and across the aisles walked over to offer peace to Danny and the rest of us. Father Farrell came down from the altar and rigidly gripped our extended hands with both of his. He tilted his head and said, "Peace be with you." It reminded me of the policemen, and how often he must have to comfort devastated parishioners.

After Mass, people crowded Danny in the aisle to offer their sympathies—old schoolmates, neighbors, CYO kids and their parents, men from the Knights of Columbus. Ever polite, he listened to dozens of folks offer their condolences and talk about what a nice young man his brother was. His face whitened. He was bigger than me, and, standing next to him, I worried about catching him if he fainted. I flagged Dez and Terry, who parted the crowd and told everyone that Danny needed air. The crowd moved back, but concern kept them in his vicinity until he left the building.

Outside, we huddled in the early evening sun, too bright on our cried-out eyes. Still worried that Danny might pass out, Dez had him sit on a step and put his head between his knees until his color returned. We walked him home for the second time that day. Gav and Terry helped him negotiate the steps to his front door while Danny, on the edge of tears, repeated, "I'm okay." At the door, he thanked us and invited us back to his house after dinner—the wait for the wake.

CHAPTER 5

The Wait

After dinner, Mom packed up a family-sized Stouffer's lasagna that she had baked, wrapping it first in foil and then a layer of the good tea towels, and cradled it all in a cardboard box for me to carry to the Cunanes' house.

"Anyone there will have eaten already," I said.

"Lasagna is a nice dish for people to pick at. Plus, the Cunanes can reheat it a couple times," she responded.

I lugged the box of lasagna over to Danny's just after 7:30 p.m. Buzzcut Colin, Danny and Jack's older brother, stood at the door, greeting people. Still wearing his dress blues, he had come home on emergency leave from Langley Air Force Base. As I stepped inside, I snuck a quick glance up the steps toward Jack's room, and my insides contracted.

"The boys are in the basement," Buzzcut said. He would call us "the boys" until we were old and gray, and I usually smiled when he said it, but not this time.

Danny's family—aunts and uncles, cousins, and neighbors—crowded the main floor. A hush permeated the house. I imagined the sadness and shock sapped their voices. I dodged old folks and little kids running through open spaces and carried the lasagna box over my head into the kitchen, careful not to step on any toddlers or knock over any canes or walkers. I passed the lasagna off to the neighbor ladies who handled the incoming food. A Greenberg's Deli tray, boxes of butter cookies, tubs of roast beef and gravy, and potato salad tubs were in various phases of being wrapped, stored, or plated. I spied the iced keg sitting on the deck off the kitchen, the one Ray had readied for the Eagles game that we wouldn't be going to tomorrow.

I walked down the steps off the kitchen like I had done thousands of times. At the bottom of the stairs, the family room extended almost the length of the house. An L-shaped black pleather sectional sofa hugged the side wall opposite a large flat-screen TV, and a bar ran the width of the far end of the room. A narrow wooden cocktail table placed in front of the sofa held a pile of coasters from a bar in County Tyrone.

Danny and the others stood. It was a narrow room, so I shook hands with those nearest, and gave the chin to the others. I hugged Megan. Pale and flat without makeup, she carried a box of photos and was headed home to prepare a display for the wake.

After she left, I turned to Danny. "How are you?" I immediately regretted the words. He opened his mouth to speak but closed it quickly to stifle a sob. Eddie pointed to a couple of pitchers on the bar. I filled a red Solo cup and squeezed into a spot on the sofa.

Danny stammered, "We are not sure yet when . . . we can . . . have the funeral."

The word *funeral* reminded everyone that Jack was dead—information that no one wanted to process. If no one talked about it, it had never happened. Everyone studied their beers, and when it got too bad, we gulped them down and refilled them. Sitting there in the quiet, I tried saying an Our Father in my head but wandered off mid-prayer so many times I stopped. The pitchers on the bar emptied regularly, and we took turns carrying them out the back door and up the outside steps to the deck for refills.

An hour or so later, Gav and Terry knocked on the back door with two coolers of iced beer that they set outside in the alley for after the keg kicked. Ray and Matt arrived soon after, and Eddie announced to each arriving party, "No details yet." Sometimes his bluntness was a good thing; it spared everyone from dancing around all the questions that we had. We sat, stared, and gulped. The beer took the edge off the pain.

At some point, Matt asked, "Where's StevieB?"

"St. Dominic's," said Brendan. "He's doing an adoration to pray for Jack."

Danny smiled through watery eyes and asked, "What's that again?" I was unsure myself. Only some parishes offered adoration, and St. John's wasn't one of them.

Brendan explained, "You know how the Eucharist becomes the body of Christ during Mass? They put the Eucharist on display in the monstrance, and people worship it 24/7. It's supposed to be like Jesus being right in the room with you and praying to Him directly."

Danny nodded, not looking at anyone. "That's nice."

"It's a little idol worship-y," countered Eddie. "Seriously, that's the definition of idol worship."

Brendan snapped, "They don't worship the thing; they worship what it stands for."

"Still . . ." he tried again.

Terry gave him the hairy eyeball, tilted his head toward Danny, and said, "Have some respect."

Eddie frowned. He never passed up an opportunity to debate, but one look at Danny and he went mute. Danny's gaze wandered and stopped in a continuous cycle. At one point he rallied and spoke to everyone and no one. "The police were here. Two detectives went through his room, took out a box of papers, notebooks, even his laptop. You know, looking for clues." He hesitated. "They have a tip line. You can call, text, email. It's not specifically for my brother, but the information will get to where it needs to go. Anything can help . . . so we find out . . . what happened."

Sideways glances passed between the rest of us. Danny had seen Jack's cuts and the straight razor.

Gav said, "That's good, Danny. The police will be able to explain everything real soon."

All conversation stopped. That never happened. What was there to talk about? The Eagles? Phillies? Sixers? Flyers? CYO? I tried to think of something to talk about besides Jack, but I thought about him all the more. Last night—his red eyes, punky hair, all that vodka he drank. Jack's last text: *Thanks for always looking out for me, Tommy.* I should have talked to him sooner. Why didn't I?

The deafening quiet stretched on. What could be said that mattered? Nothing mattered. Jack was dead. The little kid who tagged along, always trying to keep up with Danny and the rest of us. One minute he was hanging out, goofing around, and the next . . . our little bro with a big heart, gone.

When Dad died, there were aspects of his dying that always threatened to set me off. Anytime anyone—Mr. Fleury, the neighborhood funeral director, or his men in suits, or family or friends—mentioned words like *burial, grave, coffin, body*, I had to tap every reserve of self-control not to punch them in the face. Images of Dad rotting in a box in the ground destroyed me. I'd kept calm by helping Mom and my sisters deal with making "the arrangements"—calling family and friends, selecting the hymns and readings, running Dad's suit to the cleaners and then to the funeral home, reserving space for the wake and the luncheon, and selecting the menu. With Jack, death images were in my mind but without any distractions.

With so many people in the house upstairs and downstairs, the keg kicked before ten, and we drank the beers from the coolers until they were gone. I was blessed to get drunk enough to stop obsessing about Jack, about why, about God, about what it all meant, about life and death. It was a medicinal load.

No one wanted to burden the Cunanes by passing out in or near their house that night. Around midnight, we all concentrated on standing and walking home upright and intact.

CHAPTER 6

Sunday Painday

On Sunday, there were no calls or texts. Nothing to add to the nothing said last night. A gigantic hangover had descended, and Jack was dead. I'd already been to Mass, so I had no reason to get out of bed and planned to stay there for the rest of the day. I sort of slept, more of a close-my-eyes-and-fight-to-keep-my-thoughts-away kind of rest.

I talked to Jack in my head. *What happened, man? Are you okay? I know you were dodging me; I know it. I shouldn't have let you, even if it meant getting up in your business. I could have talked to Father Farrell for you, got the conversation started. I let you down. I'm sorry.*

Around three in the afternoon, Mom worked hard to convince me to get out of bed. "You can't sleep all day," and, "You need to get moving, Mister," failed to motivate me, but the "Danny might need you" logic got me up. I jumped in the shower and let the hot water cleanse the alcohol that had built up in my pores over the last two days. After I dressed, I stopped in the kitchen, chugged a glass of milk, toasted a cheese sandwich, and managed to swallow a few bites.

Mom bustled around the kitchen intent on sending more food to the Cunanes. Dissuading her required more words than I had. She opened a family-size jar of Ragu, poured it into a big pot, and added a bag of frozen pre-made meatballs. She cooked ziti until the noodles were nice and soft, added them to a disposable aluminum pan, then poured in the sauce and meatballs. She wrapped the tray in foil and placed it into a brand spanking new carryall.

"You already sent them lasagna, Mom."

"You remember how it is, Tommy. They'll have a houseful for a while."

I remembered, but I still had my doubts about the pasta. I made a mental note to pick up some beer from NoNeck.

She handed me the carryall, and I hesitated. If I was honest, I wasn't in any rush to get to Danny's house. The Cunanes were waiting for the body to be released, and their intensity was growing every minute of every hour. I estimated they were at thirty-one hours of waiting, living through each second, pushing through each minute like a marathoner. I'd enter and they'd look to me. They wanted something, and all I had to offer was a pan of ziti and meatballs.

As I walked to Danny's house, I carried the pasta like Mom asked—level, so nothing sloshed over the sides. I kept my eyes on the sidewalk and the satchel, so I missed Mr. Fleury parking his black Cadillac on the street. I was on the third step, vigilant for spillage, when he came up the steps behind me.

Mr. Fleury greeted me without expression and held open the door. Inside, Mr. and Mrs. Cunane, Danny, Buzzcut, and Danny's aunt and uncle sat at the dining room table in silence. I carried in the food and mumbled a "hey," but they ignored me. Their focus was on Mr. Fleury. The wait was over, but their eyes glazed with dread.

I hurried into the kitchen to stash the food and run. It was bad luck not to go out the same door you went in, so after I wedged the food into the overstuffed refrigerator, I had to pass by the dining room again. Mr. Fleury had spread his briefcase contents—funeral planning checklists and catalogues—across the table. His chair blocked the shortest path back to the front door, so I walked around the far end of the table. Danny and I exchanged a look, and I mouthed, "Sorry." As I made my way out of the room, I overheard Mr. Fleury say the words *coffin, burial, plot*. A scream built in my head, and I walked-ran straight to McRyan's. I texted my friends as soon as I got there: *At McRyan's. Fleury is at Danny's.*

I flashed back to Wholly Thirsty, when I'd texted them and traffic was something important. I needed to scream but ordered and tossed back a shot. Over the next hour, except for StevieB, everyone showed up one by one. We sat at the same long table near the dartboard, clutching our beers for comfort and staring at the TV airing the day's football highlights. The Eagles beat the odds and won.

Matt said, "I'd bet anything Jack helped give us that win."

"You know he would," I said.

Stilted conversation wandered between safe subjects—the health of the quarterback, the speed of the cornerbacks, the division rankings, until Eddie asked me what I'd heard at the Cunanes' house.

I surmised that if Mr. Fleury was there, then the Medical Examiner's office had released the body, so they must be done with their investigation.

"Investigation," Gav said with his eyebrows raised. "It was suicide. We all know it."

"It's too much to process. Danny knows it too," I said. And then the floodgates opened.

"He's obviously in denial."

"Seriously, nobody hunted Jack down and sliced him."

"He's following the family's party line is all."

"Everything he thought was one way was something else. He has to wrap his head around it."

"Sooner or later, he'll admit the truth."

Gav reminded us that we had to look after Danny. "He'll blame himself for it, like he failed Jack somehow. That's what happens with suicides. The people left behind are tortured."

"Count me as tortured," I said. "I can't understand why he did it, and why he did it that way."

Terry said, "People do some crazy shit."

"But at church? At the Sacred Heart?" said Brendan. "How will the Cunanes be able to walk past that spot every week?"

"I doubt I can," Matt said, and everyone agreed.

And then, one end of the table was lifted, and beers not held slid and nearly toppled. It was Danny. No one had seen him enter. We all froze.

"You motherfuckers!" He spit out the words through a clenched jaw.

How long had he been there? Jesus.

We all stood. Brendan was closest to him, and Danny shoved him against the table and spilled beers. Gav and Dez grabbed Danny by the arms and told him to calm down. Struggling in their grasp, Danny snapped, "Fuck you. Fuck you all. He isn't even buried and you're trashing him. Some friends!"

Vizzie hustled over and yanked Danny by the collar, and gave him the scary whisper, which calmed him enough for the others to release him from their grip. Ray pulled out a chair for him, and Matt grabbed a beer from Vizzie. Danny sat with his hands clamped on his biceps. We all repeated and retried apologies. The hurt we'd caused sat personified at the table.

"No one was trashing Jack," Matt tried. "We loved him. We're trying to make sense of it."

Gav said, "Sorry, man. What can we do?"

We all leaned forward, focused on Danny, waiting. He sat rigid, but it took more energy to fight than he had.

Brendan gave him an opening. "Tommy says that Fleury was at your house."

Danny stared at me, stuttered to talk, trying hard not to cry. "Tuesday. Mass at ten, Resurrection cemetery. Viewing's tomorrow night, wake right after, here."

"We'll all be there for you, Danny," I said.

His head bobbed, and he stared at the tabletop. Silence at the table. He lifted his gaze, glared at me like a TV cop, and asked, "Tommy, why were you at my house on Friday night?"

All eyes were on me.

"I talked to NoNeck on Friday afternoon. Jack was his first customer and had been drinking. I worried he'd skipped work. I texted him, but he blew me off. I stopped by to check on him."

"You should have called me immediately," Danny snapped.

How could I tell Danny that tattling on Jack had seemed like a betrayal? Maybe I should have told him. "I didn't know anything. I figured if we dragged him out with us to Towey's, maybe he'd open up."

Danny, still not looking at me, said, "Continue."

My mouth was dry even while nursing my beer. "He was recovering from a vodka load, told me he lost his job."

"Wait, he lost his job? Jesus, Tommy. You should have called me," Danny said, not for the last time.

My heart felt heavy, like a lead weight in my chest. The real unspoken question was why Jack had hid it from Danny, but I understood why. I was a younger brother. Jack would never want to disappoint, but I avoided telling Danny that because it would add to the weight of his self-reproach.

Danny continued peppering me with questions. I explained, "I told Jack that he seemed to be drinking a little more than usual. You said it yourself. I said maybe he needed to talk to someone—Mr. Greenberg gave me the idea. I suggested he talk to Father Farrell."

"I don't have a clue what was going on in Jack's life, and you talked to Mr. Greenberg about him? Why didn't you talk to me? You should have told me his world was crashing in. I'm his brother, Tommy. Not you. You fucked up, and Jack's dead."

Anything I said in response would have been hurtful. Danny lived with Jack, saw him every day, picked him up from every drunken load. He knew Jack was troubled.

"I'm sorry. I was trying to help," I said.

"You're sorry, and my brother is dead."

No one came to my defense. It was as if they all blamed me too. Either that or they were relieved that Danny's anger was redirected away from them. He made it sound like it was my fault.

Was it?

Danny looked around the table. "Anyone remember Jack being an altar boy? Do you all remember him serving Mass every week? No? Oh right, Tommy here told Jack that if he didn't want to be an altar boy, he should quit. Maybe you should have kept your big mouth shut."

I swallowed the lump in my throat. "Danny, it was after my dad died. Jack hated being an altar boy."

"Maybe if he stuck with it, went to Mass . . ." Danny paused. "Father Farrell visited us this afternoon. He said that he hadn't seen Jack in a long time. So much for your great advice."

"Look, I only know what he told me Friday night. You can read my texts."

Danny grabbed my phone and scrolled through it. His eyes filled up. He gave me back my phone and stared at his beer.

"Jack should have talked to me, Tommy. You should have told me he needed help."

The crushing weight of guilt . . . it was all I could do to stand. I left McRyan's without saying good night. In the cold moonless night, I wandered home and talked to Jack, saying, "I'm so sorry. I'm so sorry."

CHAPTER 7

Good Night, Dear Jack

I arrived at Fleury's Funeral Home a half hour before the viewing started. Mom had offered to go with me, but this was something I wanted to do alone. The line waiting at the door snaked down and around the block. I stood behind the McFaddens, Megan's parents, who chatted away like we were standing in line for a movie, and I gave the evil eye to the back of their heads. I nodded to friends and neighbors but kept mum and pulled my Jeff cap low on my forehead to hide my leaky eyes. This was Jack's time.

Viewings shredded your insides. I waited to see my friend, but not my friend. I waited to see my friend's corpse. Once the doors opened, the perfume of the flower bouquets pressed against me, the smell of death. I inched forward and talked to Jack in my mind. I told him how much I missed him, how sorry I was for not knowing how to help, how thankful I was to have known him, how mad I was at him, how great he was, how much he had to live for. I talked to Nan and Dad. I asked them to look out for Jack, to show him around heaven and help him settle in. I was overcome by how much I missed them too.

The closer I got, the tighter my muscles constricted. The coffin made it real. I erected internal shields so as not to cry in front of everyone. I kept my head down, eyes on the sand-colored carpet, but Megan's father blabbered on and on. What the fuck was he talking about, a reality TV show? What was wrong with him? Steps away from Jack, he said, "It's hard on our Megan. People keep asking her why he did it. You just pray it doesn't run in the family." Mr. McFadden was a cold, insensitive bastard. I told Jack that he was lucky he was dead or he'd be stuck with horrible in-laws; I hoped he smiled.

And then, I was at the front of the line, and there he was. His eyes closed, his face pale and waxy. Jack but not Jack. He wore a suit and tie and his new tasseled loafers. I knelt at the cushioned kneeler and said some Our Fathers. I begged God, *Please take care of Jack. Please. He's probably so scared.*

Steps away, his red-eyed family: Colin, Sheila, Danny, Megan, Buzzcut, his maternal grandparents, and Colin's family from Boston, dressed in their best. The receiving line was a bizarre practice, both for the family, who had to greet people to thank them for coming, as if this was a party, and for the attendees, who had to express soul-crushing grief in a few quick pleasantries. I was unsure of where I stood with the Cunanes. Danny's earlier questioning and implied accusations haunted me.

I waited rigidly behind the McFaddens. I shook hands with Colin, and we both nodded, no words. I moved to Sheila. I tried to be stoic, but I blubbered, "I'm so sorry." She hugged me and patted my back until I regained control. Danny stood tensed with watery eyes, and we clasped hands. I apologized to him, and he thanked me for trying. The waiting crowd mandated I move down the line. I repeated, "I'm sorry," and, "We'll miss him," and it all seemed so trite and polite.

The room had filled and kept filling. It would be standing room only for the Rosary. Everyone's grief would be pressed up against me. I had to get out of there.

On the street, I sucked in fresh air, then drifted home to

mentally prepare for the wake. My heart sagged in my chest like a wet washcloth, all drippy and formless.

McRyan's closed its doors to the public, but then most of the public was there for the wake. Except for Matt and StevieB, who were coming separately, I met up with my friends on the corner outside the bar. Gav asked whether Danny and I were okay. I hoped so. We all rambled on about the viewing. How the crowd size might have comforted Danny and his family, showing them how much they were loved, but then again, how could anything comfort them? People filed past us into the bar, but we stalled on the sidewalk.

Eddie said it best: "Wakes are a funny thing. You can be overjoyed, celebrating a friend and all the good and funny things about him, and a gut-wrenching minute later you turn around to talk to him and realize he's gone."

We entered the bar with steps slowed by dread. The first barstool held a Kelly-green softball jacket; the white scripted letters on the lapel spelled out "Cunane" and across the back "McRyan's Oddballs." A Guinness, a shot of Jameson, and a votive candle in a jar reserved the barstool for Jack, and Danny's cousins from Boston sat next to it so he wasn't drinking alone. Nearby, three easels stood; each held posters that were covered with pictures of Jack over the years. Megan had done a nice job on the display. There were so many pictures: Jack as a baby, Jack in school, Jack in his Communion suit, Jack with us in a charity Wiffle ball tourney, Jack's graduation, Jack with his relatives, Jack at the shore. There were no pictures of him in front of the Sacred Heart statue. Jack smiled in some of the pictures—not all the pictures, but who did? Was he sad then? When did he get too sad?

McRyan's was filled with all the people Jack met in the course of his too-short life. We worked our way through the crowds, stopping to chat as we went. Matt, his fiancée Brigid Keller, and her mother shared a booth with some neighbors. Mrs. Keller told the story of when Jack was in elementary school and got all serious about Northern Ireland. Instead of collecting money on Halloween for UNICEF, he collected for the Sinn Féin. She said, "He had a heart of gold, that one. So sweet."

Danny, Megan, and his extended family packed a long table across the back wall, and people crowded them, offering hugs and kind words. Danny's parents sat huddled, talking to people in a glazed state.

Eddie saw me looking at them. He said, "They're medicated, Tommy. The doctors give you drugs when there's a sudden death like this. They're numbed." I was glad of it.

On a side wall nearest the bar, a buffet table held Sterno-warmed pots of sliced turkey and roast beef in gravy, large baskets of rolls, and a tray of cheeses and condiments. Baskets of chips and pretzels and small plates of cheddar cubes served with Gulden's mustard and Ritz crackers were dispersed throughout the bar. Some food was necessary for all the drinking that would be done.

Matt worked his way through the crowd and joined us at the bar. We each ordered a shot and a beer. Like everyone else who attended, from a practice started long ago, we pointed to Jack's barstool and offered to buy a drink for "that man at the end." Vizzie took our money and put it into a pot to help the Cunanes defray the cost of the wake. The pot never went to the grieving family directly—that would embarrass them; instead, they received a tiny bill, if one at all. Once our drinks were poured, we raised the shot glass in unison, "To Jack." It was the first of many.

Maybe it was the whiskey or the eerie presence of death, but the traditional Irish music playing in the background shifted and twisted the mood like the waves at the beach. Mom refused to play it at Dad's wake—too many emotions—but not the Cunanes. When "The Rising of the Moon" started, we sang all the verses—a defiant "fuck you" to death.

> There beside the singing river
> that dark mass of men were seen,
> Far above their shining weapons hung
> Their own beloved green.
> Death to every foe and traitor,
> Forward strike the marching tune,
> And hurrah me boys for freedom,
> 'Tis the Rising of the Moon.

We sucked down our beers and ordered another round, except for Matt, who returned to sit with Brigid. That man was in love, serious too, for him to be sitting with her instead of hanging with us.

A round or two later, Buzzcut tapped the microphone. He wore a civilian suit but stood at attention with shoulders back, and his head and neck erect. He said, "My family wants to thank you all for coming tonight, and for all the gifts—food, kind stories, pictures, and the love you have for my brother and our family. I have just a few words about our Jack."

Buzzcut hesitated, reining in his emotions, and the whole room paused in support. "You know, Danny and I hated Jack . . . when he was born. We didn't quite know what to make of the crying, pooping creature who forced us to share a room while he took over the third bedroom. Of course we hated him . . . until we loved him." He paused. "Most mothers will tell you that as much time as a mom spends with her baby, their first word is usually 'Da' or 'Dad.' Jack was no different, but Danny was sure Jack was trying to say 'Dan,' and that's when Jack melted Danny's heart."

Buzzcut gathered himself, then continued, "Jack had trouble with the name Colin. We explained that Dad's name was Colin and I was 'Colin too,' but Jack ended up calling me Too, and that's when he melted my heart."

Some people in the crowd smiled; others wiped away tears.

"That's not to say we were easy on him," Buzzcut said. "Typical older brother stuff. He always fell for the 'tell me something that bothers you, Jack,' which is the absolute worst thing to tell an older brother, but he was always a good sport. If he wasn't, we gave him the traditional older brother advice: Don't be a baby. But I'll tell you, we hardly ever had to say that. He was never whiny, so I'll never believe for a minute that Jack wasn't a strong man."

He took a sip of his beer. "Mom got the job at Nazareth Hospital, and the three of us grew pretty tight. Danny would drag Jack down to the rec center after school, and Jack would watch Danny and the boys play basketball. Jack told me that he was the coolest kid in fourth grade because all the big eighth graders would say hi to him in the school hallways." Buzzcut paused. "Thank you for that, guys.

"I know some of you tried to teach Jack basketball. He may have been a tad lacking in eye-hand coordination, but thank you for all your patience. You were always encouraging. So much so that Jack thought he was pretty good. So many times, he challenged an upperclassman to play one-on-one and expected to win. He'd say, 'I don't know, Too, the game just got away from me. The other fella got lucky.'"

We all laughed, but really . . . Jack was optimistic enough to believe he'd outplay a high school starter. How did he go from that optimism to giving up on life?

"I'd get home from high school and help Danny and Jack with their homework and warm up dinner. Jack used to say, 'Too is the best cook in the whole world.' I never doubted it. Then one day he said it and I caught him winking at Danny, and it shocked me. Maybe my Ellio's Pizza was not the best in the world." He smiled.

"But that was Jack—not a mean bone in his body. I was in Iraq, and he texted me all the time, which was a blessing, because I was homesick as hell. He'd send random photos of the neighborhood, anything Philly really, Wawa's, cheesesteaks, and he always signed off, 'Hurry home, Too.'

"Jack was more special than any of us knew. People keep surprising us with the kind things he did. He shoveled sidewalks in the winter and ran errands for our elderly neighbors and never took a dime. His coworkers told us that whenever Jack met a homeless person on one of their jobs, he'd give away his lunch. Jack would be starving, but he'd say, 'We've got food at home.' You see, he wasn't just my little brother; he was a kind, good man who left us too soon. My family is hurting. You are as well. If you know anything at all that might help us make sense of it all . . ." His voice dropped off, and the room quieted.

With all eyes still on him, Buzzcut continued, "Suicide is never the answer. We've left cards with the suicide prevention hotline at the door. Please take one. You never know, you might be able to help someone or . . ." He bowed his head. "Help another family avoid all this." He clicked off the mic and sat.

Those of us at the bar exchanged a look. The Cunanes were acknowledging that Jack committed suicide.

Brendan whispered, "It's good it's out in the open. Used to have to keep it secret if you wanted a Mass."

Gav talked low. "I deal with grieving people all the time, handing out the death checks. Talking about it means they're moving forward. That's good—healing, getting past it, back to normal."

"Oh, for Chrissakes," Ray said. "He's not even in the ground. Let them grieve as long as they need."

Gav turned away and stared in the opposite direction.

Changing the subject, Dez said, "The last time I was with Jack was right here on Wholly Thirsty, almost the same seat. I can't wrap my head around it. We had some drinks, some laughs. One day, he's here, the next . . ."

Terry said, "I loved him, but to drink like he did, he had to have issues."

"What are you talking about?" Dez asked. "I drank the same as he did."

"But you're a giant—four or five shots fill up your little toe. He wasn't big like you to drink as much as he did. It was a clue and we missed it."

We ordered more drinks. As Vizzie lined them up, StevieB made an appearance. He passed on doing a shot but raised his pint glass for our toast "To Jack." Danny threaded the crowd to where we stood and shook our hands with one-armed hugs. He put an arm around StevieB, froze for a moment, then cocked his head.

StevieB's posture stiffened, and he said, "I'm wearing a cilice. It's not cutting my skin or anything; it's just uncomfortable. It's a way to pray with your body—to atone for our sins."

That was new. Weird, even for him. We were at a wake—it wouldn't be right to call him on it; we just smiled and nodded at our lunatic friend.

The bar was loud and hot, and drinks flowed. At one point, I escaped to the alley out back, and Danny joined me. We leaned against the cool brick wall and gulped in fresh air that was supposed to metabolize the alcohol and enable us to drink more.

"How about StevieB?" I said.

Danny smiled. "Make sure you put some of those hotline cards in his pockets."

"Will do. Um . . . hey, we good?"

He nodded. "We found the beer he got from NoNeck, two cases of Guinness. It was in the trunk of his car with a note that said, 'For the wake.' He'd already decided Friday morning."

"Aw, Jesus."

"I don't know if you remember Sophie McGrath. She's here. Jack fell for her. I guess this was probably around the time when your dad was sick. Her parents were really strict. We all gave Jack advice to prove to the McGraths that he was all right. Ray had him studying for the honor roll. StevieB talked to him about being an altar boy. Terry, Gav, and I worked the sports angle. And then, like overnight, he lost all interest in everything, sat around the house being moody in full-blown teenage doldrums. I blamed the McGraths. He eventually came around, but maybe something was wrong with him, you know? Maybe it was more than puberty."

Almost all my memories from that year had blurred, except for the worst one—Dad dying. If Jack was a moody teenager, I was ten times worse. I said, "Maybe . . . he just never seemed that bad, you know?"

"Sophie told my mother that she loved Jack, always did and always will. Mom cried, but not a sad cry. Sophie talked to him this summer down the shore during Irish weekend. She said he kissed her on the cheek and told her he loved her. She was sure he would call."

"I don't get it."

"Right? There has to be something more to it," he said. "He wouldn't leave us all hanging."

Danny pulled out his phone and texted. He said, "That medical examiner chick said that with suicides, the office takes their cue from the family. Some families are fine not knowing any details. I keep reminding her we want to know everything as soon as they find out."

Back in McRyan's, Danny sat with his family, and I returned to my spot at the bar. Eamon, one of the Boston cousins, took the mic, and sang "Danny Boy." A swell of tears rolled through the crowd. Danny hugged Megan and buried his head in the nape of her neck.

"Oh, Danny boy, the pipes, the pipes are calling . . .
And all my grave will warmer, sweeter be,
For you will bend and tell me that you love me,
And I shall sleep in peace until you come to me."

McRyan's was dead quiet after that. Then Danny rallied and took the mic. His voice quavered. "We can always count on Red Sox fans to kill a mood."

Folks smiled. Danny continued, "I wasn't going to talk. I doubt I can without losing it, which might happen at any minute, so I'll keep this short. My brother, Jack . . ." Tears ran down his cheeks, and he wiped them with his sleeve. "My brother Jack's life was too short . . . but he lived a full life. There were so many stories, funny and heart-warming, told about him tonight. Thank you all."

Danny smiled. "Jack was a goofball with a big heart. I loved him so much." A sob escaped. "I have one of Jack's favorite songs queued up. It's a song my brother Colin and I busted on him to no end for liking, but he insisted on singing it every St. Paddy's Day. You all know the lyrics, so please join in . . ."

There were a couple of minutes of delay that upped the anticipation, everyone curious as to what the song might be. And then it played "The Unicorn."

And we all sang loud, at the top of our lungs, loud enough for heaven to hear.

CHAPTER 8

Final Goodbyes

A blanket of people, wearing shades of gray and black, rippled across the sidewalk, steps, and landing at St. John's for Jack's mid-morning funeral Mass. With the police tape cleared away, gawkers mobbed the Sacred Heart of Jesus statue. I waded solo into the crush of people, focused on the main doors, and cut through the crowd with quick handshakes and nods. Since my sisters, being older, never really knew Jack, at my request, Mom attended with the Hanlons. I kept my distance from her because the last funeral Mass I'd attended was Dad's, and her nearness would have brought it all back. I turned my insides to steel. I wanted to contain myself. No one needed to see me go full-blown wuss.

Inside the church, incense acted like kryptonite. The sharp, spicy scent scraped the inside of my nose, gagged me, and brought back all the grief and anxiety. Everything about this day—every song, every prayer, every respite, every smell— would forever trigger its memory. I spied Mr. Greenberg in the last row and waved, then took a pew with my friends and knelt. *Please God, give us peace.*

At ten o'clock sharp, with bells tolling, Father Farrell in violet taffeta vestments, accompanied by two altar boys, stood at the front of the congregation and gave the "all rise" cue. The altar boys—one carrying the cross and the other holding the incense thurible—led Father down the main aisle, stopping at the midway point. The bells quieted, and Father stood with arms extended, ready to receive the coffin. All the attendees turned toward the back of the church for Jack's reception through the main doors. Hanging on the back wall, the twenty-foot statue of Jesus nailed to the cross scowled in an agony that we all shared.

Danny, Buzzcut, and the Boston cousins surrounded Jack's shiny wooden coffin atop a wheeled bier and pushed it through the main entrance into the silent church. The Cunane brothers in the lead positions stood in front of Father Farrell. Danny, imitating his brother's military stance, stood at attention. There was silence as everyone waited for the priest to begin. The silence stretched on. The brothers cocked their heads toward Father's urgent whispers. Something was wrong. They pushed Jack back out to the lobby where their anxious murmurs echoed, then turned the coffin around and brought it in feet first.

Once the coffin was positioned in the correct manner, Father Farrell welcomed Jack. He dipped the bulbous metal aspergillum into the holy water and sprinkled the coffin. He then covered the coffin with a white shroud, smoothing the edges. Buzzcut laid a crucifix on top of the shroud. Escorted by the altar boys, Father led the pall bearers pushing the coffin and bier to the front of the church and sang, "I am the resurrection and the life; all who believe in me will never die." Father stepped up to the altar, and the Cunanes took their seats in the front pew and left Jack's coffin alone in the aisle lit by a single flickering Paschal candle.

The first reading from Lamentations captured my mood. It began with "My soul is deprived of peace. I have forgotten what happiness is," and ended with "It is good to hope in silence for the saving help of the Lord." The second reading was from Romans about how hope never disappoints. The Gospel of John was the same passage read at Dad's funeral

Mass. "In my Father's house, there are many dwelling places. If there were not, would I have told you that I am going now to prepare a place for you? And if I go and prepare a place for you, I will come back again and take you myself, so that you may be where I am." I always imagined some infinite mansion in the clouds that fit everyone who had ever died. Dad and Nana were healthy and smiling, and now Jack. I tightened up all my muscles to make the tears stop.

Father Farrell said, "As Catholics, we believe that if we follow the Commandments and live in a state of grace, that God may judge us worthy to enter the kingdom of heaven. Some of you are worried about Jack Cunane. Suicide is contrary to the Commandments, but God is all merciful."

The funeral Mass focused on our belief in the resurrection as a way to comfort the grieving, and rarely ever mentioned the person who died. It had been a sore spot for me. I had spent hours working on a eulogy for Dad, but Father nixed it, saying if he let one person do it, he'd have to let everyone. Not everyone was a good public speaker. People presumed their loved ones were in heaven, which was inappropriate. A eulogy in a Mass had to be serious, and people always wanted to slip in funny bits. His mentioning Jack by name in his homily really surprised me, but then this was a unique circumstance.

Father Farrell continued, "Yes, Jack has wronged others. Look at the grief and loss he caused, but he should not be condemned. His mental illness is like any illness. A man is guilty of sin only if he chooses to commit sin of his own free will. The Church recognizes the mental imbalance that exists for someone to commit suicide takes away his culpability. I believe that in Jack's tortured mind, he reached out to Our Lord. Jack believed, as we all do, in the words of today's Gospel that Jesus Christ is the Way. Jesus said He is preparing a place for us in his Father's house, and we believe it. Jack believed it. We must have pity on Jack's embattled soul and trust in God's mercy."

After Communion, Father stood at the bier to perform the absolution and censing. With aspergillum in hand, he sprinkled the holy water on the coffin again and asked that Jack be found worthy to escape avenging judgment. An altar boy handed him the thurible, the pungent pot of burning incense suspended from a chain. Father clanged the pot against the chain several times, swung the thurible over the coffin, and prayed for deliverance. He reminded us that the incense was a symbol of the community's prayers for the deceased rising to the throne of God. The incense, my own kryptonite, threatened. I swayed, blinked, focused, shook my head. Had the ending prayers lasted any longer, they would have been picking me up off the floor.

Once outside, I gulped the autumn air and cleared my head. Gav offered a lift to the cemetery to whoever fit in his car. Terry grabbed shotgun, and I sat in the backseat with StevieB and Brendan. Ours was one of a long line of funeral-flagged cars that wrapped around the block. The procession up Frankford Avenue was the longest I had ever seen.

The usual thirty-minute drive lasted almost an hour and seemed even longer. Stilted conversation in the car covered the usual funeral topics: the turnout , the homily, and the Cunanes' strength in keeping it together. Terry said that people had left flowers and stuffed animals at the Sacred Heart statue. Brendan said people were saying Jack's blood had stained the statue base, that the stains might be permanent. Conversation quieted after that.

At Resurrection Cemetery, the five of us hiked up a headstone-lined trail toward the grave site. A kilted bagpiper in the near distance played "Amazing Grace" while everyone assembled. Sprays of flowers with labels like "Beloved Son,"

"Brother," "Friend," "B-Ball Champ" surrounded Jack's coffin. Gav grinned and admitted that he'd sent that last one.

Father Farrell stood over the casket atop the open grave and spoke, ending with the "ashes to ashes" prayer. The winch lowered the coffin into the earth, and he threw a clump of dirt on it. Colin and Sheila, still holding onto each other, each took a clump of dirt.

Colin said, "He is not lost, our dear Jack. Nor has he traveled far. He's just stepped inside heaven's loveliest room and left the door ajar."

They dropped their dirt onto the coffin, and then the rest of the family did the same, except for Danny. With Megan standing at his side, he squatted, rolled a clump of dirt down the side of the hole, and patted the grassy earth. And then it was over. Most people walked right to their cars and drove off to wait in the line exiting the cemetery. Our group dawdled and stood near a pine tree just off the trail. Danny and his cousin Jimmy, a square-shaped Danny, wandered over to us and thanked us all for coming.

We responded with murmurs of "beautiful service" and "so sorry," except for Eddie, who asked, "Why the hokeypokey with Jack?"

Danny kicked a pinecone. "Ah, only priests go in headfirst. Fleury's man probably told us the right way and we didn't pay attention."

The way death hit families, it was a wonder anyone ever listened to Fleury.

Jimmy said, "Seriously, what's the BFD with your priest? What would it have mattered which way the coffin went in?"

Postures straightened. That was our priest he was talking about. StevieB's face reddened.

Brendan diffused the situation. "Father Farrell's all right,

Jimmy. He probably wanted to do everything perfect, you know, for Jack's sake."

"And what's with no eulogy? I never heard of a priest who forbids eulogies," Jimmy added.

"He talked about Jack," StevieB offered.

"It was a nice homily. As a eulogy, it sucked, man. It was our very last time with him."

I totally agreed with Jimmy, but I defended Father Farrell. Jimmy was an outsider. "It's just his policy. Lots of parishes skip eulogies."

Jimmy raised his eyebrows. "Harsh, man. It's callous."

Jimmy was a Cunane, and cutting him some slack was the right thing to do for everyone except for StevieB, Defender of the Church. "You a Protestant, Jimmy?" StevieB asked.

Dez grabbed Jimmy's forearm, stopping the flying fist aimed straight at StevieB's jaw. Jimmy was strong, but Dez was stronger. Terry stepped forward to help contain Jimmy, and Gav ordered everyone to show some fucking respect.

StevieB gushed apologies. "I'm sorry. I didn't mean anything by it."

Jimmy got a look from Danny and relaxed. Danny said, "Be cool. We're all on edge. Look, we have to get going—the limo is waiting. We're having the luncheon at Kelley's. You're all invited, of course."

We begged off; the luncheon was expensive to host and should be for family.

On the ride home, Terry said, "Jimmy's a Cunane; they're from County Tyrone. You're lucky Dez caught his fist, StevieB, or you'd be sipping your meals through a straw."

StevieB cringed. "The way he criticized and questioned everything, I figured he just didn't know. Really."

"He's from Boston," Gav said. "They've been through a lot with their priests. They give them a short rope up there."

StevieB gazed out the window, misty-eyed. He sat with his arms folded over his stomach and rubbed his shirt over the cilice. I assured him that Danny understood, but he ignored me.

CHAPTER 9

The Why

Danny texted me at work the next day and asked me to keep him company on an airport drive. Buzzcut had a 7:00 pm. flight. We left right after my shift ended. In the car, the three of us discussed safe things: traffic, football, weather. At the drop-off, Danny exited the car and helped his brother unload his single suitcase from the trunk. It had to be hard to have one brother leave for a job where he put his life on the line for his country the day after burying another brother. Buzzcut reminded Danny to call as soon as he had news. The brothers embraced tighter and longer than they would have a week ago. Danny begged, "Hurry home, Too."

Once back on Interstate 95, Danny turned on the news and the broadcast covered the quiet. Near Girard Avenue, an ambulance with a blaring siren raced passed us and acted as a cue; he lowered the volume and told me the woman from the medical examiner's office had called. She wanted to talk to the family, and she was coming to the house tonight.

"That's good, right?"

He shrugged. "I don't know what they can tell us, and after all my calls and texts to her, I'm not sure I want to know anything more. Any reason Jack had to do what he did is a fucked-up reason, and it'll drive me insane if we lost him for something stupid. The whole family . . . it's like we're on a precipice, and any little thing will push us over, but it's worse not knowing.

Thing is . . . the ME chick is bringing someone from the District Attorney's office."

"That sounds like something."

"Right? Mum's the word, though. Could be something, could be nothing."

He dropped me off at home. Mom was out. The house had an uncomfortable quiet to it, and random thoughts kept me edgy. Why did Jack do it? Most people probably considered suicide at one time or another. I did. My sophomore year in high school, I tried out for the school basketball team; all my friends made the cut but not me. Riding home alone on the 88 Bus, some kids from Northeast High beat me up and stole my wallet. That night, swollen, bruised, and heartbroken, I considered it. I just wanted to be with Dad so bad, but he would never want that for me. How cruel it would have been to make my friends and family endure an unnecessary death, when the necessary deaths hurt so much. Suicide was a permanent solution to a temporary problem. Maybe Jack acted too fast, like if he waited, he'd have talked himself out of it. But why was the DA's office coming to see the Cunanes? Maybe Jack did something illegal and was afraid to go to jail, maybe something at work. I really wanted a beer to take the edge off, but I wanted a clear head more. Danny might need my help to deal with whatever.

The phone rang and jarred my solitude. It was Father Farrell. We chitchatted like the old days. If only Jack had met with him . . .

"I have a favor to ask," Father said. "There is quite a pile of gifts left at our Lord's statue in memory of Jack Cunane. Can I ask you to collect them for his family? I'd do it myself, but I'm visiting at the hospital later tonight."

"Absolutely, Father. I'll be right over."

I was reluctant to go anywhere near the statue, but the

chore gave me something to do and an opportunity to help. I assembled some supplies. I brought plastic bags to hold the gifts and a bucket of water for the flowers, and, with extreme anguish, I grabbed a bottle of bleach, a scrub brush, and paper towels in case Brendan's intel about the bloodstains had been correct. Supplies in hand, I headed off to St. John's.

I'd never stood on the landing alone at night. The up-lighting created an expanse of whiteness surrounded by a black moonless night. Stillness. Solitude. The white marble Sacred Heart statue of Jesus looked down at me and seemed almost floating. Except for the pile of offerings, this was how it had looked to Jack last Friday. A chilly breeze rippled the pile, like an exhale, and tickled my neck hairs.

I approached the pile, intending to gather every single memento for the Cunanes. I wanted them to see all the love everyone had for Jack, but I ended up sorting through everything. I tossed the burned-down votives and shriveled flowers. There were so many stuffed animals. How had that become a thing? There were teddy bears wearing Eagles or Phillies uniforms or holding Irish flags, a stuffed Phillie Phanatic, and "You are number #1" foam fingers. There were rosary beads and St. Patrick's Day beads. A flask. A resin angel inscribed "With you always" sat among the piles of flowers, mostly carnations in pink, red, white, and purple. No doubt the florist in the Acme had worked overtime. Some of the bouquets had notes: "Too dearly loved to be forgotten," and, "Always in our Hearts." I gathered up all the flowers that still had shelf life and put them into the bucket of water and put everything else in a bag.

Then I faced the task I dreaded. I peeked at the base of the statue and immediately turned away. I told myself that the discoloration on the pavement and the statue base was dirt. Without looking where I poured, I emptied the bottle of bleach and scrubbed hard at the spots but kept my eyes on the Our Lord to avoid seeing any possible evidence of Jack. The scratching sound of the plastic bristles against the stone bounced off the church walls. I scrubbed until my arms hurt, then wiped all the bleached surfaces with paper towels and threw the scrub brush and towels into the trash without looking at them. If even a microscopic blood cell of Jack's touched any of the things I threw away, I didn't want to know. Stinking of bleach, I carried the bucket of flowers in one hand and the bag of salvaged stuff over my shoulder like a hobo Santa Claus and walked to the Cunanes' house.

Climbing the steps, I peeked through the front window to see if they still had company and only saw Danny and his parents seated in their living room still dressed in the conservative, polished clothes they'd worn to meet their guests. Sheila wore a navy dress with a matching jacket trimmed in gold, and Danny and his dad wore their black funeral suits. I knocked on the door. Sheila and Colin Senior remained unmoved. Danny stared at the door, as if trying to decipher a foreign sound. I knocked again.

Minutes passed until Danny opened the door. I entered, and he stood near the door, staring at the living room, mute. I said a hello and got no response. A tea service that probably spent most of its life in bubble wrap sat on the cocktail table, but the dainty teacups, decorated with peach flowers, held filmy tea and surrounded a plate of cookies still arranged in a perfect daisy. They must have gotten bad news; I needed to scoot.

I dropped the haul and explained, "I was at the church. People left memorials up there. I collected everything for you. I hope that was okay. Father Farrell suggested it."

The Cunanes talked at each other as if I were invisible. Colin yelled, "We have to do something, Sheila. Now."

"Colin, stop it. We've had a shock."

"There has to be a mistake," Danny said. "No way. Not him."

Colin stood and bellowed, "Sheila, Danny, we're going."

"They said to stay away. They'll handle it," Sheila said.

Colin ignored her and strode out of the house, and Sheila and Danny chased after him. They left me standing in their living room with the front door wide open and all the lights on. What the fuck happened here?

I closed their door and followed them up the avenue. They were pulled like a magnet toward St. John's. Sheila's heels hammered the sidewalk. I tailed them to ensure they got where they needed to go. No way they registered anything like stop signs or traffic lights.

I followed them to the rectory and stood on the sidewalk. I assumed they wanted Father Farrell to open the church building so they could pray. The rectory, a large gray building, sat close to the street, so I was able to see and hear everything. Colin banged the knocker on the twelve-foot wooden door.

Father Farrell's cook, Mrs. Gregory, a small, aproned woman of considerable width, opened the door, touched an imaginary loose hair from the tight white bun on top of her head, and said, "He's having his dinner."

"You need to interrupt his dinner," Colin said.

"You'll have to come back at a more convenient time," she replied, assuming a linebacker's stance in front of the half-closed door.

"We need to talk to him *now*," Colin shouted.

Mrs. Gregory hesitated and then disappeared into the house.

Sheila admonished her husband, "Get ahold of yourself. We shouldn't even be here. Let's go."

Minutes later, Father Farrell stood on the threshold. He tilted his head, smiled, and invited the Cunanes in, but they stayed on the stoop. "I'll open the church—you've come to pray?" he asked.

Colin, so ballsy minutes ago, winced. "Father, we met with the medical examiner and an assistant DA tonight." He paused. "The ADA said that Jack . . . filed a complaint against you. That you . . . hurt him when he was an altar boy."

Father Farrell did a double take. "Colin, Sheila, Danny . . . c'mon, we've known each other a long time. You don't believe that."

"Did you do that to my son?"

The priest's eyes softened as he spoke. "Jack had his issues, Colin, you know that. If something like that happened, he would have told you. You know that. He loved you."

The Cunanes hesitated. Colin and Danny took steps down the walkway, but Sheila stayed on the stoop, looking up at Father. It took a minute for her to speak. "Colin asked you a question. Did you abuse my son?"

The question hung in the air.

Jack abused. I froze.

Father crossed his arms and spoke slowly. "Sheila, your boy was sick. If he said these things, it was his mental illness talking. He was disturbed and you missed the signs. Please, don't blame yourself."

"I asked you a question," Sheila said. "I've raised three boys, Father. I know when someone's stalling."

Father Farrell said. "Look me in the eye, Sheila. Do you really think I'd do something like that?"

She remained still and quiet. I was too far to see if Sheila looked him in the eye, but I saw her plant her right high-heeled foot behind her. She shifted her weight and her forearm bent to a right angle. Her fingers and thumb contracted to form a fist.

In a half-second, she answered Father's question with a flying upper right-cross to his mouth. Blood gushed from his face. Colin and Danny flew up the path. Sheila's follow-up left hook missed the now-retreating priest. Father ran into the rectory. The Cunanes chased after him.

What the fuck?

I ran up the walkway and into the rectory lobby. Father had locked himself in the hall powder room. He yelled in a garbled voice to Mrs. Gregory to call 911.

The Cunanes kicked and pounded on the powder room door with their fists and the heels of their hands. They yelled to Father to open it. I grabbed Danny by the arm and tried to pull him away. He pushed me aside like I was air, and I hit the wall hard.

As I rubbed my bruised shoulder, Mrs. Gregory pulled the fire emergency switch. The deafening alarm blasted, and the strobe lights pulsed in the crowded vestibule. The Cunanes continued their attack, immune to the sensory assault.

"Jack wasn't sick. You made him that way. You're the sicko!"

"It should be you in the cemetery!"

"How many others, Father? How many others?"

The shock of it all. I couldn't believe they were talking to Father Farrell this way! It couldn't be true. Something was wrong. Grief sent them over the edge. They were mental. The flashing lights and blaring sirens prevented me from making sense of what was happening, but this was so wrong.

"Stop!" I yelled, but they ignored me. "Please! You have to go. The cops will be here."

Colin's face glistened with sweat. "Good! They can have him after we're done with him."

Danny yelled over the alarms, "We have to get him, Tommy. He hurt Jack. Give me a hand."

I was at a loss for what to do. This had to be some mistake. Not Father Farrell.

Sheila gave the door a hip check that would make any hockey player proud. She yelled, "Come on out, Father. Come look me in the eye. We need to talk." But Sheila did not want to talk.

She yelled to Colin, "Hold my arm!" Then she swung her high-heeled foot at the door, leaving a dent in the heavy oak. She kicked again and the heel broke off her shoe. Danny drove a side-body check at the door, throwing all his weight into it. The force ripped the shoulder of his shirt and suit jacket so that his bare skin showed.

Colin yelled, "I know my boy, Father. I know what you did."

The alarms had roused the neighborhood. A crowd formed but kept a distance, fearing the threat of an actual fire, until Mrs. Gregory yelled out the door that the Cunanes were trying to kill Father Farrell. The mob surged toward the building.

"We'll have a riot," I shouted at the old woman. Then I blocked the door and yelled to the crowd, "It's okay. Everything's fine. It's under control!"

People outside on the lawn leaned this way and that trying to see what was going on. Others peered in the windows. The mob might attack the Cunanes at any minute to defend Father Farrell. I spotted Ray and Dez on the lawn and motioned them inside. Between the three of us, we put our arms around the Cunanes and struggled to hold onto them like they were out-of-control toddlers.

Colin fought us and cried, "You don't know . . . what he did . . . to my boy."

Outside, as the cops and firemen were exiting their vehicles, the neighborhood swarmed the street and rectory lawn.

Ray said, "If he hurt Jack, we'll help you, Colin, but not now. There are too many witnesses."

Seconds later, police and firemen rushed up the walkway as we moved the Cunanes outside where they deflated on the stoop. Dez explained to the firemen about the false alarm.

Father Farrell emerged from the powder room and appeared in front of the throng. His bleeding face produced an audible gasp. He brushed off first aid attempts from the EMTs and held a white towel to his face.

After a hurried conversation with Father Farrell, the policemen handcuffed the Cunanes and marched them through the stunned crowd of friends, neighbors, and fellow parishioners to the waiting police cars. Sheila limped on her broken shoe, holding onto her husband for balance, followed by Danny, whose ripped jacket sleeve bunched around his wrist.

Someone yelled, "Why'd ya do it?"

Colin wept. Sheila, stone-faced, stumbled and two cops had to help her as she crumpled like a rag doll.

"Are they drunk?"

"Jesus, the whole family's fucking nuts."

"What kind of assholes beat up a priest?"

"No wonder the kid killed himself."

A teenager in a St. John's CYO hoodie yelled to Danny, "Coach! What happened?"

Danny, in cuffs, had a faraway look, hardly registering the crowd. In a voice rough around the edges, he answered with the force and stoicism of a referee. "Father Farrell . . . raped my brother."

CHAPTER 10

The Response

I sort of remembered Jack being an altar boy. Dad had been dead a short time. Jack was walking past me on the sidewalk with his cassock on a hanger over his shoulder. I might have asked him how he liked serving Mass to make conversation, not caring about his answer. He'd said that he hated it. Flippant and angry about Dad, I told him that if he hated it so much, he should quit, that life was short, blah, blah, blah. I never asked him why he hated serving. He never said anything about Father Farrell. If he had, I don't know what I would have done. Would I have stood with Jack against the man who had helped my family cope with the darkest hours of my life? Father Farrell rape Jack? It made no sense. There would have been clues. We would have known.

By Thursday morning, everyone in the parish had gotten an email from Father Farrell.

My Beloved Parishioners,

I apologize to those sick and infirm and their families who waited for me to visit last night. I was in the ER following an assault at our rectory. My body will heal, but my heart is broken. A vile accusation has been leveled against me, but I assure you that I am innocent. The allegations come from a disturbed young man and his traumatized family. Sadly, we will never know why the young man made this accusation and why he would want to hurt me and damage the reputation of our parish. I have never in my career been accused of such a thing. I love this parish and hoped to remain your pastor for many years to come. However, rather than being tried on the hill of public opinion, and in keeping with new guidelines, I have called the Archdiocese and requested an immediate investigation. Although it may seem like an inquisition, I ask you to fully cooperate. Until the investigation is complete, I will be suspended and unable to serve as your pastor. These steps are necessary to remove any cloud of suspicion and validate your trust. Have faith. I am innocent and will be cleared of these charges. Thank you for the many beautiful, blessed memories from my time at St John's parish.

Please pray for me during this difficult time, for all priests who are unfairly accused, for the mentally ill, and all true victims of abuse.

Yours in Christ,
Father Farrell

At work, I read and reread the email on my phone. I knew Jack, and I knew Father Farrell, and I had never doubted either, but someone had lied. Zombified by anxiety and shock, I barely functioned. Twice, I screwed up the receipt counts on a truck delivery. Around noon, Danny texted us all, asking that we meet at his house that evening instead of McRyan's. He wrote that it was important to clear the air, answer questions, and share information. His parents had invited our parents and friends and neighbors over too.

I arrived early at the Cunanes' to get the scoop on everything that had happened after the arrest. Danny told me that at the police station that he and his parents had explained about the assistant DA's visit to their house, but the police still put them in a holding cell like they were the criminals. The police called the ADA, who convinced the Archdiocese, who convinced Father Farrell not to press charges. The Cunanes had gotten an earful from the ADA because they had been told to stay away from Father. They were locked up until the wee hours.

Out of earshot of his parents, Danny said, "You know what's worse than being thrown in jail?" I shook my head. He said, "Seeing your mom and dad thrown in jail."

The Cunanes' invitation list must have been large. They'd pushed all the furniture against the walls and placed the kitchen and dining room chairs around the perimeter. Megan moved through the first floor smoothing out the little indentations in the carpet where the furniture had been. Bottled and canned beverages sat in iced coolers on the back deck. Casseroles and cookie trays that had been sent to the family in the previous week sat on the dining room table ready for a crowd.

The Cunanes may have expected a houseful, but many refused or ignored the invitation. Mom was one of them. Outraged at the attack on Father Farrell, she rejected the accusation. *Not our priest.* StevieB too, he texted me: *I'M NOT GOING.* No explanation, but I made a mental note to check in on him.

Plenty of neighbors and friends did show, but the Cunanes needn't have moved the furniture. Most of the attendees mingled, but some kept to themselves, like Gav and Terry, who held up the wall nearest the front door with crossed arms. After a while, the Cunanes gave up looking out the window for more guests.

Colin asked for everyone's attention. There were thirty or forty people there. Some people sat on the steps off the living room or perched on the sofa armrests. Others sat cross-legged on the floor. Those without seats congregated at the living

room-dining room divide. The Cunanes stood together in front
of their audience, shrunken from the events of the past week.

Colin spoke for the family. "Yesterday, Sheila, Danny, and
I met with people from the medical examiner and the District
Attorney's offices. Our Jack had filed a complaint with the DA
accusing Father Farrell of . . . sexual assault." He paused as the
crowd sucked their teeth. "We had no idea—no idea—anything
like that happened to our boy. Kids have their secrets, it's part
of growing up, but . . ." His lower lip curled, and a sob escaped.
"If only he'd told us . . . Last night, we went to the rectory to
talk to Father, and we lost our tempers, and he ended up with
a split lip, and we're sorry for that." He yanked a handkerchief
from his back pocket and wiped tears from his cheek.

"It was a lot more than a split lip," someone muttered.

Sheila spoke up. "Colin asked Father a yes-or-no question:
Did you rape Jack? Three times we asked, and three times
Father ignored the question."

"He said nothing?" asked Dez.

"He went on and on about Jack being depressed."

"But Jack was depressed," said Gav, and he was right.

"Of course he was, after what happened to him." Sheila
glared, and sideways glances moved through the crowd like a
pinball.

Old Mrs. McCullough sat with shoulders pressed against a
straight-back chair, holding a large glass of whiskey, and said
loud enough for the folks in the kitchen to hear, "The first thing
these priests always do is disparage the victim. They almost
never deny the accusation first. I wonder if they want to avoid
the sin of lying, or it's like how politicians never want to say, 'I
am not a crook.' It's predictable, really."

Brendan raised his hand like he was in school and asked,
"What did Jack say happened?"

Colin inhaled. "Jack told the ADA that Father was always pointing out his mistakes as an altar boy: his posture, the way he held the crucifix, his wandering attention, talking to girls too close to the start of Mass. Jack was mortified that he screwed up and was grateful Father offered to meet with him for extra training. They met in the sacristy. Father rewarded him . . . let him have some wine. He was so relieved that Father wasn't disappointed with him." He paused. "The ADA said . . . pedophiles plan; they exploit a kid's anxieties, create opportunities to be alone with them, then introduce drugs or alcohol. Jack believed the wine was drugged. He blacked out . . . he came to while Father Farrell was . . ." Colin gritted his teeth. "That was the last day my son stepped foot in church."

"It explains his whole wine thing," Danny said. "He never drank it. Not a toast at Christmas, not even a glass in front of him at the dinner table. The smell made him sick. He never said why. I just assumed . . . everyone has had a bad night with the grape."

"Did you notice your son not going to Mass?" Brigid's mother asked.

Sheila said, "With our schedules, we never went to Mass together. Of course, I asked which Mass he was attending. He would say things like, 'There's a nine thirty at St. Bernard's,' or 'St. Martin's has a six o'clock.' Jack never lied. He never actually said he went to those Masses. On the holidays, I remember him being sick—always a stomach bug. Then in high school, he volunteered to serve meals at the homeless shelter; he kept it up after he graduated. I wanted us all to be together as a family, but, you know, he was helping the less fortunate . . ."

"Is it possible Jack was mistaken about what happened, like maybe the wine distorted his memory?" Gav asked.

"There was—Jack described the . . . physical damage."

Sheila crumpled and whimpered into her handkerchief; Colin wrapped his arm around her.

Mrs. Payton, the neighborhood crank, sat in a chair with her coat on and her arms crossed, and passed on all offers of food or drink. She was a pointer; she'd uncross her arms and then point to let you know she was saying something. She leaned forward in her seat and pointed at Colin. "What specifically did Jack say Father Farrell did to him?"

Colin, still holding up the distraught Sheila, answered, "We're not going there, Betty." Mrs. Payton resumed her crossed arms.

Dez asked the million-dollar question. "Why didn't Jack ever say anything to anybody?"

"He told the DA that he was embarrassed, assumed no one would believe him," Danny said.

"Why now?" Gav asked.

Sheila hugged Danny and patted his back. Colin answered, "Jack thought he was strong enough to come forward . . . that and . . . the wedding."

Danny's eyes filled, and Megan reached over and grabbed his hand.

Colin swallowed hard. "Jack had done his best to avoid church all this time. To stand at the altar with Danny and Megan across from Father Farrell would take more strength than he had, and he didn't want Father to take that away from him. The very idea of Father Farrell blessing Danny and Megan's wedding was offensive."

"Father requested the investigation," said Matt. "Would he do that if he was guilty?"

"That was all for show," Danny said. "The DA's office notified the church last week about the complaint. They were already taking steps to suspend him."

"That Father Farrell is a real son of bitch, isn't he?" said Mrs. McCullough. "Is he gone for good, then?"

"Officially, they have to complete the investigation first," Danny said.

I'd always known Father Farrell to be a very caring, honorable person, but if he did this thing, he had to go. At the same time, to lose him . . . He'd always been there. Looking around the room at the faces of people, I doubted I was the only one feeling this way.

Eddie asked, "In the news, when other priests got busted, they had history and multiple victims. We'd have heard something, wouldn't we?"

Danny answered, "The ADA told us more about pedophiles than we ever want to know. There's one kind who has an obsessive-compulsive need to abuse. They can't stop themselves. You hear about them the most; they're easy to prosecute—lots of victims, lots of evidence. Then there's what they call an 'opportunist' pedophile. An opportunist preys when a low-risk opportunity presents itself; they're controlled enough to stop if they get spooked. Those are the most difficult cases to prosecute. It's a sociopath's articulate testimony against a traumatized kid. The ADA says Father Farrell is probably an opportunist. Problem is, with Jack's death, she might not get enough evidence to prosecute."

Terry said, "So you're saying that maybe Father Farrell had an opportunity and took advantage of Jack, that maybe he never did it before, and maybe never would do it again. That's a lot of maybes. If nobody else comes forward, if there's no other proof, how can you be absolutely sure Father is guilty?"

Dead silence. Danny glanced my way like I should say something, but, shocked and confused, I sat mute.

Colin waited for someone else to take on Terry, but no one

did. Finally, he said, "I asked the ADA whether she believed Jack. She said that assessing someone's truthfulness is not an exact science but that she believed him. Some of his behavior over the years was classic"—he lowered his voice—"rape trauma syndrome."

Sheila closed her eyes and bowed her head. Colin hugged her, and she relaxed.

"Why wasn't Father Farrell locked up as soon as Jack filed the complaint?" Dez asked.

"The ADA needed more evidence. The testifying and the scrutiny would have been hard on Jack. He recalled details, but with the wine he drank and the passage of time, some details were fuzzy. Victims disassociate during the attacks too. Who wouldn't try to block out an assault while it is happening, right? Defense attorneys know that happens and question a victim's credibility if he forgets the smallest detail, like a calendar date or the color of a floor tile. The ADA hoped to identify other victims to take the weight off Jack."

More silence. The room held former altar boys and parents of current and former altar boys. The accusation had to make them and everyone else reconsider past Father Farrell interactions and invitations. I did too.

Brendan asked, "If Jack filed his complaint and he was so worried about Father Farrell being a pedophile . . . why did he do what he did? Why . . . why not stick around?"

Through tears, Colin said, "We'll never know what was going on in Jack's head. The ADA said living with abuse sometimes overwhelms victims. They feel alone and anxious all the time. The nightmare of the assault replays in their head, the crushing panic of confronting the abusers in public . . ." He cleared his throat. "Kids carry an extreme fear that they won't be believed. Sometimes what they imagine is so much worse than what would ever happen. What he did—his suicide—it's common for people who went through what he did. They're looking for peace."

"The news story on TV last week about the priest in a Northeast parish . . . was that about Father Farrell?" Gav asked.

Colin nodded. "The ADA released that story hoping to encourage other victims to come forward. As of yesterday, none had."

The news story we saw in McRyan's on Wholly Thirsty, the things we said: *The lawyers with their hands out. The media trashing the Church. The screwed-up victims. You'd know they're full of shit if they named Father Farrell.* We told Jack we would never believe anything against our priest. His worst fear came true. Those words must have cut him deeper than his own razor. We were to blame. We killed Jack.

"Look, last night at the rectory, we know we overreacted, but we want to do the right thing," said Danny. "With Jack gone, the ADA won't move forward without additional evidence. You all knew my brother. He would never lie about something so serious. I have a stack of flyers, and I'm asking you all to take some to distribute and post around the neighborhood. We want to encourage anyone with information to contact the DA's office."

Sheila, her face red and blotchy, said, "Even if the abuse is not about Father Farrell, we have to encourage victims to get help so no one else suffers like my son. If we can help someone else, then . . ." She stopped herself.

Danny kept his head down, avoiding eye contact, as he distributed neon-yellow flyers for the DA's Family Violence and Sexual Assault Unit. The flyer read "If you or a child in your care were the victim of an assault or abuse, please contact . . ." More than half the people in attendance, including Gav and Terry, left without taking flyers.

On my way home, I imagined Jack's last night on Earth. Living with his nightmare, I told him to have a talk with Father Farrell! What an asshole I was. *Jack, you should have told me to fuck off.* If only.

As I waited on the corner for a light to change, I spied some of Danny's flyers already tossed into a wire trash can. That fast, people had already abandoned the cause. I took a detour and cut over to Brous Avenue, remembering to check in on StevieB. I rang the doorbell next to the wall niche that held a Blessed Mother statue. It was common knowledge that his parents turned in before prime time, so I was pushing the limits. The lights in the house were dim, but he came outside, and we sat in the white plastic chairs on his porch under a yellow bug light.

"You all right?" I asked. "An all-caps text, blowing off Danny's."

He gripped the arms of the chair and stared out into the street. "I'm fine. How was it?"

"Horrible. The abuse story on the news in McRyan's Wholly Thursday about a Northeast parish—it was Jack. He's the one who'd filed the complaint. You left, but it got really bad. We talked some shit about the whole thing, and Jack was right there. We pushed him over the edge."

He folded his arms. "He had a choice, Tommy."

"He counted on us, idolized us, and we let him down. It's our fault. He said it happened when he was an altar boy. You were an altar boy. Did Father Farrell ever make a move on you? He ever do anything weird?"

"Jack was mental, Tommy."

"You don't believe it happened?"

"In the grand scheme of things, it's not important what any

of us think. I'm more worried what will happen to the parish. Mrs. Gregory told my parents that Father isn't even worried about himself. He says he's been fighting with the Archdiocese to keep us open, and he's afraid they'll use the scandal as a reason to finally close St. John's and merge us with St. Mark's. The Cunanes are out of control. Attacking our priest, throwing dirt, making a scene in front of the whole neighborhood, then talking to everyone about it. Imagine how disgusted and disappointed the Archdiocese must be."

Maybe it was the way that he said it, but StevieB sounded less like himself and more like he was parroting his parents.

In a quiet voice, I said, "It's Father Farrell's fault, though. If he hadn't—"

"When these kinds of accusations go public, people stop going to church, collections dry up. Look at all the Catholic churches that closed already. St. John's could be next."

The possibility of no St. John's . . . that another part of my life would disappear like Dad, and Nan and Jack and even Father Farrell.

"We'll fight a closing if it comes to that," I said. "Our parish is strong. It'll survive. The important thing is to protect the kids from rapists."

His face scrunched like he'd bitten into something nasty.

"Look, it's not a popular topic, but it happens," I said. I showed him the flyers. "The Cunanes printed these. We're hanging them all over. There might be other boys or girls suffering like Jack who need help."

"That's lighting the match and fanning the flame! That's all everyone will be talking about now. Danny's making everything worse." Sweat on his face glistened under the yellow light.

"He's only trying to deal. I'm sure he doesn't know anything about the Archdiocese wanting to close us. You should tell him."

He said, "No . . . no. I'm keeping my distance. I might say something I'll regret. You can talk to him. He'll listen to you." The porch light flicked twice. "I better head in, Tommy—thanks for stopping by."

CHAPTER 11

Aftershocks

I went to work Friday on very little sleep. My mind had jumped all night from sorrow to torment like a flea on a dog. I ran through a whole new set of what-ifs and if-onlys that might have changed what happened. The guilt—Jesus, the guilt—on so many levels. I thanked God that Father Farrell never got me. He was part of my family. People always said that about pedophile priests. Father was part of all my sacraments, my sisters' weddings, the funerals, my graduations. His grinning face was displayed in almost every framed photo on the credenza in our dining room. He had been part of my life almost as long as Dad. Were all his acts of kindness and generosity just a con, tools to ingratiate himself into the lives of families? Was he a psycho—smiling to the public and raping children in private? How could we be so wrong?

An email was forwarded to the parish mid-morning:

His Eminence Cardinal Paul J. Dietrich, Archbishop of Philadelphia, announces the following appointment effective immediately: Father Neil Xavier Lawler, Director of Spiritual Life at the St. Charles Borromeo seminary, is reassigned to pastor for St. John's parish in Northeast Philadelphia.

Father Lawler sent a follow-up email introducing himself. He wrote about growing up in Pittsburgh, his education and past assignments. At St. Charles Borromeo, the sprawling suburban seminary, he helped seminarians develop an intimate and eternal union with the Holy Trinity. He hoped to continue his faith-strengthening work at St. John's. He wrote, "I will not be making any major changes to parish life with one exception. I ask that you recognize the new CYO Board of Directors: Peter Gavin, President; Terrence 'Terry' Joyce, Vice President; Ray Naulty; and Ciaran Mallory."

Ciaran Mallory, father of the superstar Mallory brothers, was replacing Danny on the board. I texted Danny as soon as I read the email. He called minutes later. His voice sounded cried out and heavy. "Tommy. Got your text. They never told me."

After work, I went to McRyan's and grabbed a seat at the empty end of bar, away from the door, away from the old-timers. It was all too much. I wanted to be able to help Danny, to do and say the right thing at the right time, like he'd helped me over the years, but we were in uncharted territory. I rested my elbows on the bar. A lager appeared in front of me. A baseball playoff game was on the tube: the Cardinals and the Angels. I nursed my drink and concentrated on the game to avoid the overwhelming sense of helplessness.

The Cardinals kept the Angels' pitcher working by hitting nearly a dozen foul balls. The Angels would have to go into their bullpen sooner than planned.

By the second inning, Ray, Eddie, and Brendan showed up and sat at the bar with me, followed by Matt and Dez, who stood behind us. All eyes were glued to the game.

Russ Jackson came up to bat. The announcer kept repeating his name. "Jackson this, Jackson that. Funny thing Jackson said in the locker room."

I turned in my seat and said, "Jack."

The walls that we had put in place to concentrate on the game crumbled and a shudder rippled through us.

"I am so sick about Wholly Thirsty," said Matt. "Him being right there. The jokes, like I was so fucking funny."

"I was worse than all of you," said Eddie.

Brendan ran his hand through his hair. "The guilt . . . sometimes, I feel like I can't breathe."

"Danny must blame us, but he said some stuff too." Matt wrapped his arms around his chest.

"You saw him. He's doing his best to hold it together, but he's hanging by a thread," I said. "He and Megan are going out to dinner at Macaroni's tonight. I'm hoping they have a quiet night. He needs it."

Eddie said, "Why didn't Jack just tell us? We would never have said the things we did if we knew he was the guy."

"Oh, so it's okay if it was some unknown guy but not Jack?" said Ray. "Nice. Maybe think before you shoot your mouth off."

Right, like that would ever happen. I offered, "It just never hit home before."

Our attention refocused on the TV screen. The Angels took the field again and brought out an ace who took his warmup throws. The Cardinals manager changed the lineup and put a pinch hitter on deck.

Matt gave the intel report on the new priest from Brigid's sister, whose best friend worked for the Archdiocese. "Father Lawler is very conservative. He spends most of his time at the seminary and only fills in at parishes for short stays. He tends to piss people off."

"He's pissed me off already," I said. "Axing Danny from CYO."

"Danny beat down the door of the rectory," said Ray. "What, you think nothing should happen to him?"

"There were extenuating circumstances."

"Beating down the door." Eddie repeated.

Dez said, "Hey, I'm totally cool with what the Cunanes did."

"Hell yeah," Brendan added. "If I see Father Farrell, I might have a go at him myself."

I had a few ideas of what I'd do too. I'd seen an MMA fighter on TV spit out his mouthpiece after taking a few punches and all his teeth came with it. Father Farrell smiled, all the time knowing Jack was troubled and why. He smiled, consoling us over his bloodied body and at that first Mass and the funeral. His smile should be the first thing to go.

Matt said, "I would have done way worse than the Cunanes, but what did they accomplish? Everybody is so concerned for poor Father Farrell." He exaggerated a pout.

"Well, I'm pissed off at Father Lawler too," said Ray. "I'm on the CYO Board, and you know when I found out about the changes? Same as you—in the email."

"He never told Danny either," I said. It was bullshit.

Eddie said, "Father Lawler is so new. You know he would have had to talk over the CYO decision with Gav."

So Gav knew and never said. It was a dick move on his part not to tell Danny personally. Gav always stopped in McRyan's on Fridays after work to chat up his clients, and it was noted by all that he was MIA. Coward.

The Angels rallied, almost. A sacrifice bunt by the pitcher advanced a man on first to scoring position, but the next batter hit an infield fly and ended the inning.

Our phones beeped simultaneously. Danny had sent out a group text: *A man named Magee, Father Farrell's lawyer, stopped by. Had all the deets from last night. Warned us not to diss Father or he'll sue for slander. Be careful what you say.*

We all shook our heads in dismay.

Eddie asked, "Seriously Father Farrell, how low can you go?"

I texted back a reply-all: *Who told him?*

Danny responded with: *Not important. Tell everyone. Don't want anyone getting sued.*

Eddie scanned the bar. "What do you want to bet Gav and Terry ran straight to the rectory and told Father everything that was said at the Cunanes'?"

"They didn't take any flyers last night," I said.

Ray sighed. "You don't know it was them. Let's take it down a notch."

It took me a minute. "Fuck," I said. Everyone waited for the explanation. "I stopped by StevieB's last night. He was a no-show. I told him everything the Cunanes told us. I thought he might know something because he was an altar boy. Jesus, he probably told Father Farrell!"

Brendan and Eddie threw rolled-up soggy beer napkins at me.

Dez said, "Tommy, you win the prize. You are the weakest link. You're surprised the guy who would bathe in holy water if it was an option might run to the priest with everything?"

"C'mon now, no one knows for sure," Ray said.

I told them StevieB's other news. "He told me that Mrs. Gregory is saying Father Farrell is the only reason the Archdiocese hasn't already closed St. John's. StevieB's really pissed off at Danny, says they'll close us for sure after all the stuff with Jack and the rectory fight and without Father in our corner."

"Seriously? No way!"

"They'd never close us!"

"Really?"

And then it got quiet, and all eyes moved to the game.

The pitching duel continued until the Angels' pitcher threw a changeup and the Cardinals' batter took advantage and hit a two-run homer over the left-field wall. The Cardinals took the lead.

I heard him before I saw him. Terry was one of those guys who always had a wad of keys hanging off his belt that jangled when he walked. He had entered the bar, scanned the front barstools, and glanced in the booths, probably looking for Gav. He spotted us and hesitated, but McRyan's was too small for him to ignore us. He strutted over and stood a few feet from where we huddled. He asked after Danny, and only after we told him that Danny was out with Megan did he pull up a seat.

"Some crazy shit at the Cunanes' last night, am I right?"

Everyone leveled a stare at him.

"You don't believe it, do you? The whole story is bullshit. Father Farrell and Jack . . . and Jack kept quiet all this time?"

We answered unanimously with head nods.

"Jack was delusional. Look what he did to himself!"

"He was devastated. After we all went on and on about how perfect Father Farrell was," said Matt. "Jesus, with everything Father did to him, plus all our comments bouncing around in his head, dying was less painful."

"Maybe he listened to us and realized what happens if you go throwing around accusations. I'm just not buying the whole Father-Farrell-was-an-opportunist thing," Terry said. "What if you were accused of rape by somebody who had trouble holding a job, and he was so mental that he cut crosses into his arms, and it's your word against the kid's—who should I believe?"

"But it's not just anybody, it's Jack!" I said.

"What if no one else comes forward and it comes down to he said, he said. If there's no way to prove one way or the other, no one knows what happened. What are you going to do? What good did Jack's complaint do? Just splits everybody up."

Matt said, "Maybe there's a kid not getting raped today, Terry. That's a good thing."

Terry rose and his bar stool almost toppled. "You people are morons. I'm out of here."

The Cardinals won the game and took the lead in the series.

After the game, we went our separate ways. On the way home, I swung by Greenberg's and ordered a tuna hoagie to-go. Mr. Greenberg was off; he rarely worked Friday nights. I was kind of glad, otherwise I'd be tempted to talk about Jack and Father Farrell, and it'd be like spilling family secrets, or airing our dirty laundry. Waiting for my sandwich, I thought about my last chat with Mr. Greenberg. I wished I'd listened to his advice; he was spot-on. If only I'd suggested a therapist to Jack instead of a priest . . .

My sandwich was ready; my mouth watered from the aroma of onions and oregano, but Gav entered the shop just as I was about to leave.

"Yo, Gav."

His head turned fast. "Tommy," he said and shook my hand. "Some wildness at the rectory the other night. I hear Father Farrell might lose a tooth."

He mentioned the scene at the rectory, but nothing about last night at the Cunanes'. I waited for him as he placed his order, and we left together, walking down Frankford Avenue, where the always-bright streetlights gave the illusion of daytime. I focused on the sidewalk as I strolled.

"Missed you at McRyan's tonight. Terry was looking for you."

"I've been swamped," he said.

"Big changes in the CYO."

"Danny made his bed, Tommy."

"Finding out in an email, though."

Gav stopped. "So, what, is everyone pissed off at me? I've spent every spare minute I've had reorganizing everything. Getting Ciaran up to speed, getting all the forms filed, and notifying the teams. If you want me to apologize because I didn't call Danny, you can forget it. He should apologize to me."

"You and Terry left his house in a big hurry the other night. You ignoring what Father did?"

Gav quieted, and we continued down the street. "It's a mess, Tommy. No one knows exactly what happened, including you. People are pissed off at the Cunanes. Father Farrell had to get stitches. My insurance business is all about relationships. I have to stay out of it. They're talking about closing St. John's. That'll kill the neighborhood."

I didn't understand his priorities. Was it just business? Maybe in his mind, he owed the church. His grades at St. John's got him a scholarship to our high school, where his basketball skills got him a full ride to DeSales University. But what did any of that matter? Right was right. We walked in silence until we got to his street.

"I'll try to give Danny a call," he said.

Try? Gav, for a big guy, you are a little man.

A little after eleven that night, Danny sent a text to everyone: *Engagement's off.*

Reshuffle

I called Danny in the morning to check on him and suggested meeting up at the rec center to shoot some hoops. I reminded him of something he once said to me. "Nothing mends a broken heart, but a good workout distracts."

He thanked me and said that it was a great idea, and I sent out a group text to meet up after lunch. I included everyone. If Gav, Terry and StevieB wanted to be heartless jerk-offs and turn their backs on their friends, that was their choice.

The rec center in our neighborhood encompassed a city block, surrounded by brick rowhouses on all sides. Within that city block, city planners had shoehorned three baseball fields, a playground area, six side-by-side blacktop basketball courts, and a building that housed an indoor gym and meeting rooms. We assembled at our favorite outside court, the one where the wooden team benches had the fewest broken slats, and hung our gym bags, jackets, and towels on the surrounding eight-foot-tall chain-link fence.

Danny was the last to arrive. Ray, Dez, Matt, Eddie, Brendan, and I shot baskets until he showed. He asked if we should wait for anyone else. I shook my head. He sighed and said, "Thanks for this, guys. You know how I zone out on the court. It'll be a nice escape—a good mind-body booster."

Mass was where I went to get grounded, and I asked him if he was going today.

"Yeah, but we'll be going to St. William's from now on. It's easier all around."

A stab of sadness hit me. St. William's was in the Lawncrest section of the city, almost the suburbs. It was good for the Cunanes to avoid the memories St. John's would trigger, but it was a loss for the rest of us.

During stretching and warm-ups, Matt asked what happened with Megan. Danny said, "She needs a break. She says I'm a different person than the man she agreed to marry. She's right. I am. I attacked a priest, was publicly fired from the CYO, and almost arrested. She's embarrassed."

"Yeah, but . . ." I said.

Ray said, "Time heals, man."

Danny shook his head. "It's the right thing. It had crossed my mind. I didn't have the stones. The minute I proposed was the beginning of Jack's end. How could we ever celebrate at our wedding? Every anniversary would be a reminder. I love her, but it had to happen . . . it still hurts." He wiped his face with the bottom of his sweatshirt.

We played three-on-three with one of us rotating to the bench every ten minutes. The staccato of the ball dribbled against the blacktop and the thwack of the ball bouncing off the metal rim provided a beautiful melody to drown out the emotions of the past weeks. Stretching, reaching, passing, shooting. Conversation ceased, and sweat poured in the brisk autumn air, and it was good.

Absorbed by the melody, we all reacted to the discordant bang of the rec center's door. Debbie Clark, the high school girls' CYO coach, stormed out of the indoor gym onto the outdoor courts followed by her ponytailed squad. Debbie took a basketball and threw it with full fury against the blacktop.

The ball bounced higher than the backboards. Some of the girls tried to calm her. "It's okay, Coach. We can play anywhere."

"It's not okay," she yelled. She grabbed a ball and held it on her hip. "Put your sweats on and start running quarter-court drills."

The girls moved immediately to their gym bags. As the team donned their sweats, Debbie spied us. "Danny Cunane!" she shouted, then beelined across the other courts to ours.

All of us inched out of the line of Debbie's fire, except for Dez, who froze. He was madly in like with her. He stood under the basket and smiled a teeth-gritting grin that made him look constipated. He croaked out a loud, "Hi, Deb."

His voice carried across the outdoor courts, pausing the drills by the now-smiling girls. Poor Dez. Debbie answered him with a puzzled look that made it clear she regarded him as a weirdo. Her focus was Danny.

Almost six foot herself, with black curly hair and piercing green eyes, Debbie pointed in Danny's face. "It's your fault! The rec center only assigns the CYO certain blocks of time. I had the indoor court reserved for Saturday afternoons." Pointing to her squad, she added, "We all built our schedule around it, and Ciaran Mallory just bounced us for the boys. He wants my time because he's hired a personal trainer for his sons on Saturday morning. Besides the fact that he's overtraining his kids, it's bullshit! It's like the girls' team is nothing. He's giving us the inside court Saturday mornings or an outside court on Saturday afternoons. I work Saturday mornings; my girls will get sick or pull muscles practicing outside in the cold weather! What the hell?"

"Ray, do you know anything about this?" Danny asked.

Ray, who had ducked down behind me, peeked his head

around. "I'm sorry, Debbie. I challenged them, honest, but I got overruled."

Debbie eyeballed him like she wanted to step on him and scrape him off her shoe.

"What did Gav or Terry say?" Danny asked.

"It's all about taking care of the Mallory boys and what they can do for St. John's and how we're so lucky to have them. It's bullshit. They're two boys who can dribble a ball and shoot a decent three. Neither walk on water. My girls have awesome skills too."

"Did you try Father Lawler?" Danny said.

"He asked me to be nice to Ciaran because he dropped everything and stepped in for you, you son of a bitch. If you hadn't got bounced, I wouldn't have to deal with Ciaran Mallory. I'm teaching these girls to be strong, and now I gotta tell them that the boys' team is more important, that the boys get first dibs."

"That's not true, Debbie, it's a schedule change," said Ray.

"All the boys on the team are getting collared polo shirts with St. John emblems for keepsies. Where's that money coming from? Why aren't the girls getting any polos?"

Ray said that Terry paid for the shirts from his own pocket as a thank-you to the Mallory kids. Debbie glowered like steam would come off her head.

Danny said, "I'm sorry, Debbie. I'd offer to run practices for you, but I'm not allowed. Maybe Dez could lend a hand?"

Dez's eyebrows went to the top of his forehead while his mouth held that weird smile.

Ignoring Dez and the suggestion, Debbie slapped the ball from one hand to the other. "Hey, I am sorry about Jack. He was a good kid. Did you really give Father Farrell a concussion?"

"Split lip, maybe," Danny said.

She rested the ball on her hip, gave him a half-wave, like swatting a fly, and walked back to her team.

After two hours of stress-busting physicality, we called it a day. The surrounding courts cleared about the same time. Father Lawler, the new priest, was saying his first Mass at St. John's at five o'clock, and people wanted to be there to check him out. Even Mom, as dedicated as she was to morning Mass, made an exception. Everyone would be there. Everyone except Danny.

At home, as I dressed, I questioned whether I should have offered to attend Mass at St. William's with Danny and his family. It would have been a nice way to show support. Their first time there, they'd feel so alone and abandoned. Too late now because I promised Mom I'd go with her. When it was time to leave, I had to wait while she fussed with her lipstick in the mirror. She said, "It's a shame that we have to get used to a new priest."

I said, "Well, it'll be nice not to have a pedophile hand out Eucharist."

Things went downhill from there. We left the house and walked to Mass in silence. We sat next to each other in a pew like perfect strangers and waited for the entrance hymn. I would never in a million years admit that she was right, but having a new pastor do the Mass felt like the first time my uncle sat in Dad's seat at the dinner table. St. John's had hosted other priests, but they were visitors. This was different.

And it might have made things easier if Father Lawler's first impression was dynamic or personable, but it wasn't. He was a short, heavy-set man with silver hair. He wore frameless eyeglasses and a strained smile on a pinkish face. His nasally voice screeched at an odd pitch, like Septa bus brakes. He was so unlike tall, thin Father Farrell in appearance and manner, like the difference between a ten-year-old Buick with a wonky starter and a low-mileage BMW.

And his homily! A great Mass was where I experienced that connection to God, to the universe, and I walked a little taller in my shoes for it. This Mass was not even one of the good ones. His homily was the kind that gave little kids nightmares. He kind of frothed at the mouth as he preached—impassioned, almost manic. "The Church is under attack. Satan is real. The Evil One wants to destroy our Church by any means possible. You know it; you've seen it."

He said that the devil sowed confusion and pain, and we needed to rededicate ourselves to our Catholic life and morality. We needed to cultivate an oasis of silence and prayer. I understood why he had so many temporary appointments.

Mom was laser-focused on him and nodded throughout his speech. I was mad that Father Lawler never specified whether the attack by Satan was against the Catholic Church in general or St. John's in particular, nor did he specify how. Some people would believe Satan threatened our church by working through the Cunanes; clearly, it was through Father Farrell. Father Lawler probably left it ambiguous on purpose so as not to piss off anyone on his first day, but a little specificity would have gone a long way for moral clarity.

At the end of Mass, people lined up at the main entrance to introduce themselves. We did, too, but then people said "beautiful service" over and over. I almost laughed, imagining those same folks having to confess that lie. *Bless me Father for I have sinned; I told a lie. I said you gave a beautiful service. It was horrible, and I couldn't wait for it to be over.* I told Mom that I'd catch her later. I left the receiving line and skipped out the side door.

CHAPTER 13

Hanlon's Razor

Long-time friends of my parents, Roger Hanlon and his wife, Betty, had lived next door to us my entire life. Roger worked at Nazareth Hospital, processing work requests for the maintenance department. After a beer, he would tell you about the incorrect paperwork that was submitted, who he had to call to get it right, and what would have happened if he hadn't. Talking to him was not my favorite thing, but he was good to my mother.

After weeks of rumors circulating about St. John's closing, Mr. Hanlon took it upon himself to do something about it. He sent an email announcing a Monday night "Save St. John's" meeting to the dozen or so folks who were on the snow-alert list for the 6:00 a.m. Mass. Mom had listed my email address as backup to hers—the only reason I got a copy. If this was *the* response to the closure, St. John's would soon be one more thing from my life only seen in photos.

I called Mr. Hanlon. "Hey, it's Tommy. I read your email. Organizing the meeting is great and all, but you need to get more people involved. How about I forward your email to some friends of mine and ask them to pass it along? It's all hands on deck, am I right?"

He answered in a dismissive tone, like I was a telemarketer. "Um, thanks, Tommy, but never you mind. We're fine. I called Principal Schmidt to get a meeting room; he was very helpful.

The teachers are worried about their jobs, and the parents are worried about larger class sizes and longer commutes, so we'll be busting at the seams as it is."

If all the parents and professionals from the school were engaged, St. John's had a chance. Still, there was no way I could sit at home on the day of the meeting. I needed to see for myself that the forces were mobilizing. I sent out a group text to let everyone know about the meeting to save the parish, that they had a full house, but I was going and would fill them in. Danny's reply: *You do what you have to.*

Since our disagreements about Jack and Father Farrell, and despite my sisters' calls intervening on her behalf, Mom and I had acted like two ships passing on the steps. On the day of the meeting, I popped into the kitchen as Mom spritzed and shined our appliances, and I lobbed an offer to go with her. With her back turned, she talked to me in the mirrored reflection of the toaster. "Mkay," she mumbled.

We left the house a little while later and walked to the school. The air was frigid, and I pulled my jacket tight. We passed the Cunanes' house. Vandals now hit their house regularly, so every outside light blazed, even those at the surrounding neighbors' houses. Nothing was said until we were down the block. Mom spoke first, "How many times have we done this walk, Tommy?"

"Thousands?"

"I hope there will be thousands more. All that stuff with Jack . . . no matter what, we have to do everything we can to save St. John's, right?"

"Absolutely, Mom," I said. "My whole life happened here."

Her voice broke a little. "I have so many mental pictures of your dad in and around the parish, sometimes I have to stop myself from talking to him." She grabbed hold of my gloved hand and squeezed it. "What will we do if they close us?" I put my arm around her and reassured her as best I could.

As we approached the school, we meshed with the crowd being herded inside and down the stairs to the cafeteria. My hand brushed the thick solid walls, rough with impasto beige paint. Like a seashell, decades of children's voices still reverberated off these walls if you listened.

Inside the cafeteria, a lingering hotdog aroma hung in the air. The room was arranged in four tight rows of five tables. Mom and I sat in the first row at the middle table where Roger and Betty Hanlon were seated. Their personal office supplies lay strewn across our table: a clipboard, assorted copybooks, yellow legal tablets, and a rubber-banded bunch of pens and stubby pencils. The Hanlons welcomed Mom and said a quiet hello to me. StevieB's parents, the Behans, sat at our table too. They nodded, no handshakes or big hellos, but that was the way they were.

The meeting started late given the large turnout. Mr. Hanlon strutted around the front of the room, beaming. All these people were there to hear him speak. He reminded me of the Grinch, but instead of his heart, his head grew three sizes. He played with the microphone—numerous on-off trials, tap-taps, and test-tests, then introduced himself as Roger M. Hanlon III and talked about how long he had been in the parish and on the staff at Nazareth Hospital.

He said, "Schmitty and I want to thank you all for your show of support tonight." I smiled, as did a few others. Mr. Schmidt hated to be called Schmitty because of the way his students rhymed it.

Mr. Hanlon said, "We've all heard the rumors. The Archdiocese wants to merge us with St. Mark's. Nothing against St. Mark's, but dammit, we can't let that happen!"

The volume of the applause warmed my heart. A team accomplished more than the sum of its individuals. As much as I busted on Mr. Hanlon over the years, I owed him for stepping up to the plate.

A young dad in the audience raised his hand and stood while bouncing an infant on his shoulder. "Do we know for a fact that they are looking to close us? Is it because of Father Farrell?"

Mr. Hanlon said, "They don't close you because an allegation is made. It's more that Father Farrell got suspended at the worst possible time for us. We have no idea of all the politics that goes on in the Archdiocese. He's protected us from all that. He's been working the administrators for a while now, challenging their numbers, schmoozing. He never let up on pushing back. It's important work, otherwise, you wake up one morning and your parish is closed." A soft groan moved through the room. "Without him fighting for us . . ." He shrugged in an exaggerated manner.

The young dad asked, "How long will the investigation take?'

Mr. Schmidt took the mic. He spoke in a slow, practiced manner, as if he were back in the classroom. "The investigation will take as long as it takes. Each investigation is unique. We have to be patient. It's important for all of our sakes that the investigation be thorough and accurate."

"Would it move any faster if we held back our contributions? You know—money talks," an older man asked.

"No, there's no incentive for the Archdiocese to go slow," Mr. Schmidt answered. "Please continue to contribute. Our financial health is critical. And there is good news. As of now, the school's finances are strong. We have one of the largest enrollments. Our facilities are old, but so are most Archdiocesan schools. It makes no sense for them to close us. But Roger is correct: closures happen, so if there are things that we can do to strengthen the parish and the school, we should do them."

Mr. Hanlon reclaimed center stage. "Schmitty and I have sketched out an action plan, but if anyone else has any other ideas"—he pointed with the mic to Mr. Behan—we'll get them all down on paper. We all support St. John's, so let's really show it. I've designed a 'St. John's Parish Proud' lawn sign."

He ruffled through his papers and held up his clipboard with a hand-drawn sign on a piece of loose-leaf paper. "Behan's Printing gave us a very reasonable quote of six dollars per sign. If we all put one on our lawns, the Archdiocese and everyone else will see how dear St. John's is to us all. It'll make them think twice. We can take orders at this table."

He pointed like an airline steward to the table where one of the schoolteachers was holding up an order sheet and a canvas-zippered bag with a big dollar sign on it. He asked for project volunteers. I raised my hand, as did a few others.

Mr. Hanlon continued, "We need every block in the parish to have coverage. If you can afford more than one sign, please do. We really want to blanket the neighborhood so people won't be able to spit without seeing how proud we are of our parish."

Positivity eased my worries. No way they would close us with the neighborhood bursting with support, and maybe our visibly taking a stand for St. John's would help bring us all together. I would order two signs for our lawn.

"Point two, of course, is to keep the parish finances strong. If you are behind in your obligations, you need to pay up. As long as the parish is financially healthy, the Archdiocese has no leg to stand on. If you have any ideas for fundraisers, let us know.

A Casino Night is always successful. If we can get a healthy volunteers list tonight, we can move on that pretty quickly."

Mrs. Behan stood and brandished a legal pad with "Casino Night" in block letters across the top. My name would be first on her list.

"Point three is a GoFundMe to raise three thousand dollars so we can hire a parish advocate. An advocate will represent us, the parishioners, to the Archdiocese. This worked well for the high schools that they wanted to close. We all want to get back to normal. The advocate can let the Archdiocese know what's important to our families and businesses, what we want to see happen."

Mr. Hanlon scanned the room and asked for questions. All around the room, heads bobbed, and I had a whisper of an idea to ask what exactly did we want to see happen, but it really wasn't the time or place. Everyone in the parish wanted a strong St. John's, but did everyone want Father Farrell thrown in jail? Did we all want the Church to make whatever changes were needed to fix its abuse problem? Could we even agree on what those changes were? The meeting had progressed so well. We were all so unified, that was the important thing. If I asked Mr. Hanlon to get into any specifics, my question might derail the meeting, so I sat on my hands.

Neave O'Driscoll, a coworker of mine, accompanied by her two daughters still wearing their St. John's uniforms, raised her hand. "What evidence do they even have against Father Farrell besides—"

Mr. Schmidt jumped up to respond. "I understand your interest in all of this, Neave, but let's wait for the results of the investigation. Anything else borders on gossip."

The crowd murmured, and a few shouted out comments.

"But if Father Farrell wasn't suspended, all this goes away."

"It's only one accusation. What if they put Father Farrell on some kind of restrictions? Then they don't have to suspend him."

"We're the ones who have to suffer."

Jesus. I got that they were afraid for the parish, but seriously. We didn't need Father Farrell to save the day.

Mr. Hanlon hitched his thumb on his belt, sheriff-like, and puffed up his chest with a big inhale. "Schmitty's right. The Archdiocese has their rules, and we have to respect them. Now, I promised not to say anything pending the investigation, but obviously, Neave's not the only one with these kinds of questions. All we hear is gossip. The Archdiocese tells us nothing. I don't know any of the details, but we all know what's going on here. We need to form a subcommittee, maybe with a few senior people, to work with the advocate and look into things ourselves, see what we can find out."

Mr. Schmidt's face crumpled like he'd eaten bad cheese, but the audience applauded the idea. Mr. Hanlon was no Sherlock Holmes. What the hell would his subcommittee do? Look for clues? Do what the DA, the reporters, and the Cunanes hadn't? But, *if* they did find out anything, which I seriously doubted, and everyone had to admit the truth about Father Farrell . . . well, it didn't really matter how we got there.

At the end of the meeting, I walked with Mom into the night air. She had a bounce in her step. She said that she was proud of me for volunteering. We were taking action. It remained to be seen whether any of Mr. Hanlon's ideas would work, but he gave us all a much-needed push. It was a start. We could do this.

Our path home put us on the opposite side of the street so

that we passed in front of Danny's house, which was lit up like a casino.

"As if losing their son wasn't enough, they have to clean up garbage off their lawn every day. So much for loving your neighbor as yourself," I said.

Mom scanned their lawn. "It's wrong, Tommy, it is, but . . ."

I stopped in my tracks and turned toward her. She added, "My heart goes out to them, Tommy, it does, but what did they expect?"

It escaped no one that at every opportunity, at the end of Mass, in casual conversation, at school functions, Father Lawler with his crooked smile assured everyone that there was no basis for concern about the future of the St. John parish. Sometimes, when he repeated that St. John's was safe, a nervous laugh escaped from him; sometimes, he said St. John's was safe even when no one asked. The more times Father Lawler said not to be concerned, the more people talked about the possibility, and the more doubt and panic crept into conversations. On the street, people from the neighborhood carried an anxious look like an anvil might fall out of the sky.

Mr. Hanlon tagged me as the lead volunteer for the sign project and grumbled at me to "make it happen." After organizing so many outings for my friends, this was a piece of cake. I broke out the list of parishioners who had ordered signs, grouped them by street, and assigned volunteers. Mr. Behan rushed the job and the whole order was ready the next day. I picked them up right away and distributed them to the volunteers. The gray signs with maroon letters started popping up two days after the meeting. Many lawns, like ours, had multiple signs and distracted from those houses with none. It was be-yoo-ti-ful. This was Mr. Hanlon's project, but I implemented it. I owned it. I had an *S* on my chest, but only for a day or two.

The morning after I distributed all the signs, I walked past the Cunanes' house on my way to work. In the early hours, the rising sun competed with the night sky, making it difficult to see clearly, but I spied three signs spread across their front lawn. The Cunanes had never ordered any signs. Not only that, someone defaced the middle one. I moved closer. The middle sign was whitewashed and black letters read: "Father Farrell is Innocent." *Jesus!* I ran onto their lawn and pulled out all three signs. I jumped on them and kicked the shit out of them like a crazed ultimate fighter. I tore at the altered sign, ripping the corrugated plastic until it cut my fingers. What was wrong with people?

The front door opened. Danny said, "What are you doing?"

"People are assholes."

"We were eating breakfast. Dad noticed you freaking out."

Colin joined Danny and they came out to the lawn in undershirts, sweats, and slippers. They saw the signs and read what was written.

"I'm so sorry this happened."

Sheila came outside in her bathrobe, stood on the first step, and said, "The lawn trash was bad enough, then all those damn things showed up all over the place. What is St. John's proud of anyway?"

My face flushed. What had I done? "They're supposed to . . . help save the parish," I stammered.

"That priest raped my son, destroyed his life, and people throw garbage at my house. Is that what you're proud of? It can burn to the ground for all I care."

I wilted under her glare. She stood with her hands on her hips, daring me to respond. Then she sighed and said, "Get in here. You're bleeding. You need some Band-Aids."

Danny and his dad followed me into the house.

All the air had gone out of Colin. He said, "I know you helped with them signs, Tommy. I've seen you putting them up around the neighborhood. You're worried about them closing the parish, I know, but the signs make us feel like the whole world is against us. They're everywhere reminding us again and again of . . . everything. Each of us, we all have a cross to bear, but . . . we're just regular people. We don't have His strength."

I arrived for work guilt-ridden and edgy. I headed to the breakroom and poured a cup of coffee with my bandaged hand. Someone left a copy of the *Northeast Times* in the breakroom on the table. I grabbed the sports section, and Terry's big head was plastered above the fold. The headline read: "Will This Be St. John's Year?"

In the photo, Terry wore his big-boy clothes: sports coat, shirt, tie, and even a tie pin. The article quoted him saying, "The St. John's basketball team will dominate. This year, we're fortunate to have Liam and Lucas Mallory, who are absolute phenoms at point guard. They have great ball-handling skills, an outside shot, great feints. They're focused and keep the other kids on the team in-line. I can't say enough about them."

He omitted any mention of the girls' team, but the reporter

noted that the St. John's team led by Debbie Clark would be one of the city's top contenders.

Before Jack's death, we would have been all over Terry with texts flying and joke emails and mock interviews to bust on him. Now, he was just somebody that we used to know. I took out a pen and drew dark sunglasses over his eyes.

CHAPTER 14

Danny's Out

Since his breakup with Megan, Danny had thrown himself into his accounting coursework and his part-time job at the IRS but, even so, we spent more time with him. Never in McRyan's, though. If we hung out with him, it was always at his house. Each of us had claimed our own spot on the sectional sofa in Danny's basement. We watched football, basketball, and hockey games, played video games, or shot darts. Except for the crushing grief and the absence of Gav, Terry, and StevieB, the quiet shenanigans were almost like old times.

During one of our sessions, Brendan suggested that we check out an Irish festival in Bucks County, and we all jumped at the idea of a road trip. He'd attended the festival last year and had a great time: lots of bands, beer, and Irish smiles. This year, one of our favorite bands, the Barleycorn Boys, was playing.

Coordinating everyone's Saturday schedule to include Mass was a complex logistics problem. If an Uber picked us up at 5:45 from St. John's after Mass, we'd just catch the Barleycorn Boys, who went on stage at 6:30 p.m., but Danny went to St. William's, which was the same distance to the festival but thirty-five minutes west of St. John's. If our Uber had to swing by St. William's to pick him up, we'd miss most of the show. Between family obligations, errands, or work, the rest of us had a hard time getting to St. John's on time, let alone all go to St. William's for their five o'clock Mass.

Ray suggested to Danny, "Go to Mass on Sunday or maybe skip it this week?"

"No, you know we'll be hungover on Sunday. Mass is important. It's where I talk to Jack and pray for him. I like to do it with a clear head. It's all I can do for him now."

I understood. I went to Mass every week for Dad for the exact same reason. No way around it. He'd have to travel by himself to the festival. Everyone grumbled; a road trip wasn't a road trip unless we all went together.

"You'll have to go back to St. John's sometime, right?" I asked.

Danny sighed. "It's still the scene of the crime. It's hard enough at St. William's . . . seeing the altar boys holding the chalice, going into the sacristy, looking up to the priest for a cue. I see my brother."

"Don't go there. Don't do that to yourself," Brendan said. "Imagine him up in heaven having a great time, or him looking down on us having a laugh."

All the times that I had been to St. John's, the priests and altar servers celebrating Mass never made me think of Jack or Father Farrell. What happened was an aberration—the exception.

"Look, it's okay. Really. I'll go to St. William's and meet you at the festival."

Dez's concerns went a different way. "You worried someone might give you a hard time at St. John's? You're with us, man. It'll be cool."

"No, it's not that. It's still a church. Nobody'll do anything."

Danny's mind was made up. He had to go to Mass on Saturday at St. William's, and travel alone to the festival. Still, I hated him traveling alone, so I pushed again one more time for him to go with us to St. John's. "We'll enter the side door and sit in the back. You'll hardly see anything going on at the altar."

"No. It's all right. Honest to God. I'll see you there."

We assembled outside of St. John's minutes before Mass started. We were all dressed like it was St. Paddy's Day: fisherman sweaters, Jeff caps, and clothes in shades of green, from lime to Hunter, accented with plaids, harps, and shamrocks.

Eddie said, "Jesus, Dez, if your clothes were any louder, we wouldn't be able to hear the priest."

Laughing, we turned to enter the church, but heard a loud "Yo!" from the sidewalk. It was Danny. He hurried up the steps with his head turned to avoid seeing the Sacred Heart statue. "Was in the library working on a paper," he said. "Lost track of time."

"You okay?" I asked.

"No. No, I'm not."

We huddled and tried to console him. With eyes cast down, he listened to our whispered platitudes as we entered the building as a group, surrounding him; still, he shrunk in on himself, slowing the pace.

Eddie whispered, "Follow the glow off Dez's jacket."

Danny smiled, but we still had to propel him up the aisle.

So much for my plan. The few open seats were toward the front of the church and had an unobstructed view of the altar. The organ music rang out and bounced off the rafters announcing the start of the Mass, and with no options, Brendan hurried into the first open pew, then Danny, me, and Dez. In an almost genius move, Ray and Eddie took the pew in front of us, but being the shortest, they blocked nothing. If we'd arrived earlier, we could have changed seats and put Dez in front, but the cantor was already in the second line of "Alleluia! Sing to Jesus."

Father Lawler paraded up the center aisle to the front of the church escorted by two altar boys. He turned to face the congregation and performed his one-eighty scan and gave the opening prayer; he spied Danny and hesitated mid-arc. The altar boys exchanged an eyebrows up look.

With his head bowed and his eyes closed, Danny was oblivious to the scrutiny from the altar. From far away, he was just another parishioner listening for the voice of God. From far away, his trembling and ashen face were undetectable. I gripped his forearm and asked, "You okay?" but he stayed mum.

As Father Lawler read the General Intercessions, Danny warbled out, "Lord, hear our prayer," like a crying child. We sat for the readings, and he bowed his head and covered his eyes. I put my arm around him and patted his back. Worried, I tapped Brendan and pointed at Danny, but he frowned as if I was overreacting. Dez was hyper-focused on Debbie Clark across the aisle, so he was useless. During the second reading, still with his eyes covered, Danny rocked back and forth so that the wooden pew creaked. Now people near us were staring.

I whispered to him, "It's okay. It's okay."

We stood for the Gospel. Father Lawler read Matthew 23.

"Then Jesus spoke to the crowds and to his disciples, saying, 'The scribes and the Pharisees have taken their seat on the chair of Moses. Therefore, do and observe all things whatsoever they tell you, but do not follow their example. For they preach but they do not practice. They tie up hard-to-carry burdens and lay them on people's shoulders, but they will not lift a finger to move them. All their works are performed to be seen . . . They love places of honor at banquets, seats of honor in synagogues, greetings in marketplaces, and the salutation 'Rabbi.' . . . Call no one on earth your father; you have but one Father in heaven . . . The greatest among you must be your servant. Whoever exalts himself will be humbled; but whoever humbles himself will be exalted.'"

The congregation sat for the homily. From the lectern, Father Lawler eyed our pew. In his bagpipe voice, he said, "The verses tell us that so-called leaders can be selfish, quick-tempered, and not worthy of respect. Now, Jesus isn't saying not to use the term 'Father.' The term is used throughout the Bible referring to biological fathers. Priests are called Father because we give spiritual life. The title 'Father' does not mean priests have the same status as God, of course not. By virtue of the sacrament of Holy Orders, priests are anointed by the Holy Spirit and given a sacred power to act in place of Christ—"

Danny stood, and in a loud, clear voice, called, "That's why these rapes keep happening. We call priests 'Father,' and we pray the Our Father, and they get special orders from the Holy Spirit to be Jesus on Earth, and we give them the houses with the servants. It goes to their head, and the kids . . . they're intimidated and controlled by it all."

An audible gasp escaped from the congregation. I yanked the back of his coat to get him to sit, but he ignored me. What to do? It was like the night at the rectory all over again. He'd make a scene and be all regrets tomorrow. I should never have suggested he come.

Danny gripped the pew in front of us and added, "We need to change. Jesus would want that." He sat.

I snuck a peek at the surrounding pews filled with familiar faces. Some stared while others glowered and sucked their teeth. Megan, on the far side of the church, hid her red face behind a church bulletin. I understood her reaction. People came here to pray; they had stuff going on in their lives and needed peace and healing, and Danny had to start something. Father Lawler was a douche, but it was unfair to give him a hard time. Father

Farrell was the one to blame. On the other hand, Danny had been through so much. People should understand. God would.

Father Lawler gazed down from the lectern and gave a nod to the ushers. He said, "This is a celebration of the Holy Eucharist."

Mass stopped and all eyes followed two elderly ushers in polyester suits, who hurried to the end of our pew, extended a hitchhiker's thumb toward the door, and said, "Let's go."

Oh my God. Kicked out of Mass! All of us sat, red-faced and wooden, like an extension of the pew. It was like we were back in school, and we were the bad kids getting pulled out of First Friday Mass.

"Seriously, you're kicking me out?" Danny asked for all to hear.

"He won't do it again," I said. "He's . . . he's stressed. His brother . . ."

The usher said, "Sorry, son. He can come back if he behaves himself."

Danny frowned and admonished the man, "Only if the priests behave themselves first."

This was our fault. We had pushed Danny to come. I didn't know what to do.

Danny stood, so I turned my legs to let him pass. Dez had to stand and step out of the pew. The ushers, who almost came up to Dez's chest, stared up at him, and one of them said, "Don't give me an excuse."

Danny stood in the aisle, and the ushers grabbed his arms in front of everyone. Danny wriggled free from their grasp. Other men from the congregation jumped from their seats, ready to assist the ushers, but Danny said in a loud voice, "Don't touch me. I'm leaving."

He was making this worse than it had to be. With his head held high, his shoulders back, he marched like a soldier down the center aisle toward the exit, the gigantic crucifix looming above. I wanted to follow him to see if he was okay, but everyone would think I condoned what he did. I was working to save the parish; I wasn't going to storm out of it.

Father Lawler resumed his homily. Ray turned around in his pew and pointed to the exit and lifted his shoulders. Eddie, Brendan, and I shook him off like a pitcher to a catcher, but Dez, in his loud green outfit, gave him the okay, and the two of them stood and strode out in the same slow march down the center aisle just as Danny did. Eddie, Brendan, and I looked at each other in a panic.

Brendan whispered, "If we leave now, the Mass won't count. We'll go after Holy Communion."

He made sense. Danny lost his temper was all. It was understandable.

During the Collection, Matt and Brigid, who sat on the other side of the church, stood up, worked their way through a crowded pew, climbed over the kneelers and escaped. They marched out of the church arm in arm, almost in the exact heartbeat-like cadence of Danny, Ray, and Dez. Jesus! They were walking out too.

All eyes were on us—Father Lawler, the congregation—watching, waiting. Pressure mounted on Eddie, who was sitting alone in the front pew. He kept turning around, checking to see that we were still there. Finally, he said an audible, "Aw shit," stood, and marched down the aisle.

Brendan bowed his head. My face flushed. Perspiration dripped down my back under my sweater. The next twenty minutes took an hour. As people lined up for Holy Communion and gave us the stink eye, we snuck out with our collars pulled up perp-walk high.

CHAPTER 15

On the Way to Middletown

Up half a block, Ray and Eddie climbed into the van that we hired for our trip to the festival. Standing in front of a house with a grouping of "St. John's Proud" signs, Matt and Brigid hugged Danny. Maybe I should have walked out with Danny. Maybe he shouldn't have made a scene. I kicked a stone on the sidewalk like I was kicking a field goal and it landed near his feet.

The van held six passengers: Ray and Eddie sat in the third row, Danny, me, and Brendan in the second, and Dez, who needed the leg room, sat shotgun next to our Sikh driver. I buckled my middle seatbelt, crossed my arms, and stared straight ahead. I was at a loss for what to say to Danny. I snuck side glances at him; he sat with his face turned to the window. Brendan slid the door closed.

Eddie said, "That first beer is going to taste good. Am I right?"

Brendan ignored him, leaned over me, and spoke to Danny. "So, what just happened? Are you leaving the Church?"

Danny shrugged and continued looking out the window. "I guess so."

I said, "You don't mean that." It came out as a command, not a request. "You're dealing with a lot of stuff. You overreacted."

"You disagree with what I said?"

"You went overboard," I said. "There's a time and place for

everything. The Church has its faults, but it's like family. You don't walk away."

Danny glared at me. "You tell me when we can have a meaningful discussion with the pope and I'll be there. Last time I checked, it's not a democracy."

"Meet with Father Lawler. Apologize for the outburst and talk it out. You'll feel better," I said.

The car was quiet again.

Danny turned back to face the window. An ice wall had crystalized between us. In the twenty years or so that we had been friends, we'd argued from time to time, but this wasn't playground stuff. The driver merged onto the Boulevard, a twelve-lane highway deemed one of the most dangerous in America, challenging a speeding pickup with a screaming horn. The others shifted in their seats.

Brendan tapped Dez on the shoulder. "You leaving too?"

From the front seat, Dez said, "Going to church keeps me strong on the inside like going to the gym keeps me strong on the outside. I don't run into fires by myself, but I agreed with what Danny said. A little surprised by how he said it, but it was for the right reasons."

"Hold on now—the Church has some shade in its history, but it always heals itself. It's not perfect, but it gets us where we need to go," I said. "You know that."

Dez sat motionless.

Ray said, "I disagree, Tommy. The word 'change' is not in their vocabulary."

"I'm with Tommy. All the shit that happens in life and all the shit that can happen . . . turning away from the Church is asking for more bad. Why would you do that?" Brendan asked.

"Bren, I believe in God, not necessarily in the Church," Ray said. "God's not malicious."

"That's the point. Maybe you're pissing Him off. You don't know, do you? No one does. Are you leaving too?"

"Yes."

"How can you say that, Ray?" I said. "You're on the CYO Board."

"No, I resigned after that scheduling thing with the girls' team. Without Danny there, I'm outnumbered. They never listened to anything I had to say anyway."

"That's why you're leaving?"

"Yeah, Tommy, I'm that shallow." Ray rolled his eyes. "I want to help kids, that's why I volunteered for the CYO. We should be teaching kids to be assertive. Instead, we tell them to obey a priest with the same reverence they would give God. Danny's right. Absolute power corrupts absolutely."

"Look at all the good Catholics have done in the world. They can fix this," I said. "You can't change anything if you leave. And what if everybody walks away? At least if you stay . . ."

He stayed quiet. I tightened up my crossed arms. "If Danny hadn't walked out today, you'd be going to Mass next week, admit it."

Ray sighed. "I believe everyone should try to be a better person, and the church guided me in the past, but not anymore. I have no respect for anything a priest, bishop, cardinal, or pope has to say. I'm not as religious as you. I've always had issues with it."

"Issues, issues, there's no issues in the Catholic Church," Eddie said sarcastically.

I said, "What about you, Eddie? You're not leaving, right?"

"I am . . . for now."

There was silence for a couple of stoplights. Almost at the city border, we passed Byberry where the old insane asylum once stood. How appropriate. We crossed into Bucks County, and Brendan turned to Ray and asked, "So what are your issues?"

"I don't want to upset anyone. It's personal." Ray talked to the back of my head. His breath created warm air currents against my neck.

"I'll tell you mine if you tell me yours," said Eddie. I wanted them both to shut up; there were some things that couldn't be unsaid.

"Okay. The resurrection," said Ray.

The van erupted:

"Jesus! And I'm sitting next to you."

"What the fuck?"

"Are you kidding me?"

"The resurrection?"

"That's like everything!"

Ray said, "Well, it's hard to know if a person is dead, especially back in the day. Sometimes they dig up a bunch of coffins to move an old cemetery. The coffins pop open and the insides of the lids are all scratched up; people were put in too soon. Even today, people will wake up in the morgue. I have no doubt that Jesus was holy, but Him being dead for three days, coming back to life, and then beaming up to heaven? No way."

I barked, "We believe it because we have faith, Ray."

"No. Faith means connecting to something infinite, not turning off your brain. Look, no one knows what happens after we die. I like to think some kind of cosmic force inside of us is never really extinguished, and there's some kind of afterlife, but I have an issue with the story about Jesus being dead and coming back."

Thank God a Sikh was driving; a Christian driver would have dumped us out onto the side of the highway, and rightly so. The shock created a quiet that swallowed up the van until Ray and Eddie both talked at the same time, and then stopped, and started again. Each wanted to comment on how the ancient ushers at Mass had morphed into hard asses. Eddie told Dez, "I had your back if the old man tried to take you out."

It was funny, but neither Danny nor I laughed.

Brendan broke the returning quiet by talking about the Irish festival. "There's a ten-dollar cover, but you get to see a half a dozen bands. Last year, the food was good, and the drinks were fast. What more could you want, am I right?"

The van dropped us off in front of the hall. The temperature was cooler than in the city. The suburbs seemed creepier than usual; it was the combination of the desolate fields in the distance and the quietness beyond the hall. While we inched along the queue outside the building, everyone was chitchatting, but Danny and I said little. Our church was the best option to help Danny live with his grief. Instead, he lashed out, blaming the whole church for the sins of one man. Walking away because the church was imperfect was illogical; nothing in this world was perfect. Catholics had a duty to persist. My friends let me down. They missed the bigger picture. Faith was never easy. People gave their lives for it.

Once inside the building, the jovial atmosphere of the crowd offered the smallest comfort. A stage was set up at one end of the room, and a bar and food tables were set up along the side. After the first calming beers, the six of us semi-separated. For the most part, Danny and I stood near the bar but not together. He drank in his space and I in mine. As the bands packed the dance floor, or roused a couple of hundred people in sing-alongs, or both, Danny and I drank.

The others popped up from time to time and encouraged us to join in the fun. Dez hung out with some fireman buddies telling stories. Brendan ran into some cousins and joined their crowd for laughs. Eddie and Ray chatted up two women, and Danny and I drank. It should have been great fun. I should have been on that dance floor, or singing that song, or chatting up the cute girls, but I wasn't.

Around ten, the band played that song that Jack had sung on stage with the Scooby Dudes, and everyone in the place belted out the lyrics "I get knocked down, but I get up again." My eyes filled with tears, and I wiped them with the neck of my sweater. My friends zigzagged through the crowd to check on Danny, who had turned to face the wall. Dez put his arm around Danny's shoulder and signaled to the rest of us that he was okay. The song ended, and they all backed off into the crowd, unsure but willing to give him space to recover.

Danny walked over to me. We eyed each other through half-mast eyelids, holding our beers as ballast. In a voice that he failed to make quiet despite the crowd, he said, "Fuck you, Tommy. You and your stupid signs. I'm not apologizing to Lawler or anyone else for what I said. You're an ass if you think I should and a bigger one for asking me."

A fire grew inside me. "Fine. I'm an ass. You got your friends to turn their back on God. Proud are you? Spitting on the cross, on the graves in Belfast and Derry? Maybe you're leaving, but I'm not."

And then I lit the match. "Someone has to pray for Jack."

He came at me like lightning. Two shoves sent me flying backward. I crashed into a table, upsetting trays of soft pretzels and sending them flying. I beelined for him. Dez grabbed me in a midair tackle and held me back from Danny, who was held in check by Dez's firemen friends. On the dance floor, Eddie and Ray covered their eyes, embarrassed. Two large bouncers went nose-to-nose with us, asking who was paying for the pretzels. I fished out a twenty-dollar bill from my wallet. Not to be outdone, Danny also threw a twenty at them. The larger bouncer pocketed both twenties, then eighty-sixed us both.

I was drunk and angry, where black was white and tears and fists fought for their turn. Danny was too. Dez grabbed Danny's shoulder in one hand and my shoulder in the other and pushed us out the door. The others followed. Furious, they told us we were assholes, white trash, embarrassments. Everyone was having a great time and no one wanted to leave, Eddie especially, who said he really liked the girl he met. Dez stood with Danny and talked, and Brendan did the same with me, and each camp worked for a truce. They kept it up, shaming us, until we finally agreed that we could get in the van without killing each other.

Inside the van, Brendan took the middle seat to stop anything from starting, but a black hole settled over us and sucked out all lightness.

Twenty minutes into the ride, I broke the silence. "I'm sorry."

Danny sighed. "Tommy, I'm done."

My heart hurt. *Done with me or done with the church?*

"I need St. John's. It's where I . . . talk to Dad . . . the only way I know . . . to help Jack." My voice trailed.

Danny leaned forward, resting his elbows on his knees. His forehead touched the back of the driver's seat. Maybe he considered what I said, rolled it around in his mind, or maybe he fucking hated me, or both. After a while, he turned and gave me the slightest nod.

CHAPTER 16

What Just Happened?

The morning after the Irish festival, I stayed in bed. I had a hangover and that what-just-happened feeling you get after a car accident with the what-could-still-happen anxiety.

Every so often, Mom tiptoed in the hallway and paused outside my door. I wanted to wait until she was out of the house, but the need for carbs and caffeine propelled me to the kitchen. I assembled a mug of tea and a pile of toast with extra butter, but as I sat down at the kitchen table, she pulled up a chair. Ugh. She sat with her elbows on the table and her hands folded almost in prayer. I shoved most of a slice of toast into my mouth.

She leaned forward and said, "I saw StevieB yesterday. Did he tell you?"

"I haven't talked to him in a month or two," I mumbled.

"He said it had been a while, but that he'd give you a call. He was at Jack's again praying. I was out at the cemetery to see your father."

What the heck was he up to? I chewed and stared at the vapor rising off my mug.

"You two were close. You should call him."

I shoved more bread into my mouth.

She said, "I talked to your dad about what happened in Mass."

I did not want to do this. The full weight of her attention was on me.

She continued, "I know about peer pressure; you showed backbone. It's hard to stand up to your friends. You chose what's right over what's cool. I'm proud. Your dad is too."

I looked up at her. "They're right about some things, Mom. They're taking a stand. After Father Farrell gets tossed, they'll find their way back."

She leaned forward even more; the table pressed against her stomach. "And what happens if Father is cleared?"

"That'll never happen, Mom. He did it."

She waited to respond. "Jack was sick. I know you cared about him, but he died by his own hand, Tommy. Not Father Farrell's, his own. If it's a choice between him and Father, shouldn't we believe the sane man?"

Every muscle in my body contracted. I stared at her hard. "If Father Farrell comes back, then I'll walk out too."

"Don't you dare say that." She stood with fire in her eyes. "Sometimes the only thing that gets me through the day is knowing that one day we'll all be together. How can you even think it's okay to walk away?"

I took a deep breath. "Look, I still believe, Mom, but the Church has to get rid of its rotten parts."

"Father Farrell never did anything to you, right? You would have told me."

She stilled until I answered.

"So what?" I said.

"Well, he had plenty of opportunities if he was that way, and nothing ever happened. Look into your heart. Look at all the outreach and charity he's done. He's devoted his life to God. Give him the benefit of the doubt. For Chrissakes, your dad would have known if Father was a sicko."

"Don't play the Dad card, Mom. He always told me to do the right thing."

"But everyone loves Father Farrell. You're saying everyone's wrong, and you're right. You know, your friend Terry supports him. He told Roger Hanlon that Jack was a messed-up kid. Danny helped Jack get that nice job with the city. Father went out of his way and put in a good word with that committeeman, and look at what happened—he got himself fired."

"I'm sure Father reached out to that same committeeman to cut Jack loose as soon as he filed his complaint."

"You're inventing conspiracies, Tommy. There are only two people who know what happened. Who are we to sit in judgment? What if Father is innocent and he's kicked out of the priesthood? Is that fair?"

"That's his cross to bear, Mom. Better his than another kid's. We should err on the side of caution."

"Everyone says that without him advocating for us, they'll close St. John's. Is that what you want?"

"Of course not."

"Look, let's not argue. Remember, after your dad, we didn't know how we would go on, but we did. The Cunanes, and all of you boys, will get through this too. Time heals. You have to let it go. Put it in God's hands. Whatever happens with Father Farrell, it's God's will."

I stayed quiet. Mom's eyes scanned my face. For all my mother's toughness, she pleaded, "Hold your ground, right? Talk to the boys, tell them to have faith. It'll all work out."

The Eagles played the late game against the Seahawks, and Danny had group-texted suggesting we catch the game at the Shamrock bar. Was I invited, or was he too hungover to change his distribution list? I had to go. I had to know where I stood. I also had to escape mother-hover.

The Shamrock was part of a national chain decorated in the plastic Paddy school of design. It was bigger than McRyan's, almost three times the size and with a dozen more beers on tap. The menu was longer than my arm and had enough pages to fill a small book. McRyan's might have been smaller, but at least its trophies were actual local teams and the photos were of real neighborhood people. The Shamrock was off the beaten path for anyone from St. John's, and I assumed that was why Danny chose it.

Six of us settled into a large booth. I sat closest to the wall and furthest from Danny. Initially, all focus was on ordering and scoping the place, but once the waitress delivered our beers and appetizers, calm pervaded. Danny focused on his beer and then, with a side glance at me, said, "Last night . . . you all right?"

"I had salt crystals in weird places from crashing into the pretzel table, but other than that. You?"

He flashed a smile. The air was cleared, sort of. He let his beer and food sit while he shredded a cocktail napkin. Something had to be said about what happened at Mass, but I kept mum, grateful just to have a seat at the table.

Brendan finally broke the ice. "So, about the walkout at church yesterday . . . I'm not allowed to hang around you guys anymore."

There was a delay, and then everyone laughed. Brendan said that the news of the walkout had circulated fast. "I got tired of hearing my own name. My parents almost always call me by one of my brothers' names, but it was all 'Brendan Michael this' and 'Brendan Michael that.' Not just my parents, but everybody in my family—aunts, uncles, cousins, with the texts, the voice mails, the emails, right up until I left the house today. I could never leave the church even if I wanted to, which, to be clear, I don't. I wouldn't have a minute's peace."

He asked Danny how Colin and Sheila were taking it.

Danny shrugged. "My parents understood why I did it, but the lawn trash got bad last night."

Everyone chimed in with "That's terrible," and, "Who does that?" Danny took a long sip and said, "I helped Dad install a new video security system. That should help."

Ray said that his parents told him he was too smart for his own good, but they considered his walkout a phase, part of growing up. Some of his uncles and cousins had left the church, but they all came back after they married. Danny cringed at the marriage comment, but he didn't say anything.

Dez had gotten a full-on interrogation from his family. "They understood why I did it—supporting a friend, taking a stand—but no one's happy about it. My dad is big on having a moral compass. He said it's too easy to get caught up in the day-to-day, and you need something like church to help you remember what's important."

"You got off easy. I have to go back, or I have to move out," said Eddie.

Danny grimaced. "I'm sorry, man. Go back. Just because I did—"

"No. It's okay. I was going to have to move out someday." Danny, sitting next to Eddie, leaned back and gave him a one-armed hug.

"I think you all need to reconsider. Me, my family, we're not naïve about what happens, but we're not letting some pervert priests ruin everything," said Brendan. "Leaving the Catholic Church—you're throwing the baby out with the bathwater."

"It's not that easy, Brendan," Danny said.

But it was that easy. Brendan was right. I loved being Catholic. I liked the routine, the sense of peace I got from prayer and Mass. I liked going to Mass; it made me want to be a better person. I would feel depressed or overwhelmed by life, but then I took the Eucharist and God was with me, and everything was okay and I was all better. Father Farrell was the problem, not Catholicism. A part of me was glad they'd gotten some flak for the walkout, maybe enough to reconsider their actions, but the rest of me was miserable. Alone, surrounded by friends.

At halftime, Matt showed up and pulled up a chair to the end of the booth close to Danny. He gave him his undivided attention, wanting to know how he was, and whether Father Lawler had contacted him about what had happened.

"You made a lot of sense in church. Brigid and I will be parents someday, and we don't want to have to worry, ya know? Brigid and her mother are nervous about how and where we're going to get married, but we'll figure it out," Matt said.

Danny apologized for putting the couple in a bad spot. Matt downplayed the whole thing and proceeded to talk up the Shamrock like a salesman. "Look at all the beers they have. They have Redzone TV. You can see all the games at once. These appetizers are delish."

Danny bought into Matt's spiel. He scanned the joint and said, "I like this place too. There are lots of bars we should check out instead of going to McRyan's all the time."

I loved McRyan's. I wanted us to go back there, but everyone else jumped on Danny's idea. Ray talked up a bar near Holy Family University called the Library Bar that had a good rep. Eddie suggested Emmet's, a bar near the El—so divey that it might be cool—and Dez mentioned a brewpub further up on Frankford.

Matt asked, "Are we talking pub crawl?"

Danny smiled. "They're all close to the Avenue. We could take the bus?"

"Let's do this!" said Matt and outlined a plan. His enthusiasm helped Danny's mood. He looked not happy, but less sad. Everyone raised their pints and cheered next Saturday's pub crawl. I smiled on the outside.

Drinks at the Shamrock had been spaced out and countered with food, so after the game, no one was drunk but we were buzzed enough to take an Uber. The driver dropped us off at a central location. Since Danny and I lived so close, we walked home together.

The November air was sobering. Our neighborhood revered the holidays, and Christmas lights—multicolored or white, constant or blinking—peppered the houses and lawns, which was why it took a couple minutes for us to register the red and blue flashing lights on the police cruiser in front of the Cunanes' house. Once we did, we ran at full speed. Danny was first in the door, and I followed in a wild-ass panic.

With his reading glasses perched on the edge of his nose, Colin sat at the dining room table, staring at the laptop screen, and pecking at the keyboard. Sheila and Officer Williford stood behind him, looking at the screen like they were hypnotized.

"Dad, what's wrong?" Danny yelled.

Sheila said, "We got the little bastards. On the video."

We gathered around the laptop. Everything on the screen was gray and white like an old television show. There were five of them, skulking and laughing on the sidewalk, too far from the camera to identify. One flung two drawstring kitchen trash bags onto the lawn that exploded on impact, sending chicken bones, paper wrappers, and garbage everywhere. Another with his back to the camera baptized the lawn using a Mickey-D's milkshake, and they all bent over, laughing. Emboldened, the group ran onto the lawn and kicked at the trash to disperse it, and we got them full-face on-screen: the Mallory brothers and their friends. Their St. John's polo shirts peeked from beneath unzipped jackets. A final indignity showed them peeing all over the front stoop. Colin and Sheila averted their eyes.

While Officer Williford filled out a complaint form, Danny said, "Ray called it. They think they can do anything they want and get away with it."

Officer Williford asked the Cunanes if they wanted time to consider pressing charges. Sheila was certain, but Colin turned to Danny and said, "You okay if we do this?"

He nodded.

Colin said, "We're filing the complaint, Officer."

Colin made a show of pushing the Send key with his index finger to forward a copy of the video file to a police email address, and Sheila initialed the complaint.

While Mr. and Mrs. Cunane escorted the policeman to the door, Danny pointed to the basement and asked me to stay. He said, "This'll hurt the CYO. I have to call Terry. I need you to keep me from losing it."

He relied on me to help him, and that meant something. Once we were seated downstairs, he instructed me, "If I start to lose it, mute the call. If I do lose it, hang up."

He dialed and put his phone on speaker. The call went to voice mail, and he left a message. "Terry, you need to call me. The Mallorys are getting arrested."

Within seconds, Terry returned the call. "What for?"

"They threw bags of trash at my house and peed all over our front porch."

"I don't believe you. I know these kids. They're good kids.

They would never do something like that. I get it, Danny, you hate St. John's, but whatever problems you have, leave the kids out of it!"

"They did it."

"Says you. Who's going to believe a crazy Cunane?"

Danny's face went red. "We have it on video, asshole. We already gave the file to the cops."

Dead air. Then Terry said, "Pull the complaint back. C'mon, they're just kids. Look at all the good they're doing for the team. You can't do this to them. It's your fault. You and your family brought this on yourselves. What did you expect?"

Danny leapt from his seat, and I put the phone on mute.

"He's an asshole, Danny. Don't listen to him," I said.

As Terry yammered on, Danny picked up a pillow and punched it, sending it flying across the room. He latched his fingers, rested them on top of his head, and stared at the ceiling lost in thought. Minutes passed. He nodded and I took the phone off mute. He said, "Terry, we're filing the complaint."

"You know they'll get suspended . . . you know what that'll do. Haven't you already done enough to St. John's?"

Holding the Mallory brothers accountable was the right thing to do, but it was one more reason for people in the parish to hate the Cunanes.

Danny enunciated, "They need to own up and pay the price."

"This will ruin their reputation. For what—a momentary lapse in judgment? They're probably scared shitless. We'll talk to them. They'll never do it again. I promise. What would it take for you to drop the charges and keep this on the QT? How about I get them to apologize?"

"Nope," Danny said, and he disconnected the call.

CHAPTER 17

Diving

The pub crawl started at noon in Emmet's, a bar underneath the El in a strip of storefronts between a shoe store and a Family Dollar. The bar had once bustled, servicing factory workers on shift breaks, but the factories were long gone in this part of Northeast Philly. Failing stucco on the outside front wall showed underlying patches of the stone and mortar. Inside, a massive oak teardrop-shaped bar dominated the room. A fireplace, its Pennsylvania bluestone almost hidden by taped-up political flyers, sat wedged in the corner. The dim lighting shrouded decades of wear and tear but failed to hide the way the cracked vinyl on the barstools pinched your cheeks or how the bar's scratched and dented surface mandated care in resting a glass. Drains in the floor allowed the place to be hosed down, which might have been done recently, given the Lysol smell. A television blaring a game show hung angled over the center of the bar. At the farthest barstool, a lone patron with a beard and man-bun sat staring at a short glass of brown liquid.

The bartender scowled as the six of us took our seats on the curve of the bar. "We don't serve food," he barked.

"Not here for it," answered Eddie.

"Got a special, a buck a beer, tap beer: Pabst or Natty Light. Cash only."

We all ordered Pabst, which was served in eight-ounce

glasses. The bartender poured the beers, took the money, and kept an eye on the TV.

"The place has potential," said Eddie. "At a buck a beer, even for a short glass, our money has some serious staying power."

Many dollars later, we talked to the bartender, Bob from Port Richmond, like he was an old friend, albeit a tight-lipped one. A retiree, he only worked days. His title might have been bartender, but he got paid to watch TV so the owner could keep the liquor license and his hopes for gentrification alive. Bob told us not to bring any friends to the place. He hadn't taken the job to work hard.

The man at the far end of the bar watched us befriend Bob, then ambled over with his drink in hand. Bob pointed to the man and said, "This is Godfrey."

Godfrey wore a ripe Villanova hoodie and baggy khakis held up by a belt that cinched the frayed waistband to his too-thin frame. He petted his thick dark brown beard with his fingers and offered to sell us some loosies. He got no takers and would have ambled back to his seat, but Danny engaged him. "So, you a Wildcats fan?"

Godfrey frowned, looked down, and then pointed to his shirt. "Forgot I's wearing this. I studied philosophy there. Took some time off, working on my thesis."

"No kidding, what's your subject?"

Godfrey came to life like Frankenstein's monster, a little jerky and wobbly at first, and then fixated on Danny. "Early Christianity."

A collective groan sounded.

"Aw, Jesus," said Eddie. "Godfrey, how about those Eagles?"

Godfrey ignored him. "Specifically, the marketing of early Christianity." No one encouraged him, but he continued any-way. "The disciples considered it their holy mission to maximize converts, so they had to sell it." He slow bounced his head in an exaggerated manner, like a drinking bird toy.

Brendan gave me an elbow and did the finger circle near his head, but Danny said, "What do you mean, 'sell it'?"

Godfrey's face contorted; he had an audience. "Sell the Greeks and the Romans; they were the target market. They believed in super-beings who lived in the clouds and interfered in human lives every now and again—the Gospels gave them what they wanted to hear. The Virgin Mary being impregnated by an unseen God, and Jesus raising Lazarus from the dead, turning water into wine, rising from the dead and ascending into the heavens—all those stories tapped into and eventually took over the Greek and Roman markets. Paul's letters sealed the deal."

I did not want to get into a religious debate, not after last week. We were here to have fun. Godfrey pissed me off, but he was a few bricks short of a load, so I kept quiet.

Matt snickered. "So, the first Christians were like salesmen?"

Godfrey froze as if listening to sounds that only he heard. After a minute or so, he said, "In effect. You have a big winter solstice celebration that you all love, oh wow, that happens to be Jesus's birthday. Like your spring celebration for the pagan goddess Eostre? Wow, that's what we call the celebration of Jesus's resurrection. That message flexibility built phenomenal Q Scores. I'm not making any kind of judgment. They did what they needed to do to spread the message and save souls."

"Look, I know squat about any pagan goddesses, but Jesus's birthday and the solstice overlapped, so it made sense that they combined the celebrations," said Brendan.

Godfrey brought his glass up for a sniff. "No one knows when He was born, but based on the star, the shepherds, and the census, the least likely time of year for His birth was winter."

This guy was really pissing me off.

I said, "So you're saying the Gospel is bogus? Millions of people over thousands of years believe in the Gospel, but all the stories were part of a marketing campaign?"

"They wrapped the Jesus message in the kind of stories their audience liked to hear. Jesus never walked on water; it's impossible. Maybe a sandbar, but the facts are irrelevant. His message to love one another is what's important, right? You agree?"

"But you're making it out like it's a con. That's crazy," I said.

"Well, I am bipolar, but so what? They said Jesus was crazy, and Galileo, Pythagoras, Tesla, and Michelangelo. Doesn't mean I'm wrong." He sniffed his drink and talked to me over the top of his glass. "Besides, no one knows who wrote the Gospels."

I nearly sprayed my beer. "The apostles and their disciples."

"Some of it was written a hundred years after Jesus lived."

Ray responded, "He's right. The Gospel is not an eyewitness account. Another reason that we shouldn't take the Gospel as gospel."

I mocked Ray. "Oh, you were there?"

Ray turned to me. "Just because you want something to be true doesn't mean it is."

My face flushed. Fuck Ray. I pushed my barstool back, but Dez and Eddie shook their heads, letting me know they'd stop a fight. I didn't want to fight anyway. Plus, maybe Ray jumped on Godfrey's bandwagon so fast because he had second thoughts about leaving the church. I bit my tongue and stayed calm.

Danny said to Godfrey, "You said a hundred years. That's a pretty big lag time. They told Jesus's stories over and over until someone finally wrote it down?"

Dez finally spoke. "There were lots of gospels floating

around back in the day, and they had a big meeting and a pope decided which ones were legit."

Everyone stopped talking and stared at him. "What? I had Father Garner for Theology."

As soon as he said it, I remembered studying the synod of something in the year 300 something. I said, "The point is they got rid of any fake gospels."

"Tommy, the point is how much had the stories changed over all those years," said Danny.

"Who's got the balls to change a Jesus story? I don't buy it," I said.

"You really believe people back then told the same word-by-word replay for a hundred years?" Danny shook his head. "Hey, Godfrey, hurry up with the thesis. I want to read it, man. It sounds illuminating."

Godfrey twitched and shuddered. Bob signaled timeout to us, but it was too late. Godfrey moved closer to Danny. Inches away, his voice grew louder. "Villanova rejected my proposal, but it's not heresy if it's true. My ideas are sound. I will write it. It's a free country. I can write it if I want."

Danny deflated. "It's cool."

Maybe I smirked; I probably did. Godfrey's lunacy proved me right without me having to say anything. Eddie gave the nod that meant it was time to go. As we headed for the door, Danny invited Godfrey to join us on the crawl, but he declined. The rest of us exchanged what-the-fuck non-verbals.

Outside, the winter sun bobbed and weaved behind gray clouds, keeping the air cold. We stood on the corner pulling our coats tight and banging our feet together as we waited for the 66 bus. I asked Danny why he'd invited Godfrey, and he said, "He reminded me of Jack." The what-the-fuck looks returned.

Brendan said, "He didn't look like Jack or talk like Jack."

"Or smell like him," said Eddie.

Danny said, "It was the way he worked so hard to hold it together. I notice it now."

He was right. Where was my compassion . . .

Matt's plan had us traveling from Emmet's bar to the Library Bar, the farthest bar to the north and then working our way south on the Avenue toward home. Once on the bus, it took a while to warm-up after the deep freeze. We had left the eccentric Godfrey in the bar, but things he said rattled around in my head, and maybe not just mine. Chitchat on the bus was minimal.

About six blocks into the ride, we passed the Burren, a small bar that may have been a gas station in a former life. The Burren would never be somewhere any of us would hang out, but Matt stood up in the aisle like a maître d', one arm folded and the other extended, and announced: "I don't know about you all, but my PBR buzz is wearing off. How about a quick one at Chez Burren?"

Inside, the Burren was what I'd expected. The place was bare bones: a bar, a few tables, mismatched chairs. A single TV airing a sports talk show broke the silence of the room. Based on the odor, hidden somewhere in a backroom was a deep fryer that got a regular workout. There were maybe a dozen barstools, more than half occupied by lone men drinking. The men, of various ages, stared at the TV, or their drink, or into the nothingness. Maybe they gave us a glance, maybe not. I hoped the stench of this place smacked Danny upside the head and made him realize how stubborn he was being. Jesus, what were we doing here?

We ordered shots and beers and carried them to a sticky-topped table. At least the Jameson loosened the grip of winter's chill.

Danny eyed the bar's patrons. In a quiet voice, he said, "Stoney Aloneys. That's what Jack used to call men like that. They drink alone; they lost their friends, or maybe they never even had any. They're stoned or their hearts turned to stone. If it weren't for you all, that'd be me, a Stoney Aloney."

I folded my arms and gave him the tilted head stare my mom gave me. He knew what to do if he didn't want to be a Stoney Aloney. He turned his attention away from me and stared at his beer. The others offered up, "We got your back bro," and, "No way, Danny, not you!" and, "Don't go there, man."

Brendan busted on Matt. "Nice bar." With a nod to Danny, he added, "So glad you brought us here."

Matt busted right back, "I picked it special for you, Brendan. It's your kind of ambiance." He pronounced it *am-bee-ants*, and it lightened the mood.

"Jack's on your mind today, huh?" said Dez.

Danny nodded. "He usually is."

"You know how I remember him? That last night in McRyan's. Him laughing. I told him about the first time I ran the hose on a tanker truck. It was a fire at an abandoned building in Juniata. The mist those things give off makes it hard to see. I hosed down eight bystanders and four firemen. Knocked one of my buddies right off his feet."

We all laughed.

Matt said, "I told the story, no gory details spared, about the first time I was in a delivery room as a nurse trainee. I asked for oxygen—for myself."

After that, the jokes and stories rolled out. Snorty laughs

and double-overs brightened Danny's mood, but I caught him sneaking peeks at the Stoney Aloneys.

We finished our drinks and moved to the exit. Before we left, I risked a visit to the restroom. As I walked the cramped corridor to the back of the building, Dez called out to me that I was a braver man than him. The smell hit me as soon as I entered. Balled-up paper towels and toilet paper littered the floor. There were two urinals and a stall, and behind the stall door, a man was on his knees yacking. I hated the sound. The yacker probably drank too fast or too long, or ate something from the kitchen. I planned to get in and get out as fast as possible, but the yacker beat me to the lone sink, so I had to wait for my turn. He washed his hands, then cupped them under the faucet, rinsed out his mouth, and splashed his face. I avoided looking at him as a way to pretend the yacking hadn't happened and let him keep his dignity.

As I washed my hands, he dried off his face with the pulpy paper towels, then said, "Tommy Dunleavey?"

His face had a yellow tint. His distended, almost pregnant belly pulled at his Eagles T-shirt spotted with yack splashes. Long hair escaped from a ponytail. "It's me. Mickey Cunningham." He smiled through brownish teeth and swayed on his Chuck Taylors.

Jesus. I was glad he told me. I shook his hand. "Mickey. The ponytail threw me," I lied.

Mickey and I had been paired up at freshman orientation and had some laughs. We'd been in homeroom together, too, but he transferred out at some point. "Hey man, are you all right?"

"Ah, what do doctors know. Hey, I heard about Jack Cunane . . . about the priest." Still swaying, he pointed at me and slurred, "A priest got me too."

I froze. My eyes widened.

"That's why I left. Father Bannon, remember him from gym class? They apologized and shit, but it's not something you get over, ya know?"

Father Bannon. What the fuck? I remembered the priest from school, a boxy, muscular man, always pulling on his moustache. He coached the wrestling team. He left right after the season before the school year ended. I never gave it a second thought.

"Jesus, Mickey, I'm so sorry. I had no idea. Are you okay? Did you talk to someone, get counseling?"

He waved his hand at me like he was bouncing an invisible basketball off my chest. "What are they going to say? Sucks to be me." He was hammered. Plastered. Shit-faced.

"How about I get you a ride home? Let me give you a hand," I said.

"Nah, I'm good. They take care of me here." He put his hand on his hip and held it in place with his other hand as he leaned on the sink. "I've never seen you here."

"I'm on a pub crawl. I'm with a group: Danny, Ray, Dez, Matt, Eddie. You remember them, right? Come say hi."

He held onto the sink to steady the wobbles. "Still hanging with the cool kids. Nice." His smile turned upside down. His eyes stared at the filthy floor tiles. "You gonna be here for a while?"

"Just here for the one."

"I'm a little under the weather, Tommy. I'm going to stay in the stall. I don't want them to see me like this. Tell everyone I said hi, okay?"

This could have been Jack's path.

"Mickey, I'm not leaving you like this. C'mon . . ."

He concentrated on his balance and turned away from me. As he closed the door on the stall, he said, "It was good to see you, Tommy."

I was dismissed. I rapped on the door. "Mick, let me give you a hand. Mick. Mick."

It wasn't like I could climb under or over the stall and drag him out, and arguing with a drunk . . . forget it. He didn't want anyone to see him hugging the bowl. Who would? What could I do? I walked out and left him there.

They were all waiting for me at the door. The bus was coming and we had to hurry. Mickey said to say hi to everyone, but if I told my friends that I'd seen him, I would have to mention the yacking, and he wouldn't want that, so I said nothing. I was not avoiding the Father Bannon rape story and a raft of anti-Church guff. I was protecting his reputation. Really.

CHAPTER 18

What'll It Be?

Designed to match the contemporary style of Holy Family University's large-windowed buildings and the surrounding traditional rowhouses, the Library Bar was an expansive brick building. Even though it was across the street from the college campus he attended, Danny said that with studying, working, and Megan, he had never spent any time there.

A hostess offered to seat us, but we headed to the bar. The interior was bright, with white walls and ceilings, and pot lights bounced light off a gleaming hardwood floor. The bar itself spanned the width of the building. A large adjacent dining room was sectioned off by half walls lined with books and decorated in garland. The approach of Christmas generated a positive vibe. The bright beehive provided an ideal beacon for students and staff on a wintry Saturday afternoon. But while this place crackled with cheer, Mickey was probably still on his knees bent over a toilet bowl in the Burren.

Dez scouted a single-file path for us through the boisterous crowd. Danny at one point stopped and caused a minor traffic jam. For never spending time here, everyone seemed to know him. Dudes in university hoodies—the expensive ones with embroidered logos—came over to shake his hand. There were some sympathetic comments about Jack's passing. Girls gave him taps and winks. He had a quick chat with two, who hung on his every word. At some point, Danny noticed the rest of us standing with crossed arms, observing him like scientists. He smiled and shrugged. "From class."

At the bar, Dez and Brendan leaned over two empty stools to get drinks and a menu, and the rest of us gathered around them to stake a space. We scanned the crowd like a singular advanced radar system. From time to time, heads turned to acknowledge various women. Brendan locked in on a group of three celebrating a birthday at a table nearby and asked for company. "C'mon, help a brother out."

Eddie had started dating Caroline, the woman he met at the Irish festival. He hesitated, then caved. "All right," he said. "But just as a wingman."

"C'mon, Tommy, there's three of them," said Brendan. "I helped you out at Towey's."

Danny encouraged me. "Go on, T. Nice Catholic girls, just what you're looking for."

Standing there, dressed in jeans, my drinking sneakers, and my thermal-lined Acme hoodie, I was dressed more in the style of the old-timers in the Burren than these college guys here who wore quarter zips, ski vests, khakis, and Sperrys. Even Brendan wore a nice sweater and not-sneaker shoes. I got a whiff of the Burren and snuck a few sniffs of my clothes, but it was nothing but a guilty conscience. I was mentally off my game, but they needed a third man.

The birthday girl was Maryann, based on her Little Flower High School Field Hockey jacket, and that was Brendan's opening. His sister played for Little Flower. Eddie slid into a wingman position and congratulated the birthday girl. I dawdled, then moseyed over to the table. Maryann introduced us to her friends, Alice and Jessica. All three were in their senior year at Holy Family. Maryann and Alice studied nursing and Jessica majored in business. They talked about recent internships and dream jobs. I bought a round for the table to show I had money, and they thanked me.

Eddie explained that we were on a pub crawl. Mistake. They wanted to know what other bars we'd been to, and we had to fess up to the Burren and Emmet's. They'd never heard of them. He said, "You know how some bars are so divey, they're cool? We checked. Those two bars definitely are not."

The girls smiled. Jessica asked where we went to school. I doubted she was asking about high school, and as I was the only one who had any post-high school education, my go-to perfunctory response rolled off my tongue: "I did two years at Community. Still deciding what I want to study."

"So, is it a gap five years or are you going for the gap ten?" she asked.

Man, cut off at the knees, and I just bought them a round. I countered with, "Well, I work. I do pretty decent. I'm a produce manager at the Acme." Only a slight exaggeration.

"So, are you working your way up to the next aisle? Play your cards right, you'll manage toiletries or canned goods?"

She laughed louder than it was funny. The other girls apologized and scolded her. "She just broke up with her boyfriend," Maryann said.

That was probably the worst thing that ever happened to Jessica. It was easy to go far in life if you had an easy life so far. Like she was so great! Her boyfriend obviously didn't think so. Yes, it had been a while since I was in school. I liked working at the Acme. Nothing wrong with that. She'd be lucky to get a job like mine. Businesses get bought out, reorganized, closed, but people had to eat. Jessica stayed quiet after that, and so did I.

I faked interest in the girls' conversation and plotted my escape from the table. Matt saved the day, hollering, "Pizza's here." On the way back to the bar, I passed Dez, who stood

like a Disney animatronic president, smiling next to a very tall
Asian girl who was quite a chatterbox. He nodded a lot. They
smiled a lot. Good for Dez. I neared Ray and heard fragments
of his conversation with a bouncy blonde about co-ops and
GMATs. Good for Ray. Good for everybody else.

At the bar, the pizza was not the twelve-inch plain pie that
McRyan's served. It was a flatbread, a squarish little thing with
chunks of chicken and bits of vegetables with ranch dressing
dribbled over it. I grabbed a slice that was really a three-inch
square. Danny, Matt, and I inhaled the food so we ordered
another. While we waited, Matt talked about house hunting
with Brigid, and how she wanted a fixer-upper so they could
make it their own. My friend would soon own a house. Weird.
It was such an adult thing to do.

The second flatbread arrived. As I chomped away, an older
man nudged me, then reached past and tapped Danny on the
shoulder. "Don't want to interrupt."

Danny smiled at him and introduced us. "This is my
accounting advisor, Dr. Briscoe. These are two of my oldest
friends, Tommy Dunleavey and Matt Asher."

I wiped pizza guck on my jeans before shaking his hand. Dr.
Briscoe's smile set off his laugh lines. "Pleased to meet you,"
he said. "Maybe you can talk some sense into your friend. He's
our top accounting student. He's selling himself short working
for the IRS. I'm trying to get him to consider the Big Four."

I faked a smile, having no idea what a Big Four was, and
Danny smiled at him.

"The IRS is great, Dr. Briscoe," Danny said. "It's local, nine-
to-five, and I never have to travel."

Dr. Briscoe laughed. "Or work at one of the top accounting
firms in the country and see the world, making three times what

you earn now. It's all in how you look at it, Danny. At least look into an MBA. I'm going to keep after you."

He apologized again for intruding, and I smiled again like a twit. Danny never mentioned anything about a Big Four job or traveling. His plan had been to marry Megan, work at the IRS here in the city, and buy a house in the neighborhood. But everything had changed and kept changing. Everyone had new things to do and new people to see. Everyone but me.

The teeny tiny pizza squares laid heavy in my stomach.

On the bus ride to the next bar, Dez filled us in on the girl he talked to, or as Eddie said, the girl he listened to. Brendan asked if she was American. Dez ignored him and talked as animatedly as she had. "Her name is Leah. She's adopted. She's in her senior year at Penn State Abington. She shares an apartment with friends over on Grant. She likes to talk, but she had an exam this morning and drank an energy drink; the caffeine dialed it up. She asked me about being a fireman and my family. It was easy to talk to her."

"Any tongue-ties?"

"I did okay, until I asked her out. She didn't bust on me; she just smiled and said yes. She's so pretty and really smart. She has an easy smile, doesn't she? I could listen to her talk all day."

Eddie said, "You might have to."

We all laughed, even Dez.

"Someone has to break the news to Debbie Clark. She'll be devastated," Ray said.

"Ha-ha," said Dez.

"Brendan has a date too," Eddie teased.

Brendan smiled. "Maryann invited me to watch the Eagles game tomorrow with her friends," he said and avoided looking me in the eye.

Danny smiled. "Nice."

Eddie added, "They invited me too, but I gotta find a place to live."

Brendan turned his face away from me. Eddie made the cut, but not me.

"To be honest," Brendan said, "I expected the women there would be super stuck-up. I expected to get shot down, but except for that one, the women were really down to earth."

Dez and Eddie agreed; then they all talked about how much they liked the bar, except for it being so far from home. They couldn't wait to go back. I stayed quiet.

We exited the bus in front of Rory's Tavern, a corner bar in Pennypack. Laughter and chatter beckoned from behind its weathered wood door. Inside, the crowd was mixed—Flyers fans watching the orange and black against the Red Wings, and gamblers glued to college football. Intermittent jeers and cheers broke out. Once seated, we were noticed by a table full of Flyer'd up fans.

"Brendan? Oh man, Danny, Tommy, Dez! Jeez, Matt and Eddie too!" It was Finn, one of Brendan's cousins. "Man, long time no see." Smiling, he introduced us to his friends, who all went by nicknames: Fish, Wambo, Spill, Jawnie, and their girlfriends, Ro, DiDi, and Sissy.

"Yo, nice to meet you."

"Any friend of Finn's . . ."

"How's it hanging?"

"Flyers are up by one, but Detroit has a power play with less than a minute in the period."

We watched the play and at the end of the period, Finn asked, "So what are you guys doing here? Who let you out of McRyan's?"

Danny explained the pub crawl, and Finn did his best to

sell us on the bar. "You guys should definitely make this your place. Check it out . . . uh, wood-grain paneling, pretty cozy, yeah? We got the wall of neon beer signs, a cool bobblehead collection of Philly sports figures. You don't see that every day. We got sandwiches, cold but healthy; they all come with lettuce and tomato."

We laughed.

He pointed at an old frowning woman wearing a waitress apron standing near the bar sipping a mug of coffee. He added, "Not to mention our friendly wait staff."

She air-swatted him and rolled her eyes, then shuffled over to our table. "What'll it be?"

It wasn't McRyan's, and I was more of a playoff Flyers fan, but it was okay. Shiny-clean and comfortable, I liked it the best of the bars we'd seen. When the waitress brought our round, she asked, "Heard you're on a crawl, you boys drunk-drunk?"

"Closing in on drunk, but definitely not drunk-drunk," Danny said.

"That's good."

We watched the hockey game. Conversation with Finn and his friends included the team's prospects, a plug for the Thursday night Quizzo, as well as who attended which schools, lived in which neighborhoods, and who knew who from where. On a pass by the waitress said, "You should eat something. Not here, 'cause I double as the short-order cook. You'll be drunk-drunk by the time I can get to you, but the place down the street has good food."

I had to admire her honesty. We left soon after; we really did need to eat. We said good-bye to Finn and company, promised to meet up again soon, and yelled, "Go Flyers!" as we exited.

A short walk down the avenue from Rory's and we arrived, starving, at Challee's Brew and grabbed a table. All I wanted

was an ice-cold lager and a hot roast beef like McRyan's served.
No chance. Challee's was a gastropub that brewed its own, and
that was all the alcohol they served. Craft beers, even session
beers, were thick and heavy, and the alcohol content ran high.
The only thing I had to eat was my morning Cheerios and
the flatbread; if I drank one of those beers, I'd be bloated and
hammered, so I ordered a Coke. The others ordered the local
brews: Figgy Flanders, Hoppy the Clown, Elfin Nutjob, Pogers,
Maynoothie, and a Goin' Back Dopplebock, and let me know
that I was a pussy.

The effect of the higher ABVs on the others—heavy lids and
dopey smiles—popped right away. Silliness ensued. Brendan
scanned the menu and suggested we ask for an English language
version. Danny asked around the table about the veal cheeks
over polenta—exactly which set of cheeks did they serve over
the polenta? Eddie asked about the risotto balls with parmesan
and fontina. "What is a risotto, and why would I want to eat its
balls?"

He ended up ordering the chicken quinoa wrap with
"humm-ass." Ray ordered a sushi plate. Dez got the duck
salad hoagie. Matt chose the frog legs sautéed in garlic. Even
Brendan ordered a mahi-mahi taco. I settled for the peanut
butter cheeseburger without the peanut butter.

Ray asked, "Tommy, aren't you tired of the same old, same
old?"

"Sometimes, the same old, same old *is* the best," I said.

"But how do you know?"

The waiter served the food, and everyone else raved about
it. Dez and Eddie each swore they found their new favorite
sandwich. Matt held up his frog legs and had them do the can-
can. They all laughed. The frog legs smelled delish, but they
were frogs for God's sakes. Matt said they tasted like chicken.

Whatever. Except for bits of pizza, no one had eaten all day, so anything would have tasted good. I was not impressed. My burger came with some kind of spicy sauce on it that I didn't ask for, the fries were chip-shaped instead of normal, and I had to ask for ketchup.

The table was quiet while we ate, except for Matt's phone ringing. The ABV that had contributed to his silliness minutes now brought him down. He read the text and said, "Brigid and her mom were out looking at wedding venues today." He sighed. "The pressure is on. We're blanking on what to do for the ceremony."

Suggestions flew around the table: Justice of the Peace, Judge Trueheart at City Hall, Vegas Elvis, Vegas Star Trek, various destinations with a Rent-a-Reverend. Ray said that anyone could get a license to perform a wedding ceremony. "Pick someone you respect. By the way, I'm happy to do it."

"Thanks, Reverend Ray, you'll be our fallback. Thing is, we both want our vows to be serious, but we have to figure out the religion question."

"I sympathize. I promised my dad I'd find something," Dez said. "Honestly, though, I need it. I don't run into fires by myself."

After a few minutes, Ray grabbed his phone, typed, and read the result. "Top religions in Philadelphia, according to Google. We got your Catholics, Jews, Muslims, Buddhists, Hindus, Orthodox Catholics, all of your Protestant groups: your Baptists, Episcopalians, Presbyterians, Lutherans, Methodists, Quakers, and there's African traditional. Anything strike your fancy?"

Even without telling them what had happened to Mickey, the Catholic Church was not even a consideration. Gone. Erased. And maybe because of Mickey, I lacked the words to challenge them, to keep them from walking away from who we were. Ray read the list like it was a damn menu. Like faith could be equated to a cheesesteak order, a Wiz wit or Wiz without. I understood their anger, more than they knew, but they needed to chill, not overreact and do anything stupid . . . more stupid. The way they talked; it was like they were planning another crawl—a God crawl.

Eddie said, "Orthodox Catholics are almost the same as Roman Catholics; they have their own pope though."

Danny answered, "Been there. Done that."

Looking around the table, Brendan asked, "Would you go Protestant?"

Matt said, "Well, there's Protestants, and there's Protestants. You got your Episcopalians, who are Catholic light, and then there's Southern Baptists at the other end of the spectrum who kind of hate Catholics."

"You wouldn't go Prod, would you?" Danny asked.

"Forget centuries of oppression?" Matt shook his head.

"That girl Caroline I met at the Irish festival is a Quaker; her relatives worked at the Quaker House in Belfast that helped the two sides to talk," Eddie said. "They're all about non-violence."

"Are Quakers Protestants?" Danny asked.

"I don't know, but I doubt there'd have been any Troubles if all the Prods were Quakers," Eddie said.

"Preachers creep me out, like . . . horror-movie creepy," Brendan said. "What do you even call them, 'preacherman'?"

Ray read aloud, "Says here that Quakers don't have ministers; everyone is a minister. God works through everyone."

Danny smiled. "That's really kind of nice."

Matt tapped his chin with his index finger and asked, "Did you mention African traditional?" He was joking, but Ray went into a full description. African traditional religions involved passing stories down generation to generation, a belief in a supreme creator, spirits, the veneration of the dead, and the use of magic.

"Uh-uh. No way," Ray said. "I'm not joining anything else where I have to believe someone has magic powers."

"I have to say Hindu is out. Brigid and I like beef too much. Hamburgers, cheesesteaks, filet, prime rib, we couldn't do without," Matt said.

Brendan said, "Do you hear yourself? We're Irish American Catholics. That's who we are. What, are you going to start walking around in a loin cloth or a dress or something?"

He was ignored.

"Islam forbids drinking, so that's out," Dez said.

"You know you're risking eternal damnation," Brendan said.

Eddie answered, "Some ancestor a thousand years ago met the boys from Rome and decided something worked. You're saying I'm stuck with that decision."

Brendan gave me an eye roll across the table.

"Judaism?"

"Don't you have to be Jewish? I mean, don't you have to be born Jewish. Isn't it like a nationality?"

"I know what you mean, but I've heard of people converting."

"What about Buddhism? Dez, would Leah know?"

"Why? Because she's Asian?"

"There's a Buddhist temple in . . ."

I zoned out as their voices swirled around me. I was a lost little kid, and no one was looking for me. I slid a twenty under my plate and left.

CHAPTER 19

Mickey

I'd stopped drinking early enough on the pub crawl to avoid a hangover on Sunday. I hit the noon Mass, the last one at St. John's. Attendance was sparse. I chose an empty pew toward the back and knelt to pray. I talked to Dad first. "I miss you, Dad. I need help down here. I'm all alone."

The back of my throat ached from holding in a sob, and my lip quivered. The sculpture of Jesus, hanging behind the altar, with His hands and feet nailed to the cross and the crown of thorns piercing His head, reminded me for the millionth time of all that He endured, and I talked myself out of a pity party. God never abandoned Jesus; He was with Him for every step. I was being a pussy. I followed up with an Our Father and begged, "God, please give me strength to do Your will."

After Mass, I had nothing to do and no one to see. The Eagles were playing at one. I could have texted Danny to see where he was watching, but I didn't, nor did he text me. I still had a hankering for a hot roast beef sandwich, so I walked to McRyan's. Vizzie welcomed me. I drank an ice-crackling cold lager and ate a hot roast beef sandwich with set-your-nose-on-fire horseradish. Heaven. After my sandwich, I sat alone and watched the game. Further down the bar, two old-timers also watched, not together. At halftime, I bolted for home.

Mom was in Delran babysitting my niece at my sister's; the empty quiet of the house enveloped me. I touched Dad's picture on the end table. What I'd give to watch a game with him one more time. Back in the day, we'd sit on the sofa and cheer our teams. Mom served snacks that were off-limits the rest of the week while telling us not to spoil our appetites. Today, he'd be wearing his Eagles jersey and watching with the angels. The image of him in his midnight green reminded me of Mickey.

Mickey said he'd be okay, but I knew that he wasn't. I searched on my phone and tracked him down on social media. The profile photo on his Facebook page showed him smiling, stuffed into a suit jacket at a fancy dinner reception. The only other photo was at least twenty years old, and it was a group shot at kid's birthday party, maybe his; he wore a Spiderman T-shirt and a pointy party hat. There were a couple video clips from a punk band, reposts of Eagles commentary, and some *Simpsons* memes. Not much else.

I texted: *Yo, Mickey . . . you all right? Where you watching the game?*

It was the third quarter, and I had one eye on the Eagles and the other on my phone, but Mickey had yet to text me back. I should never have left him yesterday. I should have made sure he got home okay. If the Burren was his bar, he'd be there, so at the end of the quarter, tired of waiting, I got into the car. On my way, I got the following text: *This is Mickey's mom. He is in Jeanes Hospital—room 242B. He's alert, if you can stop for a visit?*

Oh Christ.

I met Mickey's mom outside his room. "Thank you for coming, Tommy. I didn't realize you two had reconnected. I remember your name. You were the first person that Mickey met at the high school. You were so nice to him. You introduced him to all your friends. Thank you for that."

Freshman year was a lifetime ago. I had no memory of introducing him to the St. John's crew, but I'm sure I did. It just didn't seem like that big a thing. With tears in her eyes, she said, "I'll be in the lounge around the corner. I'll let the two of you talk."

I peeked inside Room 242. Mickey lay on the nearest hospital bed. His yellow skin contrasted with his blue gown and white blanket. Wires and tubes connected him to various bags and machines. A sign over his bed read, "No Fluids." His head rested on two pillows, and he stared straight ahead, ignoring the small flat-screen TV mounted to the top of the wall. The Eagles announcer, giving the play-by-play, competed with the beeping monitors. The scene reminded me of Dad's last days.

I knocked on the open door. Mickey conserved his energy as he turned his head toward me. His lips were chapped and flaking, but he managed a grin. With slowed speech, he said, "Tom-my Dun-leavey. We ran into each other . . . I forget where."

"Yesterday. At the Burren."

He sighed. "It's why I'm here."

I sat in the curved orange plastic chair next to his bed. "What happened, Mickey?"

"My liver's shot." He scratched his arms and legs. "Fluid buildup, itches like hell. It's the booze. I need a transplant. I don't have a lot of time left."

"Fuck."

"What are you gonna do?" He hacked out a cough. "I want to thank you, Tommy. You were a friendly face at a bad time in my life. It meant a lot. I transferred out without ever saying good-bye to you. That always bothered me. I'm sorry about that."

Back then, if I registered his leaving, it was for a high school minute.

He shrugged. "I don't know if you know . . ." His lips pressed, then he spoke. "A priest got me, like Jack Cunane. Father Bannon."

"You mentioned it yesterday." Anger simmered in my gut. If I were anywhere else, I'd punch the wall. "I'm so sorry."

He grasped the side bars on the bed, trying to sit up straight. I added pillows and helped him adjust his position. Once settled, he said, "He kept me after gym class, but, being the new kid, no one missed me. You St. John's boys looked out for each other; you were lucky."

He rubbed his face with both hands, like giving it a quick wash. "The priests apologized and all, but . . . it's always in your head, you know?"

Fucking priests. Bad enough they raped him, but he should have had the best of care, not end up like this. "I'm so sorry you had to go through that, Mick. I didn't know." I added, "Jack never got over it either. He never told anyone."

He took a deep breath. "Talking about it . . . it's almost worse than . . . if you talk about it, then it happened, so you hold it in, cope with whatever gets you through the day. I used alcohol . . . Listerine got me through freshman year."

He massaged his forehead.

"You couldn't tell your parents?"

"The shame—debilitating. I figured it was my fault. Not true, but . . ." He hesitated and cleared his throat. "I lived with my mom after they divorced. I gave her a hard time about moving to the city. I told her I hated school, hated everything, and she told me to deal with it. Try slipping into a conversation with your mom that Father Bannon made me touch his dick." He flashed a half smile. "Finding the words . . . is so hard. I told a priest in confession—in the booth to avoid the face-to-face. He lectured me about hormones and fantasies . . . told me to say three Our Fathers."

"So how did—"

He pulled his ponytail straight and released it. "Mr. Beam, the math teacher. He worked out in the gym sometimes. He walked in. I was glad that he saw, so I never had to say . . ."

He pulled the blanket up to his chin and asked to me to add an extra one from a nearby shelf. While I was in class listening to lectures on *Beowulf* or trigonometry or photosynthesis or Aquinas, a priest had raped my friend at the end of the hallway.

"I'm glad Bannon got caught. Is he in jail?"

He nodded.

"I hope he rots. They're investigating Father Farrell, but it's his word against Jack's, and Jack's gone. We're not letting up, though. We put up flyers all over the neighborhood, so if it happened to any other—"

"No one's going to call," he cut me off. "I just told you how hard it is to tell. Imagine a priest pinned you down while he got his freak on . . . you're gonna call a 1-800 number? Describe the grunting priest, the dripping jizz, move on to how you begged for it to be over and cried for your parents, wanting to die? Maybe mention how you can never stop crying, not really, not on the inside. No one's calling, Tommy."

Images came into my head. Images I tamped down and pushed back. All the times I'd shot my mouth off any time the abuse issue was discussed, like that night in McRyan's; I was so fucking ignorant. But Mickey was wrong, and I told him, "You have to see by now that keeping quiet made it worse. People want to help."

He squinted his yellowed eyes. "What? You think telling is

cathartic, righteous? Once it's out in the open, the real terror sets in of what people think."

"Reporting it still has to be the best way to go, right?"

"Jack told the DA. How did that work out for him?"

That hurt. "Not so good, but maybe he saved some kids from going through what he did."

"Are the kids saved, Tommy? Did they lock up that priest?"

"Not yet," I admitted. "Some people don't believe that it happened, but lots of us do, and Jack made it easier for anyone else who comes forward."

"Tommy, you don't get it. You stop one bad priest and another one comes along. For most Catholics, as long as it doesn't happen to them or theirs, they don't care, or maybe they do, but not enough."

"Stop it. That's so not true."

"You know how I know? After everything that happened, they go on exactly the same. Nothing changes."

"That's not true . . ."

Mickey had a coughing fit. I reached over to ring for the nurse, but he waved me off. He wheezed as he spoke. "How do they do it, Tommy? I'd love to be able to go on like nothing happened. The booze helps, but it's killing me."

"Mickey, do what you have to do to get the transplant. Otherwise he wins, man."

He tried to focus through heavy eyelids. "I got no fight left in me."

Tears welled in my eyes, for Mickey, for Jack, for all the kids. "You're not alone, Mickey. I'll help you. Whatever you need."

Maybe God wanted me to find Mickey . . .

"Thanks, Tommy. It was good to see you. I'm kind of tired now."

He lowered the bed and I stayed until he closed his eyes.

Mickey was wrong. I believed with all of my heart that the Church cared, that people cared, but caring didn't solve the abuse problem, and no one seemed to know how to stop it. At home, I texted everyone, even Gav, Terry, and StevieB, to let them know Mickey was at Jeanes and wasn't doing too good. It was fifty-fifty they would remember him, but he needed our support. We'd have to get past our differences and pull together, keep his spirits up while he fought the good fight until a transplant came through. This was doable. We could do for Mickey what we couldn't do for Jack.

The responses weren't too hopeful, mostly question marks, but it was likely that they'd been drinking.

In Jean or in jeans?

Any relation to Randall?

Mickey's fine, he's so fine.

Whatever. I'd resend the details in the morning.

But it was too late. The first text of the morning came from his mom: Mickey had died in his sleep.

In the newspaper, his obit described him as being "at peace." The ceremony was private. I sent a card, letting his family know that a Mass would be said in his memory, and afterward, I prayed that they took no offense.

CHAPTER 20

StevieB

Another avoidable death. I went through the motions of living—wake, wash, work—and worried deep down that I was a death magnet. I texted my friends to let them know about Mickey's passing, but I left out the details. Mickey was at peace; that was all that mattered. I stayed in most nights and vegged in front of the television. I was fine with it. Perfectly fine. Anyway, Danny and the others were riding a bus I didn't want to ride.

At home in the evening, Mom fussed over me. I never explained, but she assumed there had been some falling out with my friends. "You know, you stand up for what's right and people are going to give you a hard time. It hurts, but that's okay. You find out who your real friends are."

She'd push Tastykakes or scoops of ice cream at me and offer to turn off her shows and watch whatever I wanted. One night, a TV show had a main character with a ponytail like Mickey and I told her about him, finding him in the Burren, what happened, and how much he suffered. I spoke haltingly, doing my best not to lose it. She hugged me and said, "You've had to deal with so much death. It's not fair. What a waste he chose to live his life that way."

She didn't get it.

I had been in self-imposed lockup for a week or two when Father Lawler announced in Mass that the church would be open on Tuesday nights for a public recitation of the Rosary. He hoped that the midweek prayer would offer "a weekly respite to connect to our Lord." I needed some respite, so on a cold Tuesday night, I bundled up and headed out to join the mostly white-haired parishioners. I prayed for Mickey and Jack and all the other victims, and my loneliness eased as I talked to everyone I knew in heaven.

I apologized to Mickey. Had I noticed that Father Bannon kept him after class? No . . . maybe. Mickey and I talked less and less as the school year went on, but those things happened. One memory I had was of Mickey sitting in a bus shelter, leaning against the plexiglass walls. He had made himself small, his arms wrapped tight across his chest and his legs crossed. I had called hello to him a bunch of times until he reacted. I'd said, "Are you deaf?"

I was such an asshole. I asked Dad, Nan, and Jack to look after Mickey. I missed them all so much.

As I stood to leave, I spied StevieB standing alone in the back of the church near the confessionals. The last time we'd talked was that night when he criticized the Cunanes for their victim outreach. He had piled on some pounds. He wore an Eagles green parka with attached gloves dangling from the sleeves; it gave him the silhouette of the Michelin man.

He walked over to me, and his girth blocked my exit. "Tommy, long time, huh? Good to see you here. Great idea, this prayer session, huh?"

"StevieB."

He frowned. "I got your text about Mickey. I called the hospital, but I was too late. I'm sorry. What was the matter with him?"

The fucker. Really? Okay, it was nice that he'd called on Mickey, but he hadn't called me or Danny in months. "Yeah, well, he was sick. His liver failed. Alcoholism. He never got over being raped by Father Bannon."

He stared at me, and I moved past, leaving him standing there.

———

That Thursday, Mrs. Grover, the head of the Casino Night set-up committee, invited all the volunteers to a meeting in the church basement. More than a dozen men of various ages attended. Locals 19 and 158 were well represented, based on the jackets, so the set up and teardown would be a piece of cake. A successful Casino Night would bode well for future fundraisers. Being part of this effort, helping my community, got me out of my head. I was almost in a good mood.

In the middle of Mrs. Grover's spiel, the double doors screeched open and StevieB ambled into the room. His corduroys trilled a *weep-weep* sound as he walked. He took the last seat at the table, the one next to me. He pulled the chair out and full-face cringed as the metal chair legs scraped across the linoleum floor. We were airplane-seat close. Once he settled, he turned to me and said in an unquiet voice, "Hi, Tommy."

I gave him a chin.

During the meeting, I kept my eyes focused on Mrs. Grover, which meant looking past StevieB. On an easel stand with paper, she sketched how the room had to be set up and reviewed the timelines and schedules. Every once in a while, StevieB turned to look at me, but I kept my eyes focused on the easel as if Mrs. Grover was briefing us on a plan to save the world.

I had to cold-shoulder him. There was too great a chance that he'd criticize the Cunanes or say something in support of Father Farrell. By not talking to StevieB, I eliminated the risk of punching him out on church grounds. Fuck him for making me look rude. And fuck him for blowing us off all this time. Talk about callous. That was the trouble with Holy Rollers— they were so focused on checking the boxes that they forgot to practice what they preached.

I planned to bolt as soon as the meeting ended, but Mrs. Grover, a real Chatty Cathy, delayed my departure to ask after Mom. It took forever to ease out of the conversation. All the other attendees had left except for StevieB, who stood by the door, rocking on the soles of his feet, waiting like a puppy.

"StevieB."

We exchanged nods and left the building together. Outside, the streetlights lit the sidewalk through the bitter gray fuzz of winter's air. StevieB slipped on his gloves, zipped his parka, and tightened the hood. I pulled my Jeff cap tight, dug my hands into my jacket pockets, and lifted my shoulders to warm my ears. We set off for home. I had to slow my pace to match StevieB's thigh-rubbing, labored gait.

He said, "You're mad at me."

"Where have you been? Last time we talked was after the meeting at the Cunanes'."

"I've been here. I'm around. Trying to deal. Like you."

"I told you about at the meeting at Danny's, about Jack and Father Farrell, and then a minute later everything got back to Father's lawyer."

"I never repeated anything, Tommy. I swear to God."

If StevieB swore, then he was telling the truth. I was glad he was not the squealer, but I wasn't letting him off easy. "Danny said you haven't talked to him since the funeral."

"It was just easier not to. I said enough at Jack's funeral without piling on or saying the wrong thing. The worst day of his life, and I insulted his cousin and almost started a fight, do you remember? I'm so ashamed. I pray for him and his family every day and every night, Tommy. That's better for him."

The goofball. Here I'd been having my own pity party and he was in bad shape too. Of course, StevieB spent the last months on his knees praying for the Cunanes.

I said, "He asks about you. You heard he lost it in Mass? He got tossed, and the rest of them walked out in support."

"They're grieving." He pulled the strings on his hood tighter. "They'll come back, right?"

It was so cold it was hard to move my lips to speak. "I doubt it. They want changes. I love the Church with all my heart. It's gotten me through some tough times, but even I have my doubts about some of its priests. Father Bannon? His collar was a cover that gave him access. Look at all the oddball priests we had in high school. Maybe it wasn't so much of a calling they had, but that they couldn't get jobs anywhere else."

His eyebrows lifted almost to his hairline. "Tommy, I can't believe you said that." Just as fast, he was serious. "You're staying, right?"

"My whole life is this church. But you get where they're coming from, right? Kids have to be safe. No kid should have to deal with what Jack and Mickey did."

He sighed and his eyes teared, no doubt from the cold. We were at his house already. As he trudged up his front walk, I called after him, "Hey, the boys' CYO team has their first playoff game Friday night. Do you want to go?"

He turned and smiled. "Okay. Thanks, Tommy."

On Friday, StevieB and I walked over to the rec center to see St. John's play Holy Child. Inside, fans packed the scarred wooden bleachers, and I had an odd, end-of-an-era feeling. In the past, the whole gang would have been here for a CYO playoff game, and now, except for Terry coaching, it was just StevieB and me. And then there were three.

The St. John's fans sat on one side of the gym, and Holy Child's fans on the other. An announcer, the same old man from back in our day, clicked on the mic to introduce the varsity teams waiting at the main entrance. As he announced each name, the player ran through the doors to applause from their side of the gym.

"From St. John's, starting point guard, Liam Mallory."

Liam entered to thunderous cheers. I spied his brother, Lucas, next in line. I said in a too loud voice, "Why the hell are the Mallory brothers playing?"

As soon as I said it, the surrounding spectators shot me dirty looks.

In quieter tones, StevieB said, "Unless they do something overt during a game, like fight or hassle a ref, the punishment is up to Father Lawler."

"The things they did to Danny's house. It was no Mischief Night toilet paper job. It was disgusting. They should have been suspended."

Those eavesdropping nearby hurled stink eyes at me, but I didn't care.

StevieB leaned his elbows on his knees. "Father Lawler talked to them. They were sorry. We forgive; that's what we do."

I lowered my voice. "What? Did he tell them to say a couple of Hail Marys? You think they learned their lesson? They didn't even clean up the mess."

He stared off in the distance. End of conversation. Nothing weird about that. StevieB being StevieB.

With the teams in place, the tip-off started a fast-paced

game. Terry walked the sideline like a college coach in the
Final Four. He challenged the ref's calls, took frequent time-
outs, yelled play calls, and gave exaggerated hand signals. He
barked orders, trying to direct the kids' every move, so that
some players paid more attention to the sidelines than what
was happening on the court. Not the Mallorys. They hogged
the ball, took most of the shots, and berated their teammates
with finger pointing and sneering.

The score seesawed, each team struggling to take control.
The gym vibrated from the crowd's cheers and jeers. With less
than one minute, St. John's was up by one and forced a Holy
Child turnover. The Mallorys, dripping with sweat, taunted the
Holy Child defense with feints, making them jump and stretch.
As the shot clock ticked down, Lucas drove the lane. Holy
Child's right forward stood with raised arms to block his access
and got drilled. The shot missed as the two fell to the ground, a
mass of arms and legs. The crowd inhaled in unison.

The ref called an offensive foul on Lucas, who exploded
in disbelief. He went nose-to-nose with the ref, who called a
technical and ejected him from the game. While the ref's back
was turned to confer with the scorekeeper, Liam gave the ref
the universal sign for jerking off. The crowd was on its feet—
Holy Child fans booing at the disrespect, St. John's still booing
the call. While Terry called a time-out to rein in his players,
Holy Child's coach conferred with the ref. The game resumed,
and the ref called a technical on Liam and tossed him from the
game. People around us fumed; the ref hadn't seen what Liam
did, not with his own eyes. Why'd he call the T?

Final score: Holy Child 48, St. John's 47.

The St. John's crowd booed. I said to StevieB, "They miss
Danny, huh? He never would have let them get away with that
stuff. Would have made all the difference."

StevieB said little. As much as I hated the Mallorys and their behavior, I, too, was disappointed we lost.

After the game, McRyan's would be full of people whining that we were robbed, so I suggested that we hit up Greenberg's, but the under-twenty-one whiners filled the booths at the deli. We ordered our food to-go and went back to my house. Mom had gone out to dinner with the Hanlons, so StevieB and I created a comfortable mess of hoagies, chips, and drinks spread out on the kitchen table.

In the time we'd been apart, he had become something of an eating machine. He did this weird thing now where he focused on his food, almost willing himself not to eat, then took quick piranha-like bites until it was all gone. After, he went on a mission, scraping the plate with a fork to get up every bit of fallen toppings. That explained his packing on the pounds.

It prompted me to suggest we shoot some hoops at the rec center in the morning. "So what if the guys are there."

He stood up too fast, reaching for a paper towel, and hit his head on the pendulum light fixture, sending it swinging. "No."

"You don't want to work out, or you don't want to risk seeing anyone?"

He rubbed his head. "Look, I will. One of these days. C'mon, let's talk about something else. How's work?"

I loved the guy, but he was one strange duck. I crumpled some of the wrappers and stuffed them into the trash and poured a beer. "Work's fine. It's okay. I guess. I don't know. I'm kind of stuck, like I know I should go back to school or try something else, but anything new requires some kind of training, and then I have to figure out what to study, and it's deciding for the rest of my life, you know?"

"If you do nothing, nothing changes, nothing gets better. It's not that big of a decision. People change careers all the time."

"It's something I would have talked to Dad about. Whenever I think about what I should do with my life, I think about him and how much I miss him."

"A journey begins with the first step, Tommy."

"Is that from the Bible?"

"No, it's a slogan from a travel agent." We laughed. "No joke, Tommy. Real fast, what was your favorite class at Community?"

"I liked sociology. It was only an intro course, but a lot of social work is about helping people. Like with Jack and Mickey, I wished I'd taken more classes to know how to spot someone in trouble or what to say or how to help if I did."

He hesitated, deflated a bit. Staring at the mess on the table, he said, "Sociology it is, then."

"But then I have to figure out which school. Holy Family, LaSalle, St. Joe's, Villanova . . . I don't know."

Still staring, he said, "Temple and Penn State Abington are cheaper. Since you have a car, Penn State might be an easier commute."

I regretted this already. Could I even afford it? How would I fit it into my work schedule? What jobs could I get if I majored in sociology? What did they pay? Would I like the work? Being in class again? I'd probably be the oldest person there. Maybe it was too late.

"I'm not sure," I said.

"You apply online. It'll take five minutes. Go get your laptop. We'll do it right now."

I stayed still.

"C'mon, just do it," he said.

I sat immobile. I could hear that girl Jessica from the Library Bar cackling in my head, asking if I was on the five-year or ten-year gap plan. I'd probably end up in a class full of Jessicas.

He repeated, "Just do it."

Somehow, I trudged upstairs and grabbed my laptop. I wiped down the kitchen table, set up my ancient computer, and pulled up the Penn State Abington website. I had to create an account. Okay, no big. The application started with the basics: name, address, education. Then they wanted to know if anyone in my family went to Penn State, like they were looking out for their own. I left that section blank; no one in my family had gone to college. For my activities, I listed my Acme job and volunteering at St. John's. The form had too much whitespace, so I added my high school intramural sports. How pathetic at my age. I'd look like an idiot, a loser.

StevieB prodded me to keep going. In the final section, I had to write a paragraph on why I would succeed in the major I chose. I wrote that I was more serious about success at this stage of my life and had a better understanding of what I wanted, what was important, but I had a hard time explaining why I cared about my field of study. "I want to help people" sounded sappy, and telling them about Jack or Mickey seemed like TMI. I kept it high level. I wrote that my life had been impacted by trauma, and I wanted to understand why people do what they do, how they deal, and how to make my community better. I put in an online request for my community college transcripts, and after the sixty-five-dollar application fee, I was done.

Amazed at my forward progress, I told StevieB how much I appreciated him pushing me. "Who knows how long it would've taken until I got my ass in gear."

He smiled and shrugged.

I teased him. "I'll give you back your own advice, you know, about giving Danny a shout. Just do it."

He said nothing. He was so hard on himself. While I shut down my laptop, I changed the subject and asked him about his job at his family's printing shop. "You're lucky to have both your parents. Is that what you want to do with your life?"

"My parents worked hard to get the shop established. It's a nice life. They want me to take over so they can retire and move down the shore. That's why they're obsessed with the parish merger talks. They're worried everyone will move out, the neighborhood will change, and there won't be a business to hand over."

"Gav's worried too, but Mr. Hanlon's meeting seems to have everyone really engaged in saving the parish."

StevieB stayed pensive. "Father Lawler says there's nothing to worry about, but no one knows him. My parents and a lot of others say we need Father Farrell back."

"That's so wrong."

"I know."

I froze. "You do?"

He sat up straight. "My concern is for the church. I hate what the scandals do. The slightest hint at a scandal and people get turned off. They leave and turn away from God. Look at what's already happened."

"If Father Farrell comes back, it'll be Crazyville," I said. "Danny will probably kill him. Sheila for sure. We'll all be doing prison visits and getting strip searched."

StevieB went pale, which was hard to do for an Irish man sitting beneath a pendulum kitchen light. "That would happen?"

"Strip searched on a prison visit? It's a rule," I said. "Oh, you mean about the Cunanes going after Father Farrell? Well, they're not going to give him a pass. The Boston cousins will want to pay him a visit. Buzzcut too. I'm not sure about myself. Even Old Mrs. McCullough would want to slip Father a mickey.

What's the matter? You look like you're going to puke. Are you okay?"

"No."

He squeezed his eyes closed and knocked on his forehead with his fists. He mumbled something, again and again. On the third try, I understood him to say, "It's all my fault."

I sat statue still, waiting to get a clue. He was having some kind of nervous breakdown. I got the whiskey bottle down from the shelf even though I knew he'd abstain. I poured two fingers and handed it to him; he passed, and I downed it in one.

"I should have told."

Oh no. "About Jack?"

He shook his head. Relief. Dread. I asked, "Something about Father Farrell? Someone else?"

Tears rolled down his cheeks. He wiped them away with the small take-out napkins on the counter.

"Aw, Jesus. Aw, StevieB."

"I kept quiet. I thought I was doing the right thing, but I was so wrong. All the suffering to Jack and the Cunanes, everyone, all the fallout. It keeps getting worse and worse. Everything bad that's happened. It's all my fault. I could've prevented all of this if I'd just told someone."

"Stop it, StevieB. Don't you dare beat yourself up."

I let him talk at his own pace, afraid of saying the wrong thing. His inhales eased from multiple beats to regular ones as he regained his composure. He kept his eyes shrouded as he spoke. "I was an altar boy." He paused. "It was after Mass, in the sacristy, like Jack. I thought I was the only one. Father Farrell asked me to finish some leftover wine so it wouldn't go to waste. I did what he told me."

That motherfucking Farrell! I am going to kill him.

I leaned forward. "You were a kid."

"Afterward, after he was done with me . . . he yelled at me. I let evil inside me. I let Satan use my body to seduce him. I was so scared that I hyperventilated, almost passed out. Once I'd calmed, he forgave me. He gave me penance. He promised to keep it a secret and never tell my parents."

Anger built inside, but I spoke in a soft voice. "You were a kid. You believed what your priest told you."

"I kept my distance from him, so it only happened one time. It was my cross to bear. I prayed and prayed, and over time, the memory got buried. I buried it for so long; it was like it happened to someone else." He uncovered his eyes. "That night at McRyan's with the news story, it started coming back. At the Mass after Jack died and at the funeral, Father Farrell talked about Jack's embattled soul. That's what he'd said to me back then: 'my embattled soul.'"

"Even if you had told someone, they might not have believed you, or they might have believed you and done nothing about it. You don't know what would have happened, but you can tell now. Between Jack's complaint and yours . . ."

He grabbed my wrist and squeezed it hard. "You're the only person who knows, Tommy. It's too late. I know I should, but I can't. I'd rather die. Don't tell anyone, please. I talked Jack into being an altar boy. I never imagined it would happen again. If I had told on Father Farrell back then, Jack would have been spared. Once Danny knows . . . he'll hate me. Everyone will hate me. I hate me."

"Stop it. No one will hate you. You got conned." I shook him off. "I won't tell, but you need to talk to a counselor or somebody. Jack and Mickey never talked to anyone either until it was too late. Look where that got them. The professionals—they'll know how to help you take the next steps."

He leaned back in his chair with his shoulders hunched.

"You have to stop the guilt trip. You were what, twelve? Look at Brendan's sister's kid, Timmy, he's twelve and what, four foot and change? Can you imagine him fighting off Father Farrell? Standing up to him, challenging him in front of other adults? Telling him he was full of shit? Of course not. Cut yourself a break."

He hiccupped. His face was wet from crying, and he wiped it with his sleeve. "I can't do psychiatrists, Tommy."

I twisted my lip. How many other tortured souls walked the street? If StevieB kept quiet, and no one else filed a complaint, Father Farrell would be free and clear. "If you told, it'd seal the deal for Father Farrell."

"I can't, Tommy. I just can't."

CHAPTER 21

Lawyer for the Defense

I carried the weight of the world on my shoulders, worrying about StevieB. What was the right thing to do? He never considered going to his parents, and neither did I; their unsmiling pictures were in the dictionary under cold fish. With all my heart, I believed that Danny would have nothing but compassion for StevieB. Sure, if StevieB had told on Father Farrell right away, Jack might be here today, but if no one had believed him or had done anything, we might have lost them both. StevieB wasn't ready to discuss his abuse in official channels, but he had taken an important first step and told me. He trusted me with his secret. As tempted as I was to reach out to Father Lawler or the DA's office, I kept my promise not to tell. I did text Mickey's mother to get the name of Mickey's therapist, and I gave the contact information to StevieB, but he declined. The only thing I knew to do was check on him, keep his spirits up, reinforce my support for him, and at every possible chance, keep the pressure on him to call the therapist.

The following week, in the church bulletin, Father Lawler offered a personal invitation to the entire parish to attend a Wednesday night informational meeting to update parishioners on Father Farrell. Finally! The results of the Archdiocese's investigation! Hallelujah. This was the light at the end of the tunnel. Father Farrell getting kicked to the curb would upset some, but it had to happen. Let the healing begin.

I came home from work on Wednesday, and the house smelled of deliciousness: sautéed ground meats with onions and carrots. Mom had been busy making my favorite, shepherd's pie. The meats bathed in brown sauce, topped with fluffy mashed potatoes, sat in the fridge waiting to be popped into the oven. It was Mom's lone signature dish.

"I know how much you like it," she said.

We ate in the dining room. While I shoveled the food in, Mom picked. She said, "You have a low opinion of Father Farrell, Tommy, but you need to hold your tongue tonight. Don't embarrass me. If you can't say anything nice, don't say anything at all. Don't do anything foolish, right? Promise me."

"Sure, Mom, but it's not like they're going to give him a pass."

She put her fork down and glared. "There's only one thing we know for sure: the church will do what's right. Whatever happens . . . it's God's will."

"He did it, Mom. They need to lock him up and throw away the key."

"See? That's what I mean. Don't talk like that. There will be people there who support him, and it's hurtful. Just sit and listen." She glared at me.

"Sure, okay, I'll be kind to the kooks. No fights, no f-bombs. But he is a child abuser, Mom."

She moved food around on her plate. "I don't want you going if you can't behave yourself."

"What are you talking about? This'll be great. The facts will be out in the open, and we can all move forward."

She cleared the table and kept her eyes averted from me. Even for the strongest Father Farrell defender, there had to be niggling doubts about him. People, like Mom, needed to hear the truth. They'd probably need some time to get used to the idea of what he was, but once he left, they'd forget about him. Out of sight, out of mind.

When it was time to leave, I was dressed and waiting at the door, but Mom took her time wrapping her scarf, buttoning her coat, and pulling her gloves tight. She started for the door but stopped. She went into the closet and got Dad's scarf, wrapped it around my neck, and adjusted my collar. She said little on the walk.

Inside the church, we sat near the front on the center aisle. While we waited, an usher set up a microphone stand, one of several, at the end of our pew. StevieB and his parents were in the second row; he waved and smiled nervously at me like it hurt. Dad's scarf was itchy; I pulled it off and stuffed it into my pocket.

I scoped the crowd. The Cunanes weren't there, but they'd probably met earlier with the investigators. Surrounded by all the people I'd prayed with my whole life, calm eluded me. There were Father Farrell supporters here. Would they see reason? They had to, right? My stomach knotted up around my tasty dinner; the meal pressed against my breastbone.

Father Lawler stood before the crowd at the altar with Jesus nailed to the cross as his backdrop. He waited while the parishioners settled and took the mic. "Thank you all for coming tonight, and for your support to me and St. John's during this difficult time. Other parishes having this experience often see financial and membership impacts, but not St. John's, so thank you. The Archdiocese is truly impressed with all of us. Give yourself a round of applause."

The crowd erupted in sustained loud clapping, myself included; I clapped until my hands hurt. As the crowd quieted,

Father Lawler called up Mr. Hanlon, who was seated in the first pew and introduced him as the man who led our efforts to stay the course. "Roger's sign project has been a huge success, and I know we are all looking forward to our Casino Night next month, again thanks to Roger. Let's give him a round of applause."

I clapped less, remembering the signs on the Cunanes' lawn.

Father Lawler continued. "In addition to everything else he's done for us, Roger and some friends have been doing some fact-finding about the allegations against Father Farrell. They have some information to share. Roger?"

Every muscle in my body tensed. Hanlon, not the Archdiocese, had done the research? Hanlon was an idiot. He didn't know what he was doing.

Mr. Hanlon gazed out across the filled pews like a sea captain. "As part of my Save St. John's effort, I've been leading a small group looking into the charges against Father Farrell. We all know him. We know what kind of a man he is. We have an important guest here tonight, and once you listen to what he has to say, you'll agree with us that Father Farrell should be exonerated."

Over scattered cheering, I let out an unconstrained "Boo!" Mom gave me a backhand to my gut. StevieB faced forward; his head tilted up at the crucifix.

Father Lawler cleared his throat. "I insist you all show some respect. This is God's house."

He looked right at me, and so did everyone else. I ducked down in the pew pretending to tie my shoe, which left Mom to get most of the hairy eyeballs. She whispered through gritted teeth, "Behave!"

Mr. Hanlon introduced John Magee, who had been sitting a few rows ahead on the aisle. I remembered the name; he was

Father Farrell's lawyer, the one who threatened the Cunanes with a lawsuit. He strutted up the aisle and shook hands with Mr. Hanlon and Father Lawler. The two then sat in throne-like chairs to the left of where the lawyer now stood.

Magee wore a suit and tie, although his tie was loosened just-so to not look fussy. He was a tall, broad man with a wide face. If I had to guess, I'd say he was an ex-rugby player. He held the mic in his palm like it was a billy club and shot me a look for my booing, then he turned on the charm for the crowd.

"Hello, everyone, and thank you for coming tonight. As Roger mentioned, my name is John Magee. I've been an attorney for twenty-three years. Like you, I've known Father Farrell for some time. I've reviewed the facts of his case and will present them to you tonight. Some of you may not like what I have to say, but all I can do is report my findings as an officer of the court. I'll open the floor to any questions you may have. There are a few microphones set up for you in each aisle. Once you hear the facts, you can make up your own mind."

Magee donned a pair of reading glasses and brought out an electronic tablet to read his notes. Everyone in the church sat on the edges of their pews. "I have reviewed Father Farrell's entire personnel file—all thirty years. I have read every Archdiocesan assessment, every evaluation, every piece of paper in his personnel folder. Until this recent single complaint, his record is unblemished. Let me repeat that. Father Farrell's record is unblemished."

The audience responded with clapping and "woo-hoos."

With a cane she wielded like a weapon, Old Mrs. McCullough hobbled into the aisle. She spoke slow and loud through bright red lips. "I insist that you cease repeating that his record is unblemished. Jack Cunane filed a complaint!"

Sparse applause. Magee had a foot in height and a hundred

pounds on her, but that set-in-stone McCullough scowl told him he had zero chance of intimidating her. She had the blind confidence of a warrior.

"Fair enough. Let's look at this . . . complainant. A young man who had trouble in school, and had trouble holding a job. He was a drinker and a pot smoker. The issues with this kid, laid end to end, would reach from here to downtown. The complainant had no credibility; no court of law would have ever believed him. To destroy a man like Father Farrell based on a complaint of an obviously mentally ill young man is unfair. It's un-American."

The applause volume and length drowned out the quiet booing and added further insult. StevieB turned around toward me in a panic. My fists clenched, and I half stood. Mom grabbed my hand, pulled me back into the pew, and whispered, "Pick your battles, Tommy."

Brendan's voice boomed from the back microphone. "Aren't Jack's issues evidence of rape trauma syndrome? You know, he had those issues 'cause a priest had sex with him."

The crowd hissed.

"Language, please! As Father Lawler said, we are in God's house," said Magee. "Let me say this, just because someone is unstable does not mean they were abused. Unstable people do erratic things, like make unproven allegations. I believe, as everyone here does, that before we destroy a man who has given us so much, there ought to be some proof besides some careless ravings."

What did Magee think happened to a kid after being sodomized by a priest? Fuck waiting to be acknowledged. I jumped from my seat and hurried to the mic. "You're Father Farrell's lawyer. You're not objective. You're only telling his side of the story."

"Young man, I am an active member of the Archdiocesan investigative team. I am involved in all aspects of the evidential review on this case. No stone is left unturned. My role is to represent Father Farrells's interests, but the truth is the truth. What I'm telling you all is that, as an officer of the court and based on my years of experience, this case shows how unfair these new abuse policies are. Any nut-job can say anything, throw mud on a good priest, and look what happens: surprise, surprise, it sticks. It's wrong, and it's a disgrace."

Magee received sustained applause.

"Despite the DA's best effort to try this in the press," Magee said, "no one else has come forward. No one. The DA's office only left the case open for political reasons. They can get some media mileage out of it, but I'm telling you all that this case will be closed, and Father Farrell will not be indicted. There is nothing there: no proof, no evidence, no guilt."

For a nanosecond, I almost shouted that there was evidence, StevieB, but I was more worried about what this was doing to him. I looked over at him. He sat, leaning forward with his elbows on his knees. How much more could he take?

I gripped the mic. "I knew Jack Cunane, and everyone here did too. He was a good kid, and if he said it happened, it did. He had no reason to lie," I said. "Look, even if you're not sure, are you really willing to let your kids be alone with Father Farrell?"

Magee scolded me. "I get that you have some connection to the accuser, young man, but you need to sit down. All these people did not come here to listen to you throw dirt on Father Farrell. If that's why you're here, then please leave. Otherwise, take your seat, be quiet, and show some respect to these other folks."

My face flushed. I would have told him to fuck off, but a look from my mom stopped me. I wanted to punch something or someone, but I pussied out and sat back down. Mr. Hanlon gave a knowing smirk to Father Lawler.

Mr. Joyce, Terry's dad, asked, "How long will it take to clear him?"

"I can't say exactly, but I will press the DA hard. To keep this case open is a travesty."

An older woman with Crayola-black hair asked, "Will he be able to come back to St. John's? Since he left, it's been like a death in the family."

Father Lawler said, "Father Farrell's return to St. John's is for the Archdiocese to decide. I have let them know how much you all miss him and pray for his return. You have been so welcoming to me, and I am truly blessed for all your support. But as much as I have enjoyed my experience in Northeast Philly, I do believe my calling is my work at the seminary."

More clapping. *They didn't care about the abuse, or if they did, they didn't care enough.*

A heavy-set woman in a too-tight top introduced herself as a teacher's aide at St. John's and said, "The kids miss Father Farrell. He's so charming. He'd drop by the classroom all the time, and they just loved it." *Who was she kidding?*

"Until his case is closed officially, the best thing you can do is to let him know that you support him. Send cards, letters, emails, whatever. Let him know you are thinking of him. It would mean the world to him. We'll post his contact information on the church website," said Magee.

In a slow, deliberate manner, addressing me specifically, he said, "Let me add, if Father Farrell receives any mail that is in any way perceived as threatening, the police will be called and charges will be brought."

Mr. Hanlon took the mic. "With all my heart, I believe that Father Farrell is innocent. He is a good man and a good priest, and I'm not afraid to say it. He's kept us going all these years. I believe if he were here, we would have no worries about St. John's. In fact, I wrote a letter to the Archdiocese in his defense and asked them for a quick decision. We need him back here, doing God's work."

An older man raised his hand. "If you haven't sent it, I'd like to add my John Hancock to that, if it's okay."

"You should bring the letter to Mass so that we can all add our names to it," suggested a woman in the back.

Somebody else added, "Let's have all the kids sign too."

The audience clapped. Some people stood. If I stayed, I'd be complicit. I turned to my mother and squeezed her hand, but I had nothing to say. She whispered to me to stay calm. "Don't be stupid," she begged. "Please. You promised."

"I love you, Mom."

I stood and stared down the truth twisters, standing in front of the altar. I glared around the congregation at the familiar faces and said a silent good-bye. StevieB shook his head, pleading with his eyes. I shook my head, exited the pew, and walked down the aisle beneath the gigantic crucifix hanging over the main doors and left my church. I passed the Sacred Heart of Jesus statue on the landing and whispered, "I'm sorry."

CHAPTER 22

Yo Bro

I held in a raging storm. I raced down the sidewalk. Tears leaked as I texted StevieB: *Everything will be okay. Lunch tomorrow, Acme.*

I was a block from St. John's when my phone chirped. I expected it to be StevieB, but it was a text from Danny: *I have a shot of Irish with your name on it. Come to the back.*

I cut through the alleys to the back of his house. He and Ray stood at the open door, waiting. I took the shot glass from Danny and threw back the whiskey. It burned so good. They welcomed me in and patted me on the back. Brendan had Skyped the meeting, so they had watched everything that had been said in the church real-time.

"Something was up. We had our suspicions," Danny said. "Neither the Archdiocese nor the DA had any involvement with the meeting. Thanks for sticking up for Jack."

"I left. They . . . they're . . . they want to . . . like nothing happened."

They guided me to the sofa, and I sat down, staring into space. That something I loved was so cruel . . . Grief and anger hit in waves. Images of my mom, my dad, my childhood, Jack, Mickey, Father Farrell, Father Bannon, StevieB, Hanlon, Magee, the clapping congregation.

Danny brought the bottle over and set it in front of me. "This will help for now."

"I want to punch someone. That fucking attorney . . . Hanlon . . . Lawler. Just wipe the smiles off their faces. Hanlon lives next door, for God's sakes. I have to . . . smash his windows or—"

"No, you don't," said Danny. "You don't want to do that; you'll get arrested. Worse, you'll be Crazy Tommy Dunleavey."

Touché. "I kept meaning to call."

"We missed you," Ray said. "I'm sorry you had to go through that tonight. Some things you have to find out for yourself."

It took a good half hour for the whiskey to take the edge off, and I was left with a numbed calmness. I observed the room I had been away from. Posters, pennants, and pictures no longer hung on the walls. Shelves sat empty. Danny said, "My parents are putting the house on the market. Nothing official yet. Just getting ready. Eddie and I have been looking at apartments."

The Cunanes leaving the neighborhood . . . inconceivable. "When? Where?"

"Not sure. Over the summer probably. They need some distance."

Jesus.

"How are you feeling, Tommy?" Ray asked.

If I'd have been at home, I'd have curled up into a fetal position. I ran my hands through my hair. "Still free-falling on the inside."

"That's kind of how Dez describes it. He's okay, but he's having a tough time running into fires like he used to." Ray cracked a beer. "If it makes you feel any better, some scientists say that behind all chaos is order that we can't yet see."

"Huh?"

Danny explained, "You know how Matt and Brigid are trying to plan their wedding? Ray accompanied them to a Universal Unitarians lecture and hasn't shut up about it."

I gave a never-heard-of-it shoulder lift.

"It was cool," said Ray. "They're not really a religion. People from all different faiths meet up. They believe in the inherent worth of every person, and they look for insight into the universe from all different sources, literature, science—"

Danny busted, "Seriously, did you memorize the brochure?"

Ray smiled.

Jeez, they actually followed through on the God crawl. I asked, "You liked it?"

"I liked it," Ray said. "They're all about engaging the mind. Moral clarity."

"Matt and Brigid?"

"I don't know. It's so opposite of what we're used to. No one answer or one way or one book. It's a little bit of everything. Intellectually it makes sense. Matt said it felt funny."

"Even after everything," I said, "going to some other church . . . I'd feel like a traitor."

Danny agreed. "I know what you mean. Thanks for laying down your life for my sins, Jesus, but I'm going in another direction. The first weekend I didn't go to Mass felt like I smashed a mirror and walked under a ladder next to a black cat all at once. On the other hand, what do I need religion for? I can pray for Jack. I'm a good person."

"So, you'd be a spiritual Stoney Aloney?" Ray asked. "Religion is a way to connect with people who share your values. It provides a sense of security, helps with our anxieties. That need for connection is hardwired. It's an instinct like the hive mentality for bees or an ant colony. You go solo, you'll always feel like something's missing."

"I miss being part of something bigger. I miss that connection to the parish," said Danny. "But I'm not an Aloney. I have my family, and I have you weirdos."

"Yeah, but it's easy to get wrapped up in your routines. It's hard to step away and contemplate all the big-picture stuff—living a meaningful life, being a better person. Organized religions are good at that."

"It's the other stuff. Anything beyond the here and now just seems like bullshit," said Danny.

Ray countered, "Maybe God as an old guy in white robes is nonsense, but look at the universe: it's infinite, it's incredible—black holes, time travel, gravity, quantum mechanics. Look at the Earth. No way random protein interactions created all life as we know it. There's something else."

I liked the old guy in the white robes. "Are you going back to the Unitarians, Ray?"

"Absolutely."

Danny said, "You remember meeting Dez's girl Leah? Not Catholic. Not Buddhist. She's Jewish. She got us all to enroll in a Taste of Judaism class. It's for Dez. He wants us there. You're in, right?"

I did not want to go, no way, but I didn't want to turn down the invite, either. "Like a temple or something?"

"C'mon, it's a chance to learn something new," said Ray.

"That's not weird?"

Danny smiled. "A bunch of Micks going to synagogue, what's weird about that?"

In the morning, I received my acceptance email from Penn State Abington as a psychological and social science major. I was a Nittany Lion. Orientation for transfer students was in May, and summer classes started in June. I was happy to be accepted but seriously panicked. My wobbly, chaotic life already had a full plate. I considered postponing my start date, but I really wanted to do this for all the Jacks, Mickeys, and StevieBs.

At lunchtime, a pale, shaky StevieB was already waiting for me in the back booth of Acme's café. I shook his hand and put my lunch order on the table. "How you doing, man? Let me get you a sandwich. What do you want?"

His eyes were bloodshot, and his voice raspy. "You're coming back, right, Tommy? You lost your temper. Magee set you off. Trashing Jack. He's nothing but a paid attack dog. Making out like Father Farrell's an angel and convincing everyone. We'd get to keep Father Lawler if it wasn't for him. It's his fault. You're coming back, right, Tommy?"

"I left, StevieB . . ."

"No. No. You can't mean that?"

I sat down and looked him in the eye. "I mean it."

"I'm sorry."

"What are you apologizing for? I'm taking a stand. I was a mess last night. I'm grieving, I guess, but I'm okay with it . . . sort of. I feel like it had to happen."

His posture and downcast eyes suggested he was lost in his own head. He carried guilt that was not his to carry. I worried about his sense of abandonment. "We're still friends. Nothing's changed. I'm just not going back."

He sat unmoved, staring at the tabletop. I unwrapped my turkey hoagie and cut it in two and put a half in front of him. "C'mon, eat something."

I told him about my acceptance from Penn State. I said, "Look at the positive difference you made in my life, man. You made that happen. I'd never have done it without you."

He blinked.

"How about we go over to the campus on Saturday and walk around?"

He relaxed his posture but sat on the edge of his seat. "Maybe."

"Danny and Ray asked after you."

He hugged his body.

"I didn't tell them anything," I said. "I never will unless you say it's okay. They care about you. They miss you. I wanted you to know."

I also wanted him to eat. If he ate, then he was okay. He pushed the sandwich away. "It's all Father Farrell's fault."

"He brought the problem to us, but it's bigger than him. It's all the bad priests. It's all of the kids, and everyone turning their backs."

"I can never leave, Tommy."

"I know. It's okay. You have to do what's right for you. C'mon now. Eat something. Did you call the therapist?"

"You think I'm crazy, don't you?"

"I'm worried about you is all. You're dealing with some heavy stuff."

"I know you don't get it, Tommy, but I really believe God doesn't give us more than we can handle."

"They want Father Farrell back. What'll you do if that happens?"

He combed his bangs with his hand while I stared at him. "I'll be fine, Tommy."

"Please, call the doc."

It took a minute. "I'm good." He stood and left.

He never touched the sandwich.

CHAPTER 23

An Intro to Judaism

On a Tuesday night in January, Danny, Ray, Eddie, and I crammed into Dez's SUV, and my brand-new button-down shirt wrinkled like an accordion. We were on our way to Temple Beth Israel in the suburbs. I didn't tell StevieB what we were doing; I worried he'd find a way to feel guilty about it. It was crazy, anyway. We were Irish, not Jewish, but I went because it was important to Dez. He was hoping to find something and wanted us there if he did. Besides, Danny and Ray were there for me in my time of crisis after my walkout. I could do this. All for one and all that.

As the car crossed the Boulevard, the building density dropped. Rowhouses were replaced by twins that were replaced by single-family homes. Trees and greenery replaced concrete. As we traveled west, conversation quieted. We weren't in the wilderness, but we weren't in the great Northeast either. At a red light, I spied our destination just up a hill. Jesus, we were almost there.

First-day-of-school anxiety washed over me. I knew not to walk around the place with a ham sandwich, but what if there were things I was supposed to do or not do? I didn't want to look like an idiot.

"Yarmulkes! What about yarmulkes?" I asked. Dez doubted we needed them for a class, but he didn't know for sure. I pictured us beanied up. This was all too weird. I wanted to go home. I rolled the window down some; I needed air.

All eyes homed in on the synagogue. Ray asked whether anyone had ever been here, and no one had. I had never been in any other house of worship in my life. It was one thing not to go to Mass, but a totally different thing to go somewhere else. What was God thinking, looking down on us? Like Danny had said—His only begotten Son gave up His life for us, and our response was thanks, but no thanks. My dad must be so disappointed.

We exited the car, stood on the sidewalk, and gazed up at the building. My heart pounded. The walls were curved, with large glass windows and doors whose white light brightened the night.

"If you told me a year ago that we'd all be standing here . . ." Eddie said and stopped.

A quietness passed between us. Even though we were here at Dez's request, Jack was the why. Whether we were supposed to be here or not, whether we were comfortable or not, leaving from where we were had to be done.

We moseyed up to the entranceway, the opposite of our normal hurried city pace, like a multi-legged beast almost joined at the shoulders. A placard on the main entrance said: "Given world events, all doors are locked for security purposes. Non-members with synagogue business must request access." Great. Anti-Semitic terrorists were a possibility. Fucking great. We gathered behind Danny, who pressed the buzzer to request access. A small, bent-over old man wearing a yarmulke opened the etched glass door for us, but he struggled with the weight of it. Danny leaned against it to hold it open for him, which then put me entering first! The old man seized my hand, and my heart jumped over a skyscraper.

He said, "We're so pleased that you're here tonight. Shalom."

I shook his hand with the smoothness of a robot. I managed to say, "Back at you."

Everyone else gave him a "shalom," although pronunciation varied. Danny assumed the man was the teacher and explained we were there for his class. The man smiled. His name was Larry. He was neither the teacher nor a rabbi; he was a volunteer greeter. "To make everyone who comes here feel like you're visiting family."

Like that would happen, Larry. But I appreciated his optimism.

He directed us to the classroom, and I maintained a quiet nonchalance as we meandered the brightly lit hallways, trying to take it all in. Whereas St. John's had the worship space on the ground floor, and a community meeting space in the basement, this place was spread out: meeting areas, classrooms, and two worship spaces. The décor—carpeting, earth tones, wavy-lined modern paintings in wild colors, and so many unstained-glass windows—was so different from St. John's linoleum floors, crucifixes, and Renaissance-style statues.

We were the first students to arrive. Each of us walked the perimeter of the classroom, checking out the wall art and a giant map of Israel. Weird curvy marks dominated one wall; Ray said they were Hebrew letters. I asked him what the letters said. "It's a famous Jewish saying. You know it, Tommy."

I shrugged.

He pointed to the letters. "Back at you."

"Very funny."

Dez said, "You know, Leah said we all might be part Jewish. She read an article that said Ireland was settled by Hebrews who came over from Spain. A lot of the town names in Ireland are based on the Hebrew language, and there's some weird burial chambers found only in Ireland and Israel."

Eddie smirked. "Is she trying to convert you?"

"Nah. Jews don't do that. It's a thing with them; you have to decide on your own."

Danny said, "Dad always said Ireland was settled by the Celts, or the Gaels, who were a subgroup."

"Leah said the history is sketchy, but the Gaels supposedly came from Galilee. She says there's another story that the Celts are the lost tribe of Dan."

"Hey Dez, raise your hands," said Eddie. "Uh, I didn't say Leah says."

"Ha-ha."

"Ireland was always getting settled or invaded," offered Ray. "We're part everything."

I moved to the large conference table with its cushy chairs and read through the handouts in front of each chair. One page listed all the "education opportunities" available at the synagogue for everyone from nursery schoolers to senior citizens. Jesus, how much did they have to learn?

Tonight's class was being taught by Rabbi Friedman. I imagined an old man with a black hat and a long beard and those curlicue things hanging in front of his ears like the Chassid over on Castor Avenue. I chose a seat in the middle of the table, figuring the rabbi would sit at one of the ends. I planned to stay quiet. I was only here to support my friends. Ninety minutes, easy-peasy, and if the rabbi kept it short, we might even get out sooner.

Other people entered the room, including Matt and Brigid, until all the seats were filled. A petite blonde my side of thirty smiled at me as she took the seat next to mine. I yanked on my collar to make sure it was straight and turned to her. "Hi, I'm Tommy Dunleavey."

She extended her hand and we shook. "Nice to meet you, Tommy. Amy Friedman."

She wore a yarmulke, so I had to ask, "Friedman, any relation to the rabbi?"

She beamed but said nothing.

"What? Is he behind me?" I turned. Slow on the uptake, it finally registered. "You're the rabbi."

She nodded. I went red. No need for a mirror, the tips of my ears burned. Everyone at the table caught it and had a laugh. If I could have melted into the chair, I would have.

Rabbi Amy began. "Just a couple things to start. This class is intended to give you a very basic overview. If, after this class, you'd like more in-depth study, our website lists other classes you can take. Tonight, most importantly, please feel free to ask me any questions you might have about Judaism. This is your time. Now, I'd like everyone to introduce themselves and explain what brought them to class."

Visions of Jack, Mickey, Hanlon, Magee, and the St. John's parishioners ran through my mind like a TV show intro. She turned to me first, grinning. "Tommy, why don't you go first?"

Silence. The fire on my face reignited. "I'm Tommy Dunleavey. I . . . uh . . . I'm Catholic, but . . . something bad happened and . . ." I struggled. "I . . . um . . . we're . . . looking around."

Rabbi Amy's face went from happy to sad like she was sorry for the bad things that happened. The other introductions proceeded without hesitation. There were three engaged couples at the table where one half of the couple was Jewish. One gal wanted to know what she was getting into. The other couple, the man said, "I love her so much. I want to know everything about her people."

He actually said that out loud in front of everyone. I was embarrassed for him. The third couple finished each other's sentences, talking about sharing family traditions. They were all so in love.

The former St. John's contingent each introduced themselves. Matt and Brigid explained that they were getting married and were shopping for a new religion. Dez said, "My girlfriend's Jewish, and I don't know too much about it. I've been kind of lost since I left St. John's. It's like Tommy says."

Danny lightened the mood. He pointed at Dez and said, "Whenever the big guy invites me to something, I always say yes."

Eddie added, "Everybody else was going. I didn't want to miss anything."

Ray told the rabbi about being fascinated with theology and visiting the Unitarian church. She said, "Beautiful. Like Abraham, you're all on a spiritual journey."

Yeah, right. I was on a blind date after breaking up with the love of my life; I was just along for the ride.

After introductions, Rabbi Amy moved to the first topic: What is a Jew? She explained that a person could identify as Jewish based on their family, culture, or religion. "There are three main branches of the Jewish religion: Orthodox, Conservative, and Reform. Orthodox believe everything in the Torah comes directly from God. Conservative beliefs are a mix of Orthodox and Reform thinking. Reform Jews believe the Torah is inspired by God and is a human understanding of the relationship between God and the Jews."

Rabbi Amy was a Reform Jew. Matt wanted to know why that made any difference. She said, "If you believe God wants you to jump, you'd jump, no questions asked, right? You'd try to jump as high as possible. You might study all the ways there were to jump and the best ways to jump. You'd make sure all your loved ones jumped and jumped the right way. Now, if someone tells you that he believes God wants you to jump, you might analyze why that person believes that, look at what the intended outcome is, and other ways to best achieve that outcome. Reform Jews believe an individual should decide what practices bring him or her to a closer relationship with God."

Even though I planned to sit on my hands, I had to ask, "How do you know Torah doesn't come directly from God?"

"Originally, the Torah could only be passed down orally, but after the persecutions and exiles, it was written down about 200 BCE. Bible scholars analyzing the style of writing, syntax, and word choices believe there were six authors contributing to the Torah we read today."

"Torah is the Old Testament, right?" Eddie asked.

"We just call it Torah."

"Maybe God told those six guys what to write. How do you know you can decide what's what?" Eddie asked.

Rabbi Amy nodded. "Remember when the Jews left Egypt? It freed them to think for themselves. Their lives were no longer controlled by one man. The last advice Moses gave was to take all things related to God to heart. Back then, they believed the heart, not the brain, was the seat of all critical thinking. Moses was advising his people to think critically about God."

It sounded squishy. If I were a Jew, I'd be Orthodox. I liked knowing the rules: Mass once a week and on holidays—check. A little charity work, no meat on Fridays during Lent—check, check. Tell me what I had to do to get into heaven and I'd do it.

"What if you think critically and get it wrong?" Danny asked.

"As Jews, we study Torah, try to live justly, perform acts

of loving kindness, but no one is perfect. We try. God knows what's in our hearts. If we make mistakes, we have to atone for those actions and seek forgiveness from those we hurt."

It seemed like . . . anything goes, sort of. Like I said, squishy, though I did like the bit about seeking forgiveness from the person they hurt, so different from seeking it in a darkened confessional. She moved onto the Jewish calendar and passed out an information packet describing each major holiday. I only recognized Chanukah and Passover. It was a long list, and one of the fiancées asked why there were so many holidays.

"Each holiday encourages us to focus on something important to God: welcoming the stranger, teaching our kids, compassion. All of the holidays give us a reason to come together and celebrate."

Eddie let out, "Party on," and the class snickered.

"Back to the calendar, which one listed here do you think is the most important?" she asked.

There were guesses around the table, but the answer was Shabbat, a Hebrew word for the Sabbath. "Shabbat starts Friday at sundown and ends Saturday at sunset, and we are commanded to make the day holy and joyous. Celebrating Shabbat involves escaping the busyness of everyday life to be in the moment and getting together with friends and family, having a nice meal, connecting with each other and with God with an open heart."

Dez nodded at that one; that was right up his alley.

My mouth had a mind of its own and shot out more questions. "So, you can be a good Jew and have dinner with your friends and family every Friday night? You don't have to go to Mass every week?"

"It would be services, not Mass. Reform Judaism doesn't mandate synagogue attendance. It is an avenue to study Torah, a way to come together as a community and connect to God and each other. It's open to everyone. You should come."

If I had a near panic attack coming to class, no way was I attending services.

"Don't look so scared," she said. "You might consider our Saturday morning Torah study. It's casual, like a book club with coffee and bagels. There's an informal lay service after if you wanted to stay. We've been studying Torah for thousands of years, but there's always something new we can open our minds to. We might look at the literal meaning of a Torah portion, or the subtext, where the section fits in the story as a whole, the historical context, the life lessons, how different Hebrew words and letters are used or written, even the numerical equivalent connections of the Hebrew words."

That seemed like overkill. The Old Testament was all be-getting, smiting, and locusts. Danny tapped me with his elbow and an open-eyed how-about-it look. I half smiled. Aww . . . fuck. I'd have to do this again?

Matt asked, "What do Jews believe about Jesus?"

"To be honest, there is some discomfort; Jews were per-secuted for centuries in His name. We believe He was a teacher or prophet. There is a spark of the divine spirit in each one of us, but there is only one infinite perfect being that we call God."

I'd always known Jesus was a Jew, but I still always thought of Him as Catholic. But He was a rabbi. He and all the apostles spent their free time studying Torah. He must have kept kosher, hung a mezuzah, celebrated some of those holidays Rabbi Amy mentioned. If He were alive today, He'd go to synagogue. How did we lose that and end up with the Vatican and popes, cardinals, bishops, and priests?

Danny asked, "Do Jews believe in heaven?"

"Because we believe in God, and that God loves us, it's hard to imagine death is final. Most Jews believe in an afterlife of some kind, and that it's open to all people, but really, the afterlife is unknowable. Anything we come up with about heaven is pure guessing; it's better to put it out of our minds—"

"It's everything!" I blurted.

"Yes, okay." She paused. "Well, one criticism is that heaven focuses on the future rather than appreciating the here and now. Jews believe each of us has a unique purpose in this life, and a responsibility to partner with God to make the world a better place. Too much focus on heaven might make it easy to slack off. Why bother, I'll be in heaven soon. The concept of heaven eases our grief, but grief can be eased other ways: honoring our loved ones by doing good works, telling their stories, pursuing the qualities you loved most about them."

When Nan was sick, I questioned the concept of heaven, but Dad was so sure that I never doubted it again. But Rabbi Amy was right; an afterlife was unknowable. Death might be a final-final good-bye. I might never see Dad again, or Jack, or Nan, or Mickey . . . for the rest of time, gone forever. My chest ached. I held back tears.

CHAPTER 24

Go High

To keep tabs on StevieB, I called or texted him every day. If I
sensed he was going to pull a Jack, I'd tell his secret. I didn't
know who I'd tell, but if it came to that, I'd figure it out. On
Friday after dinner, he told me that he was heading over to St.
Katherine's to say a novena. He said he was fine, but that he'd
be better if I went with him. I told him it was a nice try, and he
laughed.

I met Danny, Ray, and Eddie at the Shamrock, and the four
of us sat at a pub table near the bar. Danny and Eddie had been
working extra hours to build their nest eggs for their soon-to-be
apartment living, so we arrived at the mostly empty bar post-
happy hour.

"I didn't mention it the other night," said Eddie to me. "It's
good to have you back, man. Cheers."

Bottles clinked with pint glasses, but there were no smiles. I
felt like a ship without a tow line; I doubted I was the only one.

I drew lines in the condensation on my glass. "When you
all walked out of Mass, I thought you totally overreacted. I
really believed that most of the parish was on our side, furious
at Father Farrell, like maybe not all torches and pitchforks, but
something close. I never imagined that they wanted him back."

"Well, it's easy for them to be callous from the cheap seats,"
Eddie said. "Better the devil you know."

"I don't know," I said. "I think they see the collar, and they see who they want to see."

"No, you're both wrong. They don't want to think they got played, you know?" said Danny. "How's your mom taking it?"

"Not good. We argued until we got tired of repeating ourselves. Now we hardly talk. She spritzes me from time to time with her stash of holy water. The worst are my sisters and their husbands who feel compelled to give me a hard time. I stopped taking their calls, and when they visit, I leave the house as soon as they start."

Eddie asked, "What was your tipping point?"

"Losing Jack . . . talking to Mickey Cunningham gave me a push," I said. "But then they wanted the kids to sign a 'We Love You' petition to the pedophile priest. That was the final straw. It was like I was trying to flick a Bic on the beach."

Danny asked after Mickey. "I was sorry to hear about him. I had to look him up in the yearbook. You stayed in touch?"

"No. I ran into him in the Burren, puking in the men's room. I didn't say anything at the time. He didn't want you to see him like that."

I told them about how Father Bannon raped him and how difficult it was to report it, and how his drinking away the shame had killed him. They were in shock.

"That's so horrible."

"Father Bannon from gym class?"

"Jesus, how many others?"

It all hit me again, and my eyes filled and my voice broke. "The night Mickey died, he told me how it would have been for Jack . . . the fight-or-flight panic attacks, holding back from everyone to keep the secret, the nightmares."

Danny excused himself to the restroom. Eddie bowed his

head. Ray sat back and stared off. When Danny returned, we ordered the first of several rounds of whiskey. With red eyes and a breaking voice, Danny said, "Something I've wanted to talk to you about . . . I want to do a fundraiser for CSN, the Clergy Survivors' Network. They've been good to my family—recommending counselors, helping us navigate the complaint process, and dealing with the Archdiocese and the DA. Maybe do a T-shirt or something."

We were all in, and then we went quiet for a while, and that was okay. Ray broke the quiet and asked after StevieB.

I said, "He knows what Father Farrell is, but he won't leave. He's upset that we left."

Eddie busted, "Oh boo-fucking-hoo."

"He's in a bad place, Eddie. I'm worried about him. He visits Jack every week. I'm trying to get him to talk to a therapist."

Danny leaned forward on his elbows. "That bad? Should I call him? The last time I talked to him was at the funeral. I tried him a couple times. Maybe we should go over there tonight?"

Uh-oh. "He's at St. Katherine's. I'm keeping an eye on him. I'll tell him to give you a call."

Eddie played with the saltshaker. "Something has to be done about Father Farrell. They really want to bring him back, don't they?"

Ray answered, "They're already planning his welcome home party."

Groans rounded the table. I said, "If he comes back, he'll be living around the corner. I can't live in the same neighborhood as him. What do I do if I see him on the street?"

"I'd love to meet him on the street," said Eddie. "Better yet, a dark alley. No witnesses. His word against mine. You know the blessing: may God turn their hearts, and if He doesn't, may he turn their ankles, so we'll know them by their limping. I'll do his kneecaps so kids always have a chance of escaping. It's like Rabbi Amy said—I'd be making the world a better place."

"I'm pretty sure that's not what she meant. It's too easy to go low, Eddie," said Ray.

"Plus, you don't want to risk jail. It sucks worse than you can imagine. Everything about it. The smell is the worst: a mix of urine, sewer, sweat, and the Delaware River. It's horrible. But to Eddie's point, okay, if we don't go low, what's the high ground?" asked Danny.

"If we do good works, something that helps the universe . . . if that should happen to clash with Father Farrell in some way . . ." Ray tapped his head.

"What?" I asked.

He stayed mum, but his brow furrowed. Conversation continued without him until we noticed him smiling. He had an idea—a little one.

Ray said that Danny had sparked the idea, talking about priests living in big houses with servants. Ray's mother had helped at a rectory dinner once and reported that Father Farrell had monogrammed china and silverware. "He's the fucking lord of the manor."

I was still clueless.

Ray said, "We start a petition to the Archdiocese. Recommend that they make the unused rooms in the rectory available to homeless veterans. Has to be veterans because you don't want him to have access to anyone vulnerable. This will help the homeless, and you know Father Farrell, he'd hate having roommates, especially men who aren't easily manipulated. It'd knock him off his high horse. He'd definitely want to move on."

"All the empty rectory space and all the homeless in the city, the Archdiocese would have done something like that by now," said Eddie. "Most priests don't want to live with people who carry their belongings in a shopping cart. They'll never go for it."

Danny said, "Any other ideas?"

We all hushed. Serious brain wheels spun, lubricated by the whiskey.

I suggested, "Everyone in the parish is worried about the finances. It's expensive to maintain the rectory. If they moved Father Farrell to another rectory like St. Mark's and then sold ours, the Archdiocese gets some cash, and he loses his castle. Maybe he wouldn't want to come back, and if he does, there'd be other priests around him, maybe they'd keep an eye on him, keep him grounded." They smiled at my suggestion.

Danny said, "I'll do the business case analysis, but we need to take it to the parish board. I'm worried they'll toss it as soon as they see my name on it."

"So, we'll get someone else to submit it," Ray said. "Let's try both ideas. What do we have to lose?"

Eddie suggested, "If he does live in the rectory by himself, how about we throw food scraps around the rectory to feed the starving rats and roaches?"

We answered with a resounding "No!"

"We should do something for the kids," Danny said. "How about like a public service thing, like Stranger Danger on social media reminding kids that all adults can be dangerous. We leave out Father Farrell's name, but we put it on the kids' radar to be careful around priests."

All the talk about action boosted our sagging spirits—well, that and the drinks.

But the plans weren't just bar talk. Danny called me three days later. He'd assembled a three-page business case outlining the estimated maintenance costs of the rectory, the current market value of its real estate, and options to relocate the "resident" to a rectory nearby. He priced out all the costs, assessed the tangibles and intangibles, and concluded that St. John's should sell its rectory and move any residents to one nearby.

Danny said, "The numbers piece was easy. The question still is how to submit it to the parish board. They might consider the proposal if it came from Gav. You think he'd do it?"

"When's the last time you talked to him?"

"Since, ya know. He's still mad at Ray for quitting CYO. Do you want to talk to him?"

"I can, but I can't explain all the numbers."

"All right, we'll do it together."

Gavin's Insurance offered evening hours during the week. Danny and I walked over to his office, a brick rowhouse on Frankford Avenue with a large storefront window. The door was unlocked, and we walked through the waiting room past a half a dozen empty chairs and a dusty plastic Ficus tree and into his office. Photographs of Gav's various basketball teams were displayed on a shelf. His insurance certificates and sales awards hung on the walls. Wearing a navy suit and yellow tie, he sat behind his executive desk in intense concentration staring at his computer screen. When he noticed us, he froze, then stood, speechless. Danny had to tell him to take a seat, and he did.

Danny slid the financial analysis across the desk, and he and I sat in the two client chairs. Gav picked up the package. "Why is my name on this?"

Danny said, "It carries more weight coming from you."

Gav read through the write-up, then returned it. "No can

do. Nothing against you, but any suggestion that the rectories merge reinforces the idea that the parishes merge."

A face-to-face forsake. He added, "I'm sorry."

We stood and left without saying anything. A swing and a miss for the good guys.

Ray drafted the "Share the rectory with the homeless" petition. Matt asked Brigid's mother to launch it. Her concern for the homeless was well-known in the parish. Her brother had PTSD from Iraq and sometimes slept on park benches. She sent out an email with a link to the petition:

> *The rectory in St. John's parish has so much unused space—eight bedrooms, four bathrooms, a large kitchen, and dining facilities. Knowing the church belongs to its people, our priests would never presume to offer housing for anyone beyond clergy, but we know Christian charity burns in their hearts. Let's give our compassionate clergy the consent they need to provide shelter to our homeless veterans. Please sign the online petition and forward the link to your family and friends.*

The message was well received. Hundreds of people signed the petition, and no one sent her any hate mail. Even Mom liked the idea; she didn't sign it, though—who was she to tell the priests what to do? About a week and a half later, Brendan reported that Father Lawler addressed the petition during Mass, saying, "It's a lovely idea, but any decisions as to the use of the rectory's space are on hold pending the Archdiocese's decision on the pastor."

Interest in the petition waned. It was a shame; we had a real opportunity to help people, and if the decision were up to

Father Farrell, or someone like him, they'd put a kibosh on the idea.

Strike two.

Going high seemed to be going nowhere. We still had the idea about doing something for the kids. On Saturday afternoon, Danny, Eddie, and I met at Ray's house. With the help of his two tween-age cousins, Moira and Aiden, we produced a two-minute video called "Weirdo Warning." Dismissing "Kick them in the nads" and other excellent suggestions, we kept the script clean and the tone serious.

Aiden: This is a Weirdo Warning.

Moira: If a coach, teacher, priest, scout leader, neighbor, babysitter, or any adult asks you to keep a secret, it's a set up. Tell everyone anyway.

Aiden: Never drink an alcoholic beverage offered by a coach, teacher, priest, scout leader, neighbor, babysitter, or any adult. It doesn't make it okay; it doesn't make you grown-up. It makes the adult offering the drink a big weirdo. Only a big weirdo wants a kid to drink.

Moira: Get your parents' permission before going anywhere or being alone with any adult, even if that adult is someone you or your parents know well, like a teacher, priest, scout leader, neighbor, or babysitter. If your parents don't know, then the answer is no.

Aiden: Your body is private. Any adult who wants to touch or photograph your private body parts is a serious weirdo, even if he or she is your coach, teacher, priest, scout leader, neighbor, or babysitter. If it happens, or if they ever show you pictures of their private body parts, call 911.

Moira: If someone does something that makes you uncomfortable, walk or run away, and if necessary, say or yell, "Knock it off!" Practice saying it. Develop a secret code you can say or text to your parents to let them know you are uncomfortable.

On the video, the camera lurched as it moved between Aiden and Moira, and the sunlight coming in the picture window created a bit of a glare, but it was decent. Ray uploaded the video to YouTube, and we all posted it to social media and asked our friends to share. Ray's cousins were popular kids at St. John's, so the video got lots of views over the weekend.

By Monday morning, major pushback against the Weirdo Warning resulted in Aiden and Moira being called to Mr. Schmidt's office. St. John's parents complained that anything involving "private body parts" was a discussion best left to parents. Others complained that St. John's kids discussing those kinds of topics in a public forum was a disservice to the reputation of the school. Mr. Schmidt demanded Moira and Aidan delete the video file, and they complied.

I was disappointed. If parents had these discussions with their kids, then hearing it again reinforced the message. I showed it to StevieB, and he said the same thing I did. Some parents, like ours and Jack's and Mickey's, never had those conversations at all and kids suffered for it. The school should be proactive. I sent an all-caps text to the group: *WHAT'S THE MATTER WITH THESE PEOPLE? FOREWARNED IS FOREARMED!* Ray texted me to chill, said I must be getting old. Mr. Schmidt's prohibition was free advertising and turned it into a must-see for the kids at the school. Probably not for all the kids, though.

Strike three.

CHAPTER 25

Won Temple

Danny sent the text midweek: *There's a Buddhist temple I want to check out.*

Everyone was in; I was the last to respond. My brain still hurt from Rabbi Amy. I googled Buddhism during a lunch break at work. It was more of a philosophy than a religion. Like in Christianity, Buddhist thought varied, from monks who believed they had to give up everything to find enlightenment (whatever that was), to regular people who believed they could find it in their everyday life.

On the ride over to the temple, I asked him why the interest. He said that Dez had told him a story about one of his first fires. A Thai man had lost everything—wife, daughter, house—but remained calm, so calm that Dez worried he was catatonic or something and asked him repeatedly if he was okay. The man nodded and said, "I'm a Buddhist."

"They believe grief and suffering come from wanting a situation to be different. To stop hurting, you have to stop the wanting. They put their whole focus on appreciating every moment, caring about others, and being moral. It feels real, ya know?"

Yeah, real uncomfortable.

Danny, Ray, Eddie, and I waited on the street corner near the temple for the two couples, Matt and Brigid, and Dez and Leah, to arrive. I should have been more at ease, having been to the synagogue, but the brownstone Buddhist temple gave me the willies. It had lived a former life as a Protestant church, evidenced by the towering pin-point steeple. Black letters over the door were in English and some kind of Asian language— Won Buddhist Temple. Having seen too many martial arts movies, I kept looking around and over my shoulders every two seconds, until I annoyed myself enough to stop.

"How'd you come to select this place, Danny?" I asked.

"I drive by it on the days I work in town. It's new and they were advertising a beginners' session. The big plus is that some Buddhist practices are hierarchal, but this one isn't, I checked."

He mentioned hierarchy whenever he talked about religions; he said that elevating a person or group of people as being closer to God was bullshit. It presumed someone actually knew what was in God's head.

The two couples arrived, and we had taken only a few steps toward the temple when Leah said, "Hold up."

We all froze like in a game of freeze tag, which made her giggle. She said, "I did some research online. There are certain customs, etiquette for Buddhist temples. I thought I'd give you the rundown. Unless you've done the same?"

No one had, so she shared. "You have to remove your shoes and hats as you enter the building. When you see the Buddha image, bow to thank him for sharing his knowledge. Always kneel with your feet pointed backward away from the Buddha, and avoid pointing your fingers at the monk or the Buddha or you look rude. Also, whenever the monk is there, bow your head and stay lower than his eye level; it's a sign of respect."

Everyone nodded. It was a lot to remember. All that bowing

seemed at odds with what Danny had said about the place not being hierarchal, but what did we know.

Then Matt hummed the theme song to *Mission Impossible* and said, "That is your mission, should you choose to accept . . ." It cut the tension.

"Okay, let's do this," Dez said and charged up the walkway to the entrance. Leah followed, and the rest of us fell in single file. The white unadorned vestibule had a wooden cubby for shoes and a metal rack with hangers for coats. Between hanging up coats and storing shoes, the going was slow. Dez stuffed his size fourteens into a cubby, then cracked the double doors and peeked into the main room. He turned and gave us an uh-oh look. The man who ran into fires gave us an uh-oh look.

He waved over Leah. She cracked the door and turned back to us with an exaggerated grimace. We leaned this way and that to get a peek as people entered, but the doors opened and closed too quickly. Dez, Leah, and Danny waved us through, whispering that they'd go in last. What was their problem?

With our heads bowed, the rest of us entered the large, white-walled room. Straight ahead, on the wall opposite the entry, a bald Asian man stood in the front of a small, raised platform that held large bouquets of flowers. The man wore a flowing white jacket, almost like a short cassock, over gray pants; he was maybe five-foot-four. Dez, Leah, and Danny, given their height, would have to do some serious bowing to stay lower than the monk's eye level.

The man smiled and directed us to select one of the yoga mats spread out on the hardwood floor in front of the platform. We sat cross-legged, taking our cue from the Asian teens already in place.

Intent on following Leah's guidance, she, Dez, and Danny entered and became human hairpins so as not to be disrespectful to the monk. As Dez crouch-walked by us with a bowed head, Eddie whispered, "You lose something, Big Man?"

Dez covertly gave him the finger.

The monk introduced himself as Reverend Lee. He explained that tonight's session was a breathing meditation for beginners. "The demands of modern life bombard our conscience and diffuse our thinking. Meditation allows us to calm the mind and connect to our inner peace."

Once the breathing meditation was mastered, he suggested we attend a loving-kindness meditation session. He said that Won Buddhism emphasized being relevant in contemporary society, using our minds, engaging the world, and caring for the earth. He pointed to a golden circle hanging on the wall behind him that he said symbolized the world's interconnectedness. My leg cramped.

The reverend told us to concentrate our minds on our breathing. "Listen and feel the breath go in and out of our bodies. Fill the lungs with air until almost bursting and then release the air slowly, squeezing the air out until the belly button touches the spine."

I concentrated so much on breathing that I forgot about my leg. Once we got into a rhythm, the reverend talked about quieting the mind. He said, "If grief, sorrow, or anger, or desires intrude, acknowledge those emotions and let them go. They may be trying to comfort a need in you, but tell them to go away for now. If they are stubborn, concentrate on your breath."

After everything that had happened, calming my mind seemed an impossible task. My conscience hosted a party for all my anxieties. *What did God really want from us? What were we doing here? Where was all this leading? Was prayer another form of meditation? How do I help StevieB? Am I doing this right? If I stopped grieving for my dad, was I abandoning him? If Mom despised my opinions on the Church, was it possible to have a normal relationship with her?* I yelled at my brain to shut the fuck up, and there were some moments when it listened. The breath filled my lungs, and the exhale swooshed. It was only for a couple moments, but I experienced a peace like being at the edge of falling asleep. Danny was into it. His eyes were closed and his shoulders hung looser. Good.

At the end of the session, the rev told us to do the breathing mediation every day so that calming the mind would get easier. We stood to leave, keeping our heads bowed. It was hard, even for me; he was so short. "Please, let us help you," he said. "What is it that you are looking for?"

Ray said something about new ways of thinking about life. Dez agreed, saying something about gaining perspective. Danny replied, "A little peace."

The rev said, "What is it that you are looking for on the floor?"

Apparently, the etiquette that Leah had read about was for a different practice of Buddhism. We didn't have to do all that bowing. Nothing was said until we dressed and moved outside, then the stifled laughter exploded. Danny and I had to sit on the steps; we were crying laughing. My sides hurt. Leah was beside herself and apologized profusely. Danny thanked her. "Best laugh in a long time."

Afterward, Leah suggested we stop at Starbucks. She was still getting to know us and didn't realize we'd normally go to a bar. To propose one after her suggestion seemed skeevy and turning down her invitation outright might have made her anxious about the whole etiquette thing. Each of us murmured "sure" or "okay."

She and Dez held hands, standing in line, and the rest of us stood behind them, trying to be casual. I was a Dunkin' or

Wawa man and had never been to a Starbucks. The menu was confusing with all of the Italian-sounding stuff. No doughnuts. No soft pretzels. I ordered a tea and a chocolate chip cookie, which set me back six dollars. I carried it over to where Dez had pushed two tables together.

Once we were seated, Leah, sitting close to Dez, said, "Despite my major faux pas, which, again, I am so sorry about, was it a positive experience?"

"I wasn't able to calm my mind for very long, but maybe with more practice I can see how it could help me deal with . . . everything," Danny said.

I seconded him, and everyone else did too. I asked if she knew if there was a limit on the number of visits before they'd ask us to convert or join the team or whatever. Leah said, "No one converts to Buddhism. You can accept Buddhist beliefs and practices, even if you practice another religion. I'm Jewish, and I have friends who call themselves JewBu. They use meditation and Buddhist teachings to keep themselves calm and balanced while they try to repair the world."

Then Eddie stammered, "Tonight was good. But . . . um . . . I happened to talk to that girl Caroline—you know, from the Irish festival. I mentioned, you know, what we've been doing. She invited us to one of their Quaker meetings. You know, if that's something, you know . . ." He blushed.

Everyone at the table silenced. A smiling-eyes look passed between us. Danny said, "Sure, Eddie. Sounds serious. Tell us more."

Meeting House

As promised, Eddie arranged with Caroline for us to attend a Quaker meeting. He liked her, liked her, so we had to go. On a bright, crisp Sunday morning, we all piled into cars and headed out to the burbs again. The GPS told us the meeting house was forty minutes away, but Eddie, worried about traffic, insisted we allow an hour travel time.

Minutes into the ride, Eddie jabbered on and on: "Ray, would it have killed you to wear a button-up? Is my tie straight? Don't be telling her any drinking stories. No cursing around Caroline. She's not used to that."

He checked himself in the visor mirror.

"Will she mind my long, loud farts?" Ray asked.

Eddie turned around and seethed. "Don't even."

"Seriously? What do you think I am?" Ray then reached under his shirt and ripped a fart sound with his armpit.

"C'mon now!" Eddie sputtered.

"Easy, Romeo," Danny said. "We won't embarrass you. We got your back."

Eddie nodded and took a couple of deep inhales and exhales.

Danny smiled. "Jesus, he's doing the breathing. Tommy, just in case, text the other car. Best behavior."

I sent the text and waited until Eddie relaxed, then I pulled up Neil Diamond on my phone and let it play "Sweet Caroline."

Three of us leaned back and sang along, while one stared at the road, deep breathing.

Reading from the website's map, Eddie directed Danny to the Quaker meeting house parking area. With Neil Diamond wafting from his car speakers, Dez drove in minutes later with Leah, Matt, and Brigid, and parked next to us. There were only a few other vehicles in the lot.

"Are we're in the wrong place? There's no one here," I said.

Danny grinned into the rearview mirror. "We are twenty minutes early."

We exited the cars and took in the landscaped grounds and large farmhouse. Eddie led us to the building in a slow march of not knowing where he was going. No one talked except for Eddie, who reminded us several times to keep quiet.

As we neared the building, Caroline waved from the front porch. I sort of remembered her. The last time I saw her was the night Danny and I fought at the Irish festival—not the best first impression. She wore her blonde hair in a side part, and it was chopped in a straight line above her shoulders so that it swished. She was cute. Up close, she had hazel eyes and a hint of a pointy chin. She saw Eddie and her face lit up.

We followed her into a large room brightened by the sun shining through the floor-to-ceiling farmhouse windows. It was some kind of activity center, with multiple conference tables set up in different parts of the room. She led us to one of the tables, and we sat in silence.

She said, "It's okay to talk here."

Eddie, next to her, introduced us, and she thanked us for coming. She spoke in a kind, warm voice like we'd been friends forever. "Eddie suggested that I give you a quick overview. So . . . Quakers believe each person has an inner light that is part of God's spirit, and we try to open ourselves up to it. We worship in silence in the meeting room across the hall. Take a seat—anywhere is fine—and stay silent for about forty-five minutes. The goal is to still our minds, embrace the fellowship of those around you, and listen. We hold ourselves open to the Light and hope that the Light will help us see something in ourselves or the outside world that needs our attention. The meeting ends when an elder stands and shakes hands with a neighbor."

It sounded like meditation but taking it in a different direction, connecting the mind and body to what God wanted, like another way to pray but with more receiving and less sending.

"If you're not talking, why come together as a group?" Brigid asked.

"Well, sometimes, during a meeting, a person might feel divinely compelled to deliver a message that benefits others in the room."

Eddie gave us a don't-you-dare scowl.

Matt asked, "Can anyone speak out?" I suspected only to tease a pinkening Eddie.

"Yes, absolutely, but it is important to contemplate the message before speaking. People will take to heart what you have to say."

Radical concept. Instead of getting tossed or being told to sit down and keep quiet and pick your battles, they listened.

"What do you mean by hold yourself open to the Light?" Leah asked.

"Be willing to acknowledge that suggestion from within that pushes you to do right, or to be better, or make the world better."

"How are Quakers organized?" asked Danny.

"There's no central authority in Quakerism, no hierarchy,

no priests, and practices can vary, but there's certain principles that we all agree on."

No priests, imagine that.

Matt asked, "Quakers are conscientious objectors, right?"

She nodded. "If the spirit of God is in every person, then violence against another person is violence against God."

It was an interesting take. Even so, I still wanted to meet Father Farrell in a dark alley. Whatever light he'd had, he'd flipped that switch long ago.

"Truth is an important value," she added. "Because we are open to the Light in ourselves and share it with each other, speaking the truth is essential, even if it's not in our own interest."

Eddie pointed to his watch, and we all stood and walked across the hall to the meeting room. With thirty-foot ceilings, it was larger than I expected. A woody smell from the centuries-old timbers permeated. White walls topped dark wood wainscotting. Rows of wooden pews on each wall faced an empty open center space. There were no banners, statues, paintings, or crucifixes, and the polished pews had no kneelers or hymnal pockets.

Caroline and Eddie sat in a row closest to the center. The rest of us took seats behind them, much better for Eddie's nerves. I forgot how we would know the service started. I couldn't ask anyone; I'd have to talk. I tapped Danny and mouthed, "Is this it?"

He nodded. We sat and stared. The only sound came as other people entered and sat. The congregation represented all ages and races and fashion styles: jeans, T-shirts, flannel shirts, business casual. What did they think about? Big save-the-world kind of things or small individual things? I hoped someone spoke; I wanted to see the Light in action.

We sat and we sat.

Finally, a gray-haired woman with a long thick braid stood. "As you know, we have an ongoing book drive to fill the new library at West Philadelphia Elementary. Last week, I volunteered to drive a carload and help stock the shelves. It was just one errand on a long list of things I had to do that day. Driving there, I was preoccupied on the logistics of getting everything done. At the school, I carried in the cartons of books. The children in the recess yard and the hallway clapped and cheered." She paused. "I was reminded how what seems like a small action to us can mean so much to another."

And then she sat and the quiet of the room returned.

I waited, gazing at faces and wondering who might say something. Who might God tap to give us a message? I gave it a shot and looked inward in case it was me. Anxiety and anger swirled: What would Father Farrell's return to St. John's do to my friends? What about the kids in the parish? I calmed my mind, like the rev had taught us. Who was to say if it was any kind of light or whatever, but StevieB came to mind and stayed there. I needed to keep an eye on him, keep talking to him, dropping by, and encouraging him to call that therapist. "Praying on it" might soothe his soul, but he needed to be able to move past, not just cope. He trusted me with his secret and needed my help, and failure was not an option.

CHAPTER 27

He's Back

After the Quaker meeting, I hung out with StevieB whenever he let me. Two things kept me hopeful: his acknowledging what had happened was a huge step. And although I hadn't sold him on seeing a therapist, after a couple weeks, he'd stopped dismissing it outright. But then we caught a Tarantino flick at the Mayfair Theater and that hope collapsed.

It was a quiet ride home. I dropped him off in front of his house like always, and I almost missed hearing it. He said, "Father Farrell's back."

"What? What the fuck? Are you kidding me? Jesus. What are we going to do?"

As freaked out as I was, he was that calm.

Through the cracked car door, he said, "Really, Tommy, it'll be okay," then he turned and shuffled up the pavement to his house.

This was fucked up. He wasn't okay. Hell, I wasn't. How was he so calm? I'd memorized the suicide warning signs. I sat and analyzed everything he had said and done over the last few days. There were no red flags, but I might have missed something, and I couldn't lose him too.

At home, I lay in bed. Sick images played in my head: the bloodied Sacred Heart Statue, the black body bag, the straight razor . . . *Please God, no.*

The next day, I texted StevieB multiple times, and he assured me he was fine and told me to stop, that I was being annoying. He had to work late with his dad on a big print run at the family's shop. Figuring he was safe for a couple hours, I swung by Danny's for a visit.

In the basement, Danny was on his laptop with a marketing textbook open next to him, and Eddie lounged on the sectional with ear buds watching a Temple basketball game on his phone. Eddie saw me and tossed his phone. "You heard? He's back."

I nodded.

"We have to do something. This is bullshit."

"Tell me where and when," I said.

Danny lifted his nose out of his textbook. "C'mon, non-violence, remember? What would Caroline say?"

Eddie and I challenged him: We'd tried taking the high road. We had to do something, for Jack.

"You'd be hurting yourselves. What are you going to do? Kick in the door of the rectory? Been there, done that, and went to jail for it," Danny said.

But if Father Farrell got to another kid . . .

Danny suggested, "Instead of risking jail, why not MLK it? Protests, signs, sit-ins, legally, with permits and shit."

Getting a permit from the city, if it got approved, would take time. Eddie and I wanted to do something now.

Danny said, "We'd talked about doing T-shirts for the Clergy Survivors' Network. We don't have to wait to do that."

Eddie and I were pumped for a more physical kind of action, but without any viable alternatives, we relented. Neither of us had our laptops, and wanting to take action right away, we stared at Danny until he closed his textbook and said, "Okay, let's design some T-shirts."

We huddled around him as he ran a search and pulled up a site. He maneuvered the shirt's layout, and we threw suggestions at him. He pulled down the Clergy Survivors' Network logo, a graphic of a white dove with the acronym CSN arched over it, and their motto "Help and Healing" beneath. Out of habit, we selected St. John's colors, a steel-gray shirt and maroon letters outlined in white. He centered the logo on the front of the T-shirt, and across the back, spelled out Clergy Survivors' Network and listed the website. Not bad and only seven dollars.

We had originally talked about selling the shirts at a markup to raise money for CSN, but now, with Father Farrell back, it was more important to get the shirts into circulation to put CSN on everyone's radar. But how?

We spitballed ideas, then amid our pondering, a jarring metallic bang-clang sounded. Someone in the alley pummeled the storm door. What the hell? Vandals? Maybe Father Farrell? Closest, I grabbed a baseball bat leaning in the corner and choked up.

The door opened. He walked into the room and the three of us stopped all movement, like God put us on pause. Gav, still in his suit and tie from work, carried a six pack under his arm. Danny finally stood, and Gav walked over to him and shook his hand. Nothing was said. He put the beer onto the cocktail table and sat down on the short section of the L-shaped sofa.

Eddie said, "You look familiar. I can't place the name."

Gav gave a conceding look.

"What's up?" Danny asked.

Gav leaned forward, resting his elbows on his knees. It took a minute. He said, "I'm sorry I had to pass on the rectory thing."

Danny opened one of the beers and handed it to him. Gav stammered and stopped, then took a swig and set the can onto the cocktail table. "I never believed Jack lied. I want you to know that. But if he told the truth, that means . . . Father

Farrell would have to be some kind of sociopath or something. He is, isn't he?"

No shit.

Danny asked, "What tipped you off?"

He took another big swig and told his tale. "He's officially back next Saturday."

We nodded.

He kept his eyes on his beer as he spoke. "The other night . . . a group of us met for dinner to welcome him back and to thank Father Lawler. Aside from the priests, it's me and Terry, the Behans, the Hanlons, Magee, Mr. Schmidt, some of the teachers from the school."

He sipped. "We're at the Torresdale. It's nice—fresh flowers, cloth napkins. We start at the bar. Terry and I are standing together. Father Farrell comes over all friendly and asks what he missed. I tell him CYO had a great season. The boys' team made the playoffs, and the girls are playing for the city championship. He says it's a shame about the boys, that we need to get a better coach. Terry's right there, for Chrissakes. You know, if Father said it a certain way, it's funny, like a bust on Terry, but he didn't say it that way. Terry, he lives for coaching, thinks he's fired. He's crushed, runs out as soon as dinner ends."

Eddie and I rubbed our index fingers and thumbs together, playing our teeny, tiny violins on Terry's behalf. Gav shrugged and continued. "Okay, but I was surprised at the dickishness. Anyway, we sit down for dinner—salmon, a couple bottles of the house Chardonnay. The whole thing costs maybe six bills of the parish's money, but Father Lawler goes on and on about how nice everything is and how there is nothing like this in seminary life. I take it like he doesn't get out much.

"Then Father Farrell leans over to Father Lawler and says, 'Such a small reward after what I had to go through, don't you agree?'" Gav looked at Danny. "No offense, Danny, but everyone there sympathizes with him, tells him he deserves ten times this."

Gav ran his fingers through his hair and shook his head as if to erase a memory. "Father Lawler thanks Mr. Hanlon for his fundraising, and he puffs up and rambles on like he does—glad to do it, anything for the church. The polite thing to do would be to thank him. Instead, Father Farrell cuts him off and says, 'You have a long way to go to catch up to how much I've raised over the years, but that's good. Keep at it.' Awkward, right? People eyeball their plates. Father Farrell says, 'Oh, don't mind me. I dedicated most of my life to the parish, but I worry. Do they even want me back?' Everyone gushes. We're so happy, thrilled, glad to be back to normal. Everyone except Father Lawler."

"Do they not like each other, or does Father Lawler know something?" I asked.

Gav held up his index finger. "Father Lawler mentions the petition about sharing the rectory with the vets. Father Farrell says that given his risk of bodily harm from even the parishioners, what the rectory needs is more security. Everyone around the table acts like it's a reasonable response, except for Father Lawler, who just stares. Father Farrell smiles and tells everyone about Danny's parents selling the house, then Father Lawler cuts him off."

Gav's nostrils flared. He crumpled the beer can in his fist, and Danny handed him another. Gav took a big gulp.

"Father Lawler says to Father Farrell, 'There's a crazy rumor going around that the Archdiocese wants to close St. John's and merge it with St. Mark's. Father, you and I both know that's not true. St. John's isn't on the chopping block, never has been. Isn't that odd?'"

The three of us let out a "What?"

"I know, right? Father Farrell flashes a death-ray look at Father Lawler, but all he says is, 'Mrs. Gregory may have misunderstood something I told her. She's an old woman. She's probably confused, but look at how it brought the parish together.'"

"The merger talk was all nothing?" I asked.

"Yeah." Gav continued, "There's stunned silence at the table. Everyone's been busting their hump to save the parish. Poor Father Lawler. Father Farrell toasts him, but we were all too shocked to say anything."

Gav leaned back in his seat. "If Mrs. Gregory was confused, then everyone around the table was too. Father Farrell told us all some version of the merger story."

"Gav, are you saying Father Farrell is a big, fat liar?" Eddie asked.

Gav sighed and turned to Danny. "I'm sorry. I'm so sorry."

Danny nodded but said nothing.

"So, everyone knows what he is now," I said. "They'll give him the boot, right?"

"No. The consensus is that Father Farrell exaggerated the threat to the parish to keep us together during the investigation, and it worked. From their perspective, there's still no evidence that they were wrong about him."

"But you know, Gav. You know what he is. Think of the risk," I said.

He sank lower into the sofa and answered, "I'm one guy. What can I do? Father Farrell's old and probably going to retire in a couple of years anyway." He stared at his crumpled beer cans. "I'm having dinner with Father Lawler next week; maybe he can suggest something."

Suggest something? The answer was obvious. At a minimum,

Father Farrell had to be called out for the lying scumbag that he was.
He needed to be defrocked and locked up.

No one challenged Gav. Priests had told us how to live our
lives: what would happen to us after we died, and what we
needed to do to be gifted with eternal life, and we all did as we
were told. Gav still depended on a priest to tell him what to do.

The laptop beeped, signaling a low battery, breaking the
silence. Danny plugged it in and banged some keys. "We were
designing a T-shirt for the Clergy Survivors' Network," he
said, "They've been helpful. People need to know about them,
especially now."

"Put me down for fifty," Gav said. "You still have some
friends in CYO, Danny. I'll pass some around and put the rest
in my office as a giveaway."

"Buying yourself some penance?" asked Eddie.

Gav rolled his eyes. "All right, I deserve that."

Danny said, "If we really want to promote CSN to the parish,
how about giving shirts away at the girls' basketball game? It's
the city championship; there'll be a heavy turnout."

It took some convincing, but Gav agreed. Eddie and I
volunteered to distribute the shirts since Danny's appearance
at the CYO game might cause trouble.

"We should hand out a pamphlet or something to spell out
all of the services they provide too," Danny added. "Is that
doable?"

"It's still a sensitive subject." Gav hesitated. "Nothing
explicit, right?"

"What if no one wants a shirt emblazoned with CSN?" I
asked. "We might not get any takers."

"Oh no, the shirts will go," said Gav. "A free T-shirt is a free
T-shirt."

Mom and I had developed a roommate relationship where we discussed things about the house and little else. She worked the rosary beads whenever we watched television and audibly prayed before and after every snack and every cup of tea. I suspected she only behaved that way if I was home to see it. I ignored it. After the Torresdale dinner where Father Farrell's mask slipped ever so slightly, left-handed comments meandered through the neighborhood. One night, she said loudly in my direction that Mr. Hanlon had said that maybe everything had been too much of a strain for poor Father Farrell.

"I couldn't be happier."

"You've a cold heart, Tommy. I feel sorry for you."

That's the pot calling the kettle. I bit my tongue; it was her worry and anxiety talking.

With the shirts Gav donated and what the rest of us chipped in, Eddie and I had 150 shirts to give away on game day. On Saturday, we loaded up his car and headed to the Palestra, the storied gymnasium, in West Philadelphia. I had invited StevieB, but he was working. We passed St. John's, and I read the marquee aloud, a quote from the Gospel of John 14:6: "I am the Way, the Truth, the Life. No one comes to the Father except through me." I sneered, "I bet he thinks that quote is about him."

Eddie snickered. "The old lady next door can't wait to give Farrell a big hug. She's the wrong age and sex, but I'm betting he'll cop a feel."

I groaned.

He added, "Speaking of the man, I almost want to go to the five o'clock Mass to see his lying act, see if he says anything about the merger . . . or Jack."

"No way. You know we'd pound him."

"Yeah, it'd be hard not to."

An hour before game time, we lugged all our stuff inside and set up in the gym lobby. Eddie skirted a folding table with a banner he'd drawn on butcher paper. It read "St. John's" in giant silver and maroon letters. I propped up the table tents that we'd made from a cut-up poster board. On one, we pasted the CSN mission statement and contact information; the other read "Free Tees." Neither of us had any artistic skill, but we managed.

Eddie acted as barker—"Free T-shirt, get your free T-shirt, St. John's colors"—and I handled distribution and answered questions about CSN. I explained that their mission was to advocate for and offer counseling to people who had been abused by clergy. Some people took a pamphlet, while others pivoted away in a fast one-eighty. Most people just took a shirt. Gav was right. A free T-shirt was a free T-shirt.

Once all the shirts were gone, we packed up our stuff and squished into a space on the bleachers. Between the St. John's swag and our T-shirts, one side of the gym was a fierce sea of steel-gray and maroon in contrast to St. Mark's navy and white on the other side. Gav, sitting in the row behind the team, saw us and waved.

An emcee introduced each player to cheers and applause. The starters took the court, the ref threw the jump ball, and the teams exploded into action. Dressed in a maroon blouse and gray suit pants, Debbie Clark strolled the sideline. Her team was perfection on the court. The St. John's girls finessed shooting, unselfish passes, cool heads on the foul line, and endless energy meant an easy win. As the seconds ticked down, streamers spiraled from our side of the gym. Final score: St. John's over St. Mark's, 70 to 50. The winning team jump-hugged in jubilation. After the two teams lined up and shook hands, two pony-tailed St. John's girls poured the water jug over Debbie's head.

Parents and friends surged onto the gym floor. A *Northeast Times* reporter corralled the team to photograph them getting their trophy and had to wait while Debbie hustled into the locker room to dry off. Gav handed her something that made her smile, then waited with the team for the photo. He signaled to Eddie and me, giving us a thumbs-up. I wasn't sure how to interpret that until Debbie returned from the locker room, took her position with the team, and received the Philadelphia Archdiocesan trophy wearing one of our T-shirts.

After the photo, Eddie and I hung around to congratulate Debbie, and listened to a reporter interview her. The reporter asked about her secret to success. Debbie said, "I don't micromanage. I want my girls to think for themselves. I teach strategy, skills, mental focus, but then it's up to them. They took what I taught them and ran with it."

We headed to the exit. Having arrived early and parked close to the entrance, we escaped the parking lot ahead of the crowd. Still, we hit I-95 well after four. Riding home, I rested my head against the seat and wore a contented grin. I watched a great basketball game. I was happy for Debbie and the St. John's girls' team. And anyone who might need CSN's services . . . well, maybe we made it a little easier for them to get help. Eddie called Danny, who was on his way home from Holy Family, and put him on speakerphone. We told him about the game and had a laugh about Debbie wearing the T-shirt in the team photo. We were still chatting and had just exited at Bridge Street, a couple blocks from the parish, when my phone buzzed.

It was a StevieB text: *If anybody has the right to kill him, it's me.*

Aw shit! I punched in StevieB's number, but the phone went to voicemail. Damn. I texted: *Don't do anything, please. On my way.*

Shit, shit, shit!

I hollered at Eddie, "Get to St. John's right now! Hurry! We have to stop StevieB. He wants to kill Father Farrell!"

Danny, still on speaker, heard me. "I'm on my way. I'll be there as soon as I can."

CHAPTER 28

Challenge

Eddie drove fast and furious until stopped by a light. He turned to me. "StevieB wanting to kill Father Farrell—it's not just about Jack, is it?"

I hesitated, then shook my head.

The light wasn't changing. We waited and waited. The freaking lights were stuck again! Eddie pulled over at the corner, parked illegally, and we raced from the car. With the return of Father Farrell, the crowd for five o'clock Mass was larger than normal and grew as people arrived from the game. Eddie and I zigzagged through the parishioners on the landing, looking for StevieB. He wasn't anywhere in sight. Into the building, we hustled down the center aisle. Eddie scanned one side and I checked the other. We bobbed and weaved around the crowd, searching. Mom, sitting with the Hanlons, wanted to know what I was up to, and I explained that I was looking for StevieB and kept walking. I jiggled the handles on the confessionals; they were all locked. Eddie checked the restrooms. We were on a mission. I cared zip about what happened to a pedophile priest, but I did not want StevieB to do something he'd have to pay for with the rest of his life.

I phoned him again, but he didn't answer. Where the hell was he? If he wanted to ambush Father Farrell, he might be lying in wait near the rectory. I headed for the side exit. As I pushed open the door, from the corner of my eye, I caught a green blur from the altar.

"Eddie!" I called over.

I pointed to StevieB in his Eagles green parka; he must have been in the sacristy. He walked to the center of the altar and genuflected. He saw me, turned, and walked quickly in the opposite direction but came face-to-face with Eddie. I dodged people and hurried over to them. If we had to, we would restrain him.

"Eddie, Tommy, you came back," StevieB said, looking around the pews.

I said, "We're here for you. How about we get you home?"

"I have to be here today," he said, then broke from us down a side aisle and entered a center section pew. Eddie and I followed him and sat on either side of him as he knelt to pray.

I leaned over and whispered, "What were you doing in the sacristy?"

He blessed himself and sat. "Waiting for Father Farrell. But the kids were there."

"You spike his wine or anything?"

"No. One of the kids might drink it."

"What were you going to do?"

He closed his eyes. "God will forgive me, Tommy. He won't be able to hurt anyone else."

Behind StevieB's head, Eddie gave me a Jesus Christ, he's nuts look. He leaned over and whispered, "You'd lower yourself to his level. You're better than that."

StevieB patted the front pocket of his parka. "It'll be quick."

I lunged for whatever he had in his pocket. StevieB grabbed my wrists and pushed me away. A tug-of-war raged. All that weight he'd gained these last few months was working in his favor because he gripped my wrists so hard that I thought he'd break them. Eddie tried to help. He reached across and pulled StevieB's arm, but StevieB twisted his body to block Eddie. The move sent Eddie falling onto the kneeler, his head slamming on the pew in front of us. It was enough to stun StevieB. I freed myself from his grip and removed a six-inch steak knife from his front pocket and shoved it into my own.

StevieB helped Eddie up and apologized to him, but then turned to me. "Give it back, Tommy," he pleaded in a hard whisper. "I have to make this right."

"Forget it."

The entrance hymn sounded and the crowd stood. While everyone watched Father Farrell's procession, Eddie and I kept our eyes on StevieB. Still, I sensed the priest's presence, ugly and menacing. Father advanced up the aisle, and StevieB reached again for the knife, but Eddie and I held onto his forearm.

I said, "You'll have to fight me for it. You're not getting it, so stop."

After Father Farrell passed by our row, I asked, "You carrying anything else?"

He crossed his arms and pursed his lips.

The music stopped. At the altar, Father Farrell took his place and stood, smiling with his hands raised like the Sacred Heart of Jesus statue on the landing. I flashed to the day we found Jack. Blood red smears on white marble. Crosses cut into arms. *Thanks for looking out for me, Tommy.* I used the deep-breathing stuff the rev taught us, a few prayers, and anything else not to rush Father myself. It would be so easy. A quick jab. I pushed it out of my mind and focused on StevieB.

In urgent whispers, Eddie and I tried to reason with him. "What are you doing here, man? There are other Masses. You don't want to hear anything this lowlife has to say."

He crossed his arms. He was staying. I suspected he had a back-up plan. If he rushed the altar, we'd have to tackle him. It wouldn't be pretty; StevieB was a big guy, plus I'd have to make myself want to save Father Farrell.

A tap on my shoulder. I jumped; it was Danny. He motioned for us to make room and sat with us. StevieB froze in Danny's presence; all of his bravado dissipated. I whispered to Danny and told him about the knife. He leaned over and said, "I wanted to hurt him, too, StevieB, but Jack wouldn't want that. There are other options."

StevieB nodded with his head turned away from Danny.

Each of us took turns urging him to leave, but he refused. Other than to stand or sit or kneel, he hardly moved a muscle, although his eyes scanned the periphery. After the second reading, he whispered to me, "A lot of people are wearing the same shirt as you guys."

I took a gander. He was right. The game had run late, and with the slow exit from the Palestra lots, anyone coming to Mass had gone from the game straight to the church. In low tones, I said, "They're the shirts we gave out at the game, the Clergy Survivors' Network."

It seemed rude to God to do otherwise, so the four of us stood, sat, knelt, and recited the prayers like it was any other Mass. But I was spiritually detached; my actions were by rote. The Gospel was from John. Father Farrell delivered it in a gentle tone like he was coaxing a toddler. "Remain in me, as I in you. As a branch cannot bear fruit all by itself, unless it remains part of the vine, neither can you unless you remain in me. I am the vine; you are the branches. Whoever remains in me, with me in him, bears fruit in plenty; for cut off from me you can do nothing."

I took the passage to mean we all needed each other, and we

needed God. But the way Father Farrell read it, emphasizing "me" and "I," it was like he was saying we needed him to survive. In his butter-wouldn't-melt-in-his-mouth homily, Father Farrell discussed how the act of bearing false witness separated the sinner and the sinned against from the vine. "Lies diminish the sinner in the eyes of God and isolate the victim who is hurt emotionally and spiritually. I have personal experience with this, but I have maintained my faith and am blessed to return to you."

Danny white-knuckled the seat. StevieB's face reddened as he stared at Father. The fuse was lit and they were ready to blow, either of them, even me, at any moment. I pointed to the side door, but they ignored me.

When the Holy Communion hymn began, I calmed. Mass was almost over. We were all still kneeling for the pre-Communion prayers when StevieB made his break. He pushed Eddie aside like an NFL running back and cut through the center section of pews to get in Father Farrell's communion line. The three of us chased after him through a slow-moving crowd. He had a lead. We caught up, but he was already in line. Danny motioned for "cuts" to the man standing behind StevieB. The man hesitated, and Danny jumped in line and let in Eddie and me. People behind us grumbled, but what could they do? Eddie stood right behind StevieB, then me, then Danny.

I whispered to Eddie, "He gets up there, I'll step left, you step right."

Panic set in. Danny had to be a tinderbox. Eddie was jonesing to take action. What the hell was StevieB planning? Did he have other weapons? We'd be in front of Father Farrell in minutes. I still had the knife. I'd be only inches from him. Images of Jack and StevieB, it would be so easy. As the line moved, I whispered to StevieB as much for my own benefit, "Don't do anything to him, right? Don't do anything."

StevieB ignored me, but his slightest action would light the match and send the rest of us into complete pandemonium.

We crept forward. Sweat dripped down my neck and swamped my pits. Father Farrell's voice repeating "Body of Christ" grew in volume. I remembered the little rev's instructions about hosing down my yin. I ordered my yang to pump it up. *Breathing. Inhale, exhale.* I was shaking. Body of Christ . . . Body of Christ . . .

StevieB got to the front of the line. I took a step left and Eddie went right.

Father Farrell removed the wafer from the chalice and held it up to StevieB, saying, "Body of Christ."

StevieB said, "Amen," and took the wafer in his hand. Odd—he'd always been a tongue man. He placed the wafer into his mouth, but he didn't step away. "Everyone knows what you are, Father. And everything you did. Everything."

Father Farrell had another wafer ready; he glanced at Eddie and me and then back to StevieB. I was inches from him. I quaked. The knife in my pocket. I ran my finger along its serrated edge. The gigantic Jesus on the cross over the altar peered down at me.

I said, "We all know."

Eddie mouthed, "Fuck you."

Father Farrell smiled. Nothing got to him. StevieB turned to go back to the pew. Eddie and I took only a few timid steps, on alert, ready for whatever, as Danny came face-to-face with Father Farrell. The priest flinched but held up the wafer. "Body of Christ."

Danny said, "No, it isn't. Not in your hands."

If he hoped for a reaction, he was disappointed. They stared at each other, and Father Farrell said, "Please move along for the benefit of the other communicants."

Back in the pew, StevieB knelt to pray, and Danny, Eddie, and I sat and exchanged wide-eyed looks. My pulse raced; my body trembled at what almost happened. He was so close. Regret set in. We gave him some lip. Big fucking deal. We were spineless, weak. We didn't do anything. We didn't get him to confess, express remorse, nothing. Absolutely nothing. He was Teflon. Sure, at least none of us killed him, but the kids were still endangered. Father Farrell's "Body of Christ" repetitions droned on. With him back in the pulpit, there'd be another kid, another StevieB, another Jack. He had to go, but how? I wanted to scream, loud and long. I scanned the aisles, half expecting and half hoping the ushers would toss us, given Danny's presence, but no. I wanted out of there more than anything, but StevieB never left Mass until the final note of the recessional hymn.

Father finished his Eucharist tasks, directing the altar boys in this and that. Seeing the kids scurry at his instructions made me touch the knife again. We stood for the Communion prayer, and then Father stepped up to the lectern and asked the congregation to be seated. People around us smiled up at him, so happy to see him. Not all, obviously. Danny and Eddie refused to look at him, and StevieB sat erect, staring at the wood grain on the pew in front of him.

Father adjusted the mic. "It is so nice to be back with my St. John's family." Applause reverberated, and he beamed. "So many of you have been so kind to me. As a priest, I sacrifice my life to Christ to serve the needs of His Church. I give, give, and give again, that's what I'm asked to do. People don't always appreciate the rigors of priestly life. My reward is your gracious welcome. Thank you."

More clapping.

"I am so proud of you all. You're good, observant Catholics.

You know that the church is the one place to find the fullness of truth and joy. By the grace of God's goodness, we all persevered through a very difficult time." He paused. "There are a handful of people here today still struggling. Confused, embattled souls who came to hassle us. In our hearts, we knew they'd be here. The Church is always under attack. That is our lot, but as Christians, we turn the other cheek. That is what our Lord asks. By showing compassion, we open our hearts and invite them to return to the fold."

StevieB started a rocking motion. Even as Danny and I tried to calm him, I gripped the knife handle in my pocket. Father turned this all around. He was so saintly, and we were lost sheep . . . it was bizarro world. Below the pew level, Eddie leaned back and gave him the finger with both hands.

Father Farrell smiled. "Father Lawler was so impressed with our parish. He was effusive in his compliments—your commitment and dedication. The Archdiocese too. We are an example for others to emulate."

He paused. "I do have to say, though, I'm not quite sure what to make of so many of you wearing those T-shirts today. Are you making some kind of statement, or . . ."

His voice trailed off, and he scanned the murmuring crowd. "You do know that CSN is an anti-Catholic organization."

What?

People in the pews looked to each other with narrowed eyes and tilted heads. A few, like me, pulled out their phones for a quick Google search. Despite what Father Farrell said, the website was all victim outreach, nothing anti-Catholic, but nearly everyone removed their T-shirts or covered them with their coats. Docile and obedient, they embraced the priest's words as absolute truth. Eddie and I slid down in our seats.

People would be pissed off at us for giving them the shirts.

"I take it by your expressions you didn't." He gripped the edges of the lectern, leaning in as he spoke. "CSN wants to destroy the Catholic Church. Statute of limitations? Throw it out the window. No evidence, no problem. Priests are guilty. They hate us. If they had their way, I'd be rotting in jail. That's who they are."

Spittle flew from Father's mouth. "If you thought you were helping victims, think again. It's all about the money. Our community means nothing to them."

His face reddened. "Their atheist lawyers use the donations to fuel their own gravy train. They're amoral, hostile people, full of rage, bent on twisted notions of revenge. These are treacherous times, folks. Something can sound caring and good, but that doesn't mean it is."

He caught himself, and his voice quieted. "I apologize if I sound harsh, but the Church is at a critical juncture and to see so many of you wearing those shirts, supporting that organization, it just . . . please consider your actions. The sin of ignorance is still a sin. Ask yourselves, are you with the Catholic Church and her priests, or are you against us?"

He told the congregation to bow their heads and pray for God's blessing. "Mass is ended. Go in peace to serve the Lord."

The recessional hymn sounded, and Father Farrell strode down the center aisle, escorted by two altar boys double-timing to keep up. Instead of standing in the lobby to greet exiting parishioners, he walked straight to the rectory. Shambling from the pews, the mostly quiet crowd exchanged *what just happened* looks. Maybe they expected gratitude from the reinstated priest. Certainly not a diatribe. A wary few muttered:

"He's probably a little oversensitive about CSN, you know,

after all he's been through."

"He doesn't seem the same."

"It gets to them, you know, with all they have to give up."

"The weight of the world."

CHAPTER 29

Headway

We were the last congregants in the church, only standing to leave after an usher in the back cleared his throat. A slow walk out the side door. We bookended StevieB and paused near the street.

I said, "You need to get checked out, StevieB. Friends Hospital has a crisis center. You're going tonight."

He insisted he was okay.

"The knife in my pocket says different. You fought us for it. You wanted to kill him."

He stuck his hand out.

"It's my parents'. I need it back."

"Right, there's no blood on it, so put it back in the kitchen drawer. You're gonna save it for next time?" Eddie moved in close to him. "A beatdown is one thing, man, but to go all stabby? What if we didn't stop you?"

StevieB's eyes filled with tears and he turned away. "I didn't do anything."

Danny said, "You came close, StevieB. There's been too much blood spilled already. You let Father Farrell get to you."

Let Father Farrell get to you. The words sucker punched StevieB. He crumpled and avoided our gaze. "I'm so sorry, so sorry." He bowed his head and cried. "I almost did it, didn't I? In my head, it made sense, but . . . I must be nuts, right? There's something wrong with me. I'm scared."

I was scared too. "After everything, we're all a little nuts. It'll be okay, but you need to see a doctor. Seriously. Otherwise, I have to tell your parents . . ."

He shot me a look. I added quickly, "About what happened in Mass."

"I wish I had talked to someone," said Danny. "I wouldn't have ended up at the rectory that night. Or Jack, if he'd gotten help, it would have changed everything. I know it'll be hard, but we'll help you get through this."

Tears ran down StevieB's face. "Only Tommy. I only want Tommy to come with."

If the other two were surprised at being shut out, they said nothing. That he'd agreed to go was the important thing. I took the mission to heart like a soldier. The four of us walked to the corner where Eddie's car was parked. Eddie lent me his wheels; StevieB got in and buckled up.

Outside the car, the two lingered, and we spoke in whispers. Danny asked, "You okay going solo? I can get my car and we can follow."

"I'm worried he'd see you and get spooked. I don't want to risk it."

Danny said, "It's a good thing what you're doing, Tommy."

I shook it off. "What if they put out a restraining order on him, stop him from going to Mass? If he doesn't have Mass—"

"There are worse things," Eddie said. "They might keep him. You know, commit him with strait jackets and shock treatments and stuff."

"He needs help," said Danny. "They're the professionals. Whatever they do or say, that's what he needs."

He was right, but still . . .

On the short ride to Friends Hospital, StevieB kept repeating, "Why did he have to come back, Tommy? Why?"

The refrain echoed in my head. I parked the car and reassured him that he was doing the right thing, that it'd take time to heal, but he'd be stronger and better able to cope. As we walked through the parking lot to the entrance, he whispered, "Will you tell the docs . . . about Father Farrell? I can't . . ."

I nodded and patted him on the back.

We met with Karl, the counselor, a short square man built brick-solid with a Semper Fi tattoo on his forearm. He asked StevieB questions as part of a mental health assessment: any drug or alcohol problems, family issues, trouble holding a job, trouble with the law, history of psychiatric issues, history of violence. Everything was a no until that last one. StevieB signaled to me. I stammered out the worst parts, "He was an altar boy . . . our parish priest . . . sexually assaulted him. Earlier, he texted me that he had the right to kill our priest. I tracked him down at Mass . . . he'd brought a knife. We came straight here."

Karl frowned, then asked StevieB more questions. "You said you had a right, but did you ever say, 'I'm going to kill that priest'? Did you injure or attack the priest? Verbally threaten him? Did you confront him face-to-face?"

"Only the last one. I told Father I was going to tell," StevieB answered.

"So no direct threat. You had the idea. We call it ideation. Where's the knife?"

I handed it to Karl. "Not the sharpest thing, huh? It'd do the trick though."

He asked me to wait in the lounge while he took StevieB to meet with a psychiatrist. I texted Eddie and Danny and let them know we'd made it. Maybe it was the artificial lighting, the antiseptic smell of the place, the other walk-ins, seeing my friend disappear down the corridor, or everything that had happened, but I was majorly on edge. I needed a distraction and found an assortment of brochures on a display rack. I shut everything else out and buried my nose in them: *Opioids: Break the Cycle, Am I Bipolar, Dealing with Dementia, Pennsylvania's Mandatory Reporter FAQ, Living with OCD, Schizophrenia and You, What to Pack for an Inpatient Stay.* Not knowing how messed up he might be, I pocketed a copy of that last one.

StevieB eventually exited the exam room, and he was free to go. He stayed quiet until we got into the car. "He said I have PTSD, gave me a script for Xanax, for anxiety, and wants me in for twice-a-week sessions. I don't know, Tommy, I can't imagine talking about what happened."

"You told me. It can't be harder than holding everything in, right? You don't have to go alone. Make your appointments for late afternoon and I'll drive you."

He wavered, and I laid on some Catholic guilt. "StevieB, you owe it to Jack."

During his second week of treatment, StevieB's parents discovered he was in therapy. His family's health insurance company had sent them an e-notification outlining what charges were and weren't covered. I picked him up for an appointment and arrived as his parents were in mid-harangue: What was wrong? Why did he need that kind of help? What did he say to the shrink that he couldn't say to them? Who knew about this and what would people say? Why wasn't he talking to a priest for goodness' sake? StevieB shrunk in on himself, so they badgered me.

When neither of us answered, his mom wept. His dad put his arm around her. "Love, I'll call Father Farrell. He'll advise us."

"All the stress he's been under . . . he has so much on his plate already," Mrs. Behan said.

"He'll find time for us."

The Behans believed Father Farrell had been called by God and acted in the person of Christ to do good works. There were no words that could convince them not to call the priest, so I dragged StevieB out to the car and we hit the road. He held on to his seat and rambled, "I should go back. They're upset. I should forget all this. I can deal. What will Father Farrell say to them? What if they find out . . . it would ruin everything for them. I should go back. They're upset—"

"Calm down. You need this. Don't worry about Father Farrell. You think he's going to fess up? Not in a million years. What's the worst thing he'd say? That you're nuts? I told you. We all are. Take a couple of deep breaths—it'll help you relax."

He quieted, a good sign. "The doc will tell you how to deal with your parents. It'll work out. How is therapy, by the way?"

"Not that bad. The doc had me write down the details that were too difficult to talk about, which made things easier. He asked a lot of questions about Father Farrell."

It took a few traffic lights for my brain to work and recall one of the brochures I had read. Under Pennsylvania law, certain professions—psychiatrists, teachers, social workers, priests—were mandatory reporters and were required to report the sexual abuse of a child, no matter how long ago it occurred. StevieB's parents were going to tell Father Farrell that their son was seeing a psychiatrist. The priest would have to consider it had something to do with the rape and that the psychiatrist would have to report it. What would Father do? Double down against StevieB like he did with Jack, or cut and run?

The *Northeast Times* photo of the St. John's girls' basketball team, with Debbie Clark in her CSN T-shirt, got picked up by the *Philadelphia Inquirer*, local television news stations, and online news sites. The picture was everywhere. Gav requested a copy and had it made into a poster that he displayed in the window of Gavin's Insurance. A ballsy move for him, but he did check beforehand with Father Lawler, who assured him that CSN was not anti-Catholic. A fact Gav was happy to share.

Father Farrell prepared a letter for Mr. Schmidt, the school principal, to distribute to all the students that detailed the failings of CSN. Gav told us that Mr. Schmidt, unhappy with Father Farrell's deceit about the parish merger, normally would have issued it immediately, no questions asked. Instead, he contacted the Archdiocese, who advised him to hold the letter, promising to take the subject under advisement.

The Sullivans, Brendan's large and fiercely Catholic family, respected the Church and its clergy, but being friends with the Cunanes, they rejected Father Farrell's CSN opinions. How could victim support be anti-Catholic? What if it had been one of their own? They wanted to ensure that help was always easy to find, so they surreptitiously left CSN pamphlets in the pews, hymnal racks, and on the church bulletin boards and replaced them as fast as infuriated Father Farrell's supporters removed them. Nothing was ever said to the family; they were known for being strong-minded and unafraid, and there were so many of them. Each side probably thought the other would relent, but neither did.

Despite Father Farrell's diatribe, CSN T-shirts were still seen in and around the neighborhood. My friends also had CSN hoodies made, and I wore mine everywhere. Word got around soon enough that challenging us was wasted breath. Just to push the envelope, Eddie and I created a banner by spray painting "CSN" in large silver and maroon letters on a queen-size bedsheet. Draping it over the arms of the Sacred Heart statue, we took pictures and splashed it all over social media. Shame on Father for telling us that CSN bothered him.

Promoting CSN was empowering, but I worried about what Father Farrell had planned for StevieB. The vaguest threat and StevieB would crumble like a cracker. I slept little and plodded through my shifts at the Acme: unloading trucks, rotating the produce, restocking, sweeping, and carrying the empty boxes to the loading dock. The store made them available to its customers, and people used them for moving. On one of my trips to the loading dock, I saw Mrs. Gregory, Father Farrell's housekeeper, taking some boxes like maybe some packing needed to be done at the rectory. I tried not to get my hopes up, but in my gut, I knew.

On Sunday morning, I was in my shorts, eating my Wheaties, when Mom came home from Mass and sat down next to me at the kitchen table. "Father Farrell announced his retirement today at Mass." She clutched a tissue. "I'm sure you're happy. You think the worst of him, but you didn't see his big heart. He didn't want a big farewell—too hard, he said. He thanked everyone for the memories, just wanted us all to live in peace. He even made a point to say more than once not to blame anyone for his leaving."

I tried to hide a smile.

"Was this your doing, Tommy?"

"No, Mom."

I called StevieB and Danny and told them, then I texted the group: *Ding, dong, Farrell's gone!* The sun shone, and it was a joyous, beautiful day in the neighborhood.

In the afternoon, Danny and the boys and I piled into an Uber with some beers and a bottle of Jameson and headed out to Resurrection cemetery. We walked up the path lined with headstones, passed by the tall pine tree, and gathered around Jack's grave. Gav started off by apologizing to him on behalf of all of us for anything ever said that caused him hurt, that we were ignorant assholes and we were sorry for it. We passed around the bottle, telling him all the things we'd done: distributing the DA's handouts, the rectory petition, the video, the T-shirts, the banner, the poster, the pamphlets. We took our time there, telling stories, getting Jack up to speed on all he'd missed, laughing through tears. Then it was time to go, and we lifted our beers for the last toast of the day. "Love you, Jack."

Around the neighborhood, the rumor mill cranked out multiple reasons for Father Farrell's departure—ill health, spiritual exhaustion, a calling to do mission work—but among my friends, our CSN marketing blitz chased him out of town. The lore of the CSN campaign took on a life of its own, growing in impact and validity with each retelling, giving us all a palpable sense of empowerment, righteousness, and atonement for Jack. Challenging the boasts would mean spilling the beans about StevieB. Only Father Farrell knew his reasons for leaving. The most important thing, what really mattered, the only thing, was that he was gone.

CHAPTER 30

The Oldest Book Club

The Archdiocese assigned a new priest to St. John's, Father
Mitchell. He was a roundish man with a bald head and a
beard, Irish American by way of Oregon so he talked funny.
Brendan said he was all right. According to Mom, he was kind
and gracious, real down-to-earth. During Mass, he encouraged
everyone to hold hands for the Our Father if they wanted. She
said that I'd like him. Everybody liked him, except for people
like the Behans and the Hanlons, who called him a hippie.
Mom said that in one of his homilies, Father Mitchell discussed
a Japanese philosophy that put a higher value on a cup that had
been broken and repaired than one that had never been broken,
because the broken one had been tested and persevered. He told
the parishioners to have compassion for the abuse victims, first
and foremost, and that the Church was taking the abuse problem
seriously and looking to put in new reforms to eliminate it.

Mom pestered me. "It's been months. Father Farrell's gone.
You should be happy. God answered your prayers. You have
no reason not to come back. What more do you want?" Her
favorite was "A lapsed Catholic is still a Catholic."

I stalled answering her, until I didn't. "Mom, they're so
wrong on so many things: their concept of the clergy, the false
moral superiority. The Church cares more about itself and
fighting change than it cares about people. I can't do it. I won't."

Seeing her cry hurt me, but I stood my ground. After college,

I'd move out, and it'd be easier for her. Until then, we'd avoid the subject. Father Mitchell allowed the rectory kitchen to be used by Aid for Friends, a group that made meals for shut-ins; Mom joined and it kept her busy.

I wasn't Catholic anymore, but I wasn't anything else either. Ray was energized by the Universal Unitarians, but it was too Protestant for me. Danny became a regular at the Won Buddhist Temple. He said the meditation kept him from dwelling on the past and helped him sleep at night. I attended with him every so often, and the practice offered peace and positivity, but something was still missing.

Matt and Brigid liked the Quakers and had been attending meetings with Eddie and Caroline. They liked the social action activities, and collected two bags of children's books after that first meeting. They planned a Quaker self-uniting wedding ceremony for the fall. Eddie liked the Quakers' emphasis on truth and honesty. No surprise. All the times I'd called Eddie out for his boldness over the years, it almost always was for speaking a truth I didn't want to hear. I liked the whole opening yourself up to the Light, but I liked talking things out more. Dez liked Judaism, especially the way they celebrated Shabbat. Leah had something to do with it, but he liked the fact that Jews always stuck to their guns no matter who was trying to push them around, and he liked the idea of being a mensch. He invited us all to one of the Torah Study sessions. Ray and Eddie passed on the invitation because they had work stuff. I still lost sleep from my last visit to the synagogue, but I said yes. Dez really wanted us to go. It was only an hour long.

On an azure blue-sky morning, Danny picked me up for a quiet drive to the burbs. We met Matt and Brigid and Dez and Leah in the synagogue parking lot, and we all walked in together. Leah, as a member, used her key fob to get us in the door. Inside the meeting room, tables were set up in a giant circle, with rows of chairs outside the circle for overflow. The only open seats were near the coffee station on the far side of the room. About forty people sat or mingled. No doubt, we lowered the average age of the group. Dez and Leah, holding hands, led the way. I put my eyes on the floor and soldiered forward in formation until we stopped.

Dez said, "Hey look, it's Larry. Hey, Larry, good to see you."

We all crowded around little Larry and took turns shaking his hand. Recognition finally hit. "The young people from Rabbi Amy's class," he said. "Shabbat Shalom."

The others hesitated, waiting to see if I'd give a "back at ya," but I managed a "Shalom there, Larry."

As we proceeded to our seats, Danny reacted with a fake double-take to someone sitting at the table and said, "Wow, small world. You a member?"

It was Dr. Briscoe, Danny's advisor, who popped up to welcome us. Danny broke into a big grin. "This is so weird seeing you today. I've been meaning to talk to you about what you said about my options."

Danny stayed talking with Dr. Briscoe, and the rest of us took our seats. Matt and Brigid sat holding hands, whispering, and Leah talked to Dez tête-à-tête. I sat next to them, talking to no one, and guarded the empty seat next to me. I was waiting for Danny. What did he mean about Briscoe's options? Staying in Philly and going to grad school, or moving on to a Big Four job out of town, or something else altogether? I leaned forward, trying to hear Danny's conversation, but he was too far away. Alone, I faded into the background and eavesdropped on the conversations of the people coming and going at the coffee station.

"Where's Reuven? He should be here."

"He's on crutches. His granddaughter is bringing him."

"Oy, what happened?"

"He fell riding his bike."

"What is he, nuts? He's lucky he's not dead."

At 9:00 a.m. sharp, a stylish white-haired woman tapped on the table to call the meeting to order. Danny hurried over to the seat that I had saved, and the six of us sat up straight, waiting for the words of wisdom to begin. The woman spoke in a strong voice.

"A Jewish grandmother and her grandson are on the beach. A great wave rises up and sweeps the young man into the ocean. She is devastated. Her sweet boy, whom she loves with all her heart, is lost to the ocean. Immediately, she falls to her knees in the sand and pleads with God for the safe return of her grandson."

This sounded like a variation of the Job story.

"The grandmother prays, 'Blessed are you, God, ruler of the universe. I have always been a good person, a good Jew. I love him so much, please return him to me.' Just as she finishes her prayer, a giant wave crashes back onto the beach and delivers her grandson to her side. She cries tears of joy, and hugs and kisses the young boy. She looks over her grandson, and then back to the sky and says, 'He had a hat.'"

Everyone in the room laughed, but we laughed loudest. The joke was so unexpected. After the laughs, people joined in some kind of prayer in Hebrew, I guess. The six of us looked at each other. Seriously, did she just tell a joke?

The discussion leader, an older man, stood in front of the room, and said, "This week, we're reading from Numbers. The Jews are in the desert and they're complaining. Egypt had better food. Why did we leave? We had fish and melons and cucumbers, and you bring us to this wilderness to die. Moses is beside himself. He despairs to God; the complaints are getting to him. Questions for discussion: Why were they complaining about the food? They weren't starving. They had their freedom. Also, why is Moses so upset at their complaining? The people have been complaining the entire trip. He should be used to it by now."

Different people in the room offered comments:

"People hate change, so they criticized the decision to leave Egypt, and even denied that they had to leave at all."

"Only twenty percent of the Jews actually left. Why? They had a slave mentality. After all those years in slavery, being told what to do, never doing for themselves, never thinking for themselves, they were afraid and anxious."

"It's one thing for Moses to tell them to do something concrete like cross the Red Sea, but now he has to get them to think independently. Moses doubts he can do it."

"The people who left Egypt had to die out. That's why they were in the desert for forty years. The next generation, those who were born into freedom—they had the right mindset to go into Canaan."

I said nothing, of course, but I understood their difficulty, having left St. John's. Hell, I had trouble leaving the city to go to the suburbs. After all their troubles, those who left Egypt never even got to experience the peace offered by the Promised Land. So sad. But their kids did. They were martyrs, in a sense; they left everything that was familiar and endured all that discomfort so their children and their grandchildren would be free and be able to think freely. Their having the guts to leave Egypt changed the course of history.

As the discussion continued, the doors banged open and the infamous Reuven hobbled into the room on crutches, chased by his twenty-something granddaughter. She ran to get in front of him to spot him if he fell. Ginger curls cascaded down her back. Then, with her arm on his elbow, she settled him into his chair. He asked for a decaf, and she turned toward the coffee station. With everyone around me seated, I stood up and stared at her. She stopped, stared back, and blushed. In my head, fireworks exploded and the choir of angels commenced.

Reuven spoke in what I assumed was Hebrew. *"Oy gevalt, Ahuvi,* who's the *meshuggener*?"

She walked slowly to the coffee station. I joined her, in linger mode. I whispered, "Eileen, we met at Towey's." I pointed to myself. "Tommy Dunleavey."

As she poured the coffee and schmeared a bagel, she spoke in a hushed voice inches from my face. "I remember. I remember you said that I'd see you at happy hour . . . and I never did. What are you doing here?"

The room disappeared and there was only her. She remembered me, and she had been back to Towey's hoping to see me.

"It's a really long story. Please don't be mad. Would you have lunch with me? Let me explain. Please."

I held my breath. She picked up the coffee and bagel and whispered, "I shouldn't."

One of the old-timers said in a voice loud enough for all to hear, "You see the way those two are looking at each other? That's how my wife and I looked at each other the first time."

She and I turned to see the whole room smiling at us. What else could we do? We smiled back.

Epilogue

There was a reason I never found Eileen Cowan on social media: spelling. Ilene Cohen and I met for lunch at the Country Club Diner. She admitted to dragging her friends to a couple of Towey's happy hours and being embarrassed that I never showed. She vowed to never set foot in the place and never expected to see me again. I told her about Jack and everything that happened. That hours-long conversation morphed into a relationship, growing stronger every day.

I continued with the weekly Torah study group, becoming a regular. Something about it felt . . . comfortable. Like McRyan's had made me feel. The folks there reminded me of Dad. Besides being the age he would have been, they made me ponder big-picture things, joked around, debated, offered life lessons, and were open to so many different opinions. Discussion leaders studied the text, then challenged us to see new perspectives. I never knew what to expect, and I looked forward to the aha moments, big and small.

Friends and family busted on me, said I was dissing Jesus, but Jesus was a humble man. Being worshipped wasn't His thing. He was a teacher. He wanted people to study and think, to help our fellow man and honor God the Father. That was all I was trying to do. He'd be cool with it. With my job, school, and Ilene, the weekly Torah study was all I could fit in my life religion-wise.

College challenged me—the coursework, presentations,

exams, and managing my time, not to mention financial aid forms, selecting my schedule, and just walking into class after so many years away. The breathing exercises I'd learned really helped my nerves. Sometimes, with a tough situation, I just had to face it. College got easier.

I still missed Dad and wished I could talk about college and my career with him, but certain images stayed with me: Jack walking down the street with his cassock. Mickey trying not to sway in the Burren's restroom. StevieB panicking in the hospital parking lot. Those images helped erase any doubts I had about my major and career path. Ilene worked as a pediatric nurse, and I planned to be a social worker after graduation. Between the two of us, we hoped, in our small way, to make the world a better place for kids. Given how much he prized his CYO coaching, Dad would like that. Mom too.

StevieB never did tell his parents or Danny what had happened. Besides dealing with trauma from the rape, the doctor also diagnosed him with scrupulosity—an OCD condition where a person felt pathologically guilty about religious issues. Healing would take a long time, but he started working out at the rec center and stopped avoiding Danny. I took it as a good sign.

Danny decided to go for his MBA. He was accepted at Wharton and found a nice apartment in Center City. On move day, the usual crew showed up to help. Organized as always, he'd already filled the cardboard boxes that I had collected from the Acme and had them stacked and ready for loading into the U-Haul he'd parked in the alley. We performed the delicate, sacred operation that was loading Old Pleather, the sectional from the family room. Once OP was braced, we all put a hand on it and wished it Godspeed. The cocktail table that had held countless beers over the years was making the trip, as were the coasters from County Tyrone. Once all the big stuff was in, we loaded the boxes, and the process moved faster than I wanted.

I kept repeating, "Did you forget anything? Are you sure?"

I was stalling, but he did forget something. He ran upstairs and came back with a hard plastic cylinder that contained the Bobby Sands poster from Jack's room. He kissed it and nestled it into a safe space on OP. Seeing his stuff boxed, wrapped, and packed made me realize no one ever really traveled a new path without taking something from their old one.

Once the truck's rear door was secured, Danny honked the horn, and Sheila and Colin came out to the alley for last hugs. I worried about them going back into the empty house, but they would be moving in a month or so and would be attending St. Cecelia's, almost five parishes away. An investor had bought their house to rent; there would be new faces in old spaces. I asked Danny about his leaving the nest. "I'm going with the flow, T. Seeing what life holds next."

Danny, Ray, and I got into the front seat of the U-Haul, and the others piled into Dez's SUV to follow us to the apartment. At the end of the alley, we turned left onto the two-lane one-way street and drove past McRyan's. Vizzie stood outside, smoking a cigarette. He seemed a little shrunken, but so did the bar. We drove a little further, and traffic stopped. The lights? No. The traffic light changed at regular intervals, but there was some kind of roadblock. I jumped out to investigate. Drivers laid into their car horns, and people leaned out their car windows yelling obscenities. I walked through the idled cars. At the cross street, a red Fiat had stalled crossing the intersection and closed off both lanes.

The driver cracked his window on my approach. He was an old Italian man. He spoke no English and talked urgently with his hands. I motioned that I would push him, but he only stared, so I exaggerated my actions. Somebody from the backed-up line of cars yelled, "This ain't no time for the chicken dance."

The man finally grasped what I was trying to say. He put the car in neutral. I pushed his car across the intersection, and he steered it into a parking lane. Once the car was out of the way, traffic moved again. Danny pulled up and I climbed back into the truck, and we continued on down the road.

About the Author

Charley Heenan has delivered newspapers, waited tables, tended bar, analyzed logistics for the military, managed a restaurant, worked in finance, and knocked on doors for political campaigns. A life-long resident of the Philadelphia area and huge Philadelphia sports fan, the St. Joseph's University graduate now writes full-time.